A nighttime swim turned deadly

I was about to let go and push back for shore when my fingers felt something strange. My arm was slung over the side of the rowboat, hanging down inside it. And whatever I felt at the bottom of that boat was far cooler than the water I was drifting in, and cooler than the mountain air. It was cold. Dead cold.

As my hand patted around, trying to get its bearings, to see by touch, the thing took shape. It had a long, mushy stem, a flat soft section. It had five thin pieces spread out in all directions. It had—oh God, it had fingernails.

Then I heard my name at long last. "Chlo!" Ruby was shouting. "Chloe! Chlo!"

Normally my heart would have leaped, hearing her call my name like that, wanting me back so loudly, so badly, so everyone could hear—but my heart wasn't even beating. I couldn't speak, didn't have the sound in me to shout back.

There was an arm in that boat. An arm attached to a cold, dead hand.

Other Books You May Enjoy

Catalyst	Laurie Halse Anderson
Hold Still	Nina LaCour
If I Stay	Gayle Forman
Impossible	Nancy Werlin
Lock and Key	Sarah Dessen
Looking for Alaska	John Green
Shadow Mirror	Richie Tankersley Cusick
The Sky Is Everywhere	Jandy Nelson
Trance	Linda Gerber
Where She Went	Gayle Forman
Willow	Julia Hoban
Wintergirls	Laurie Halse Anderson

nova ren suma

imaginary
girls

speak
An Imprint of Penguin Group (USA) Inc.

SPEAK

Published by the Penguin Group

Penguin Group (USA) Inc., 345 Hudson Street, New York, New York 10014, U.S.A.

Penguin Group (Canada), 90 Eglinton Avenue East, Suite 700, Toronto,
Ontario, Canada M4P 2Y3 (a division of Pearson Penguin Canada Inc.)

Penguin Books Ltd, 80 Strand, London WC2R 0RL, England

Penguin Ireland, 25 St Stephen's Green, Dublin 2, Ireland (a division of Penguin Books Ltd)

Penguin Group (Australia), 250 Camberwell Road, Camberwell, Victoria 3124, Australia
(a division of Pearson Australia Group Pty Ltd)

Penguin Books India Pvt Ltd, 11 Community Centre,
Panchsheel Park, New Delhi - 110 017, India

Penguin Group (NZ), 67 Apollo Drive, Rosedale, North Shore 0632, New Zealand
(a division of Pearson New Zealand Ltd.)

Penguin Books (South Africa) (Pty) Ltd, 24 Sturdee Avenue,
Rosebank, Johannesburg 2196, South Africa

Registered Offices: Penguin Books Ltd, 80 Strand, London WC2R 0RL, England

First published in the United States of America by Dutton Books,
a member of Penguin Group (USA) Inc., 2011
Published by Speak, an imprint of Penguin Group (USA) Inc., 2012

1 3 5 7 9 10 8 6 4 2

THE LIBRARY OF CONGRESS HAS CATALOGED THE DUTTON BOOKS EDITION AS FOLLOWS:
Suma, Nova Ren.
Imaginary girls / Nova Ren Suma.
p. cm.
Summary: Two years after sixteen-year-old Chloe discovered classmate London's dead body
floating in a Hudson Valley reservoir, she returns home to be with her devoted older sister Ruby,
a town favorite, and finds that London is alive and well, and that Ruby may somehow have
brought her back to life and persuaded everyone that nothing is amiss.
ISBN: 978-0-525-42338-6 (hc)
[1. Sisters—Fiction. 2. Supernatural—Fiction. 3. Dead—Fiction.
4. Reservoirs—Fiction. 5. Hudson River Valley (N.Y. and N.J.)—Fiction.]
I. Title
PZ7.S95388 Im 2011
[Fic] 2010042758

Speak ISBN 978-0-14-242143-7
Set in Cochin

Printed in the United States of America

For my baby sister,
Laurel Rose

And for Erik,
always

CHAPTER ONE

RUBY SAID

Ruby said I'd never drown—not in deep ocean, not by shipwreck, not even by falling drunk into someone's bottomless backyard pool. She said she'd seen me hold my breath underwater for minutes at a time, but to hear her tell it you'd think she meant days. Long enough to live down there if needed, to skim the seafloor collecting shells and shiny soda caps, looking up every so often for the rescue lights, even if they took forever to come.

It sounded impossible, something no one would believe if anyone other than Ruby were the one to tell it. But Ruby was right: The body found that night wouldn't be, couldn't be mine.

We had no idea—this was before the blue-flashing strobe through the pines; the spotlit glare on water; the skidding over rocks; the grabbing of shoes, any shoes, of clothes, any clothes. Before we went running through the brush and the sharp sticks cut our bare feet. Before the heart in my chest went pounding, all the while wondering, *Is this really happening?* when it was, most definitely it was. Before all that—all we wanted was to go swimming.

The boys surrounded Ruby at the edge of the reservoir, some closer than others, some with flashlights that they let dance far lower than her face, though Ruby didn't smack them away when they did it—tonight, she didn't feel like doing any smacking.

In the distance were more boys, and a few girls, the group straggling along the edge of the reservoir and into the night, but this here was the beating center. This was where to find Ruby. She stood and stretched out the length of her foot to dangle one browned, pearl-painted toe in the water. She let the boys watch her do it. Let them watch her splash.

I was there, too, watching, but no one paid me much attention until she said my name.

"Chloe could swim this whole thing, there and back," Ruby told the boys. She was talking me up, as she liked to. She was saying I could swim all the way across the reservoir—from our shore to the hazy shape of the one just visible in the distance—and she dared any of them to say I couldn't. I'd swim it, she said, and more: I'd bring back a souvenir.

The waterline was lower than usual that summer, since we hadn't seen a drop of rain in weeks. If you knew where to look, the towns that had their homes in this valley were peeking through. Here where we stood was the edge of what had once been a village called Olive, and now Ruby was saying I could pay a visit while crossing the reservoir, that I'd plunge down to the bottom where the remains of Olive still stand, dig around in their abandoned dressers, and come back to shore draped in their jewels. If anyone could do it, Ruby said, her sister could.

The boys laughed, but they should have known Ruby wasn't making a joke of it.

"I swear," she said, "dunk her in and she turns half fish. She doesn't need air like the rest of us. I've seen it. Who do you think was the one giving her baths when she was three?"

She's five-and-a-half years older than me, so she has memories I don't, can put me in places I'd swear I've never been (Lollapalooza, Niagara Falls, the Ulster County Jail that one time, to visit our mother). If Ruby said I could swim all the way across, if she said I could dive down to the bottom no one's ever put a hand to, find what's left of Olive, touch the floorboards of the houses flooded in 1914, and come up kicking, a splinter of proof in one finger, then maybe I can. Maybe I have. Ruby could turn me from an ordinary girl you wouldn't look at twice into someone worth watching. Someone special, mythical even.

That's what I got for being her baby sister.

The more Ruby talked about me, the more the boys looked my way. She made me come alive when she said my name; her words gave me color, fluffed out my hair. You could tell by the way their flashlights fell on me, by where they fell, by how long they lingered, just what her words got them thinking.

"Right, Chlo?" she said. "Tell them you can do it. Go on, tell them." I couldn't see her face as she spoke, but I'd know the smile in her voice anywhere. The tease.

I shrugged, like maybe I could do what she said, maybe.

I was on the lowest rock, the one almost submerged in water. I was down below the waterline, where I could sink in my legs and kick. Here at the edge, we might catch a glimpse of the old stone foundations, some still standing in places. A wall, crumbling. A cellar doorway, left open. Maybe we'd spy a chimney poking up out of the water, a church steeple. From shore, the dark night made it seem like I could wade across, but that was only a trick, as the bottom dropped a few feet in. This reservoir was deep enough to bury whole towns—and it had. It had destroyed nine of them. Ruby knew this; she was the one who told me.

So I could stay on this rock, getting just my feet wet, then my legs up to my knees, no more. I could do nothing and she wouldn't be mad tomorrow. But what would we have to talk about then?

I was fourteen, way younger than the boys poking at me

with the beams of their flashlights. Hanging with Ruby's friends meant I had to be careful of who was looking, whose bottle to steal a sip out of, who to let sit beside me in the dark where they knew Ruby couldn't see. Less dangerous would be the reservoir itself, too large to keep track of in the night—an oil spill instead of a mapped and measured ocean.

That's why, when she stood tall on the bed of rocks and pointed out into the night to say I could swim it right now, this dark minute, I didn't protest. She meant the width of the reservoir, about two miles across, but it looked like she meant the night sky itself, that there was a universe of time unknown and I could cross it.

Most people weren't aware of our reservoir's history; they didn't think about what had been here before. At night, it was just this indescribable thing without shape or color. This thing that could only be felt around you, when wading in, when you bent your knees and gulped air and let it swallow your head. Once under, all sound cut off. The water thickened the lower you sunk—with what, you didn't think about, didn't want to know. You had to watch your toes, because the jagged bottom could cut you, and hang tight to your clothes, if you were wearing any, because the reservoir was known to take what it wanted when it wanted it. Not just loose change and car keys but bikini tops and piercings come loose from decade-old holes. Ruby once lost a ring a boy gave her, a ring handcrafted by his father, given as a promise she never meant to keep. So for Ruby the reservoir took what *she* wanted, almost as if they shared an understanding. Everyone else had to be more careful.

This reservoir didn't belong to us, though it lapped into our backyards. It cut through multiple towns across the Hudson Valley; it lined our roads. It was there past the trees, behind chains and No Trespassing signs, dammed up and shored in, but still sparkling in every kind of weather, calling us to drop our pants and jump in. It was part of the watershed that supplied New York City—just begging us to take advantage.

I loved swimming it, Ruby knew. We liked to think of them, the city people who assumed they had lives so much better than ours even though they lived stacked up tight in their gray city, locked in their boxes, breathing their canned air, taking their baths in the pool we just swam in.

It was illegal to swim in the reservoir, but I did it anyway—we all did, and more. It was the water we puked into, when we were too drunk to keep standing; water we pissed in, secretly, in darkness; water in which some girls gave it up, thinking they didn't need a condom; water where stupid girls did stupid things.

I'd been coming here since I was a baby. Besides, I knew I wouldn't drown if I tried to cross—Ruby said.

So there I was, standing up, and clawing out of my shirt,

and then I lost my shorts, and then I was wading into the water past my knees.

I knew what she wanted: a show, for the rest of them. Ruby said I could do an impossible thing and all I had to do was act like I was about to do it, make them wonder enough to think it real. Her friends sure weren't sober; they'd remember it however she wanted them to tomorrow.

I pushed forward, plunging in up to my waist. She wound them up for me, saying, "Chloe'll make it across, no problem. Chloe'll bring us back something from Olive, just watch. Right, Chlo?" And some boys yelled, "Yeah, Chloe, think you can do it?" And other boys yelled, "No way!" and "Let's see her try!" Flashlights dancing circles around me. My name on their lips, coasting across the water. My name.

Everyone was watching, it felt like. The night was mine now, as if my sister had handed it over to me, simply curious to see what could happen.

It had all started because Ruby had invited some boys to the reservoir, and then word had gotten out, as it always did, news of a party passed along from car to car at the Village Green, phones buzzing, messages flying, girls and boys we didn't even bother talking to in daylight saying, "Ruby wants to go swimming. Did you hear?"

I was only aware of how many kids had come when I looked back to shore. Then my eyes went to him, the one boy on the rocks who wasn't yelling. I could see him up on the tallest rock, a shaggy silhouette showing how his mohawk had grown out, the hard angle of his chin turned away. A pulse of light as he sucked in on one of his brother's smokes, then dark, when he ground it out, then no light. He was the one not watching. His brother was up there, and so was some girl in a white shirt, so white it was the brightest thing I could see from out in the water, and they were watching. Their heads were turned my way. Only his wasn't.

I stopped looking. I'd play along, since that's what Ruby wanted.

"Sure I could do it," I called out to the boys gathered by the water. "Totally I could."

Ruby didn't seem worried, not one bit. It was like I never had that Rolling Rock one of her friends slipped me, hadn't chugged from her bottle of wine when she wasn't looking. As if I were an Olympic-class swimmer and had done this before, diving down to ransack swollen dressers, as if any story she told about me or about the drowned towns at the bottom of the reservoir was true.

"So are you going to or not?" one of Ruby's friends called.

"Yeah," I said. "For twenty bucks." And Ruby smiled the slight smile that showed she approved, then held out a hand to collect the cash.

I could see Ruby lit up by a flashlight. This was the summer she was nineteen. She was beautiful, everyone said so, but that wasn't all she was. Her hair was deep brown and long down the length of her back. She had a smattering of freckles, just enough to be worth counting, across her nose. She wore boots every day, even with sundresses; and she never left the house without sunglasses, the kind with the giant, tinted lenses that celebrities wear while lounging on some distant tropical beach. When Ruby slipped the glasses up on her forehead to keep the hair from her eyes, when she let you see her whole face, she got the sort of reactions a girl from a magazine might get if she flashed what was under her shirt. The stopped traffic, the stares. Ruby just had this light about her that can't be explained in words—you had to see her.

I was an echo of her. We both had the long dark hair, the sometimes freckles. We shared not just a mother, but also preferences in sugary-sweet foods and slow, sad songs; tendencies toward motion sickness and talking in our sleep; our knees went purple in cold; our hiccups could last days; and our telephone voices were nearly indistinguishable, so she could pretend to be me or I could pretend to be her if we wanted to fool you into leaving a message.

More than that, we had the same recessive earlobes, identical pinkie fingers and toes. But those were inconsequential details. Who ever called a girl beautiful because of her toes? In reality I was a pencil drawing of a photocopy of a Polaroid of my sister—you could see the resemblance in a certain light, if you were seeking it out because I told you first, if you were being nice.

Only then, all those eyes on me in the water, did I wonder if this was what it felt like to be my sister. To be looked at this way, always. To be seen.

She was gazing down at me, down from a very long distance, but straight-centered into my eyes. "You ready?" she asked, and sent a smile that was meant for me only, understood to be mine. I'm not sure how she thought I'd manage to come back with a souvenir from Olive, but I couldn't ask her, not now, not in front of everyone. I knew she was already gathering the pieces of the story she'd tell tomorrow—Ruby loved her stories—and here I was, the star.

"Ready," I said.

This would be the story of my crossing, and with the twenty bucks for my effort we'd ignore the overdue phone bill and buy dinner at the Little Bear.

This would not be the story of how I drowned at the deepest point of the reservoir the summer I was fourteen—Ruby would never let it happen.

"Okay, Chlo," Ruby called to me, "show them you can do it. Bring us back something good! . . . Go."

The boys at the edge of the water were shooting waves in my direction, getting the current going, giving me my push. And they looked at me the way they looked at her, because it was dark, because it was late, because they were confused or high or drunk or all three, and I didn't mind it, didn't mind it at all.

I started swimming.

It was night, so I knew there was no way they could see how far out I'd gone. When I was moving this fast, there wasn't a flashlight that could find me. I cast out quick past the point at which the rocky ground gave way, when I could touch my toe to the bottom and then when I couldn't, when it felt as if there was no bottom at all. I moved out into the depths where no one could catch me.

I could hear them back on shore, and then I couldn't. I kept swimming.

The water spread out all around me, familiar and warm. As I swam I didn't keep my eyes open; I knew the way. And then I felt it, all at once, how as I darted forward the water turned cold, seeming at least ten degrees cooler than before, and I knew I'd gotten close to where Ruby always said we'd find the center of Olive. Its heart, she used to say, was in the middle of the reservoir, at its deepest, bottommost point.

My legs got heavy as I kicked past the cold spot, as if the current had turned thicker there, a tugging downward pull.

It's true that a town called Olive used to be in this spot before the water got flooded in; that's in history books; that's not just one of Ruby's stories. Olive was one of nine towns buried because New York City wanted more water.

The city bought up all the land and built its dam here. It dredged out this great big hole and gutted away every last tree. People's homes and farms were taken over, then flattened. Olive was dismantled and swept out of the valley like it had never been here at all. Like it got erased.

Ruby knew more about Olive than anybody. She knew things no one else did. She said the people in the town didn't want to leave, that the city of New York tried to buy their houses, their churches and schools, their farms and storefronts, and the people of Olive wouldn't sell. People in the other towns took the cash and scattered. It was only Olive that decided to stay. Only Olive that ignored the eviction notices, like that time we got a bright orange one pasted to the door of our apartment, and Ruby simply sliced through it so she could get inside. It was exactly like then, Ruby told me—except imagine if it looked like the world were ending because the city cut down all the trees and big machines roared and took the earth from under our feet and we had nowhere to go.

Olive wouldn't budge, even when the steam whistle blew for a full hour at noon on June 19, 1914, to show that the building of the dam was at last finished. It was only the people of Olive who stood in place on the land where they were born and waited for the water to come flooding in.

"But they did go," I remember saying to Ruby when she told me this story. "They had to."

"Did they?" was all she said then.

As I swam over Olive, I wondered.

Ruby used to say that, down in what was once Olive, you could still find the townspeople who never left. They looked up into their murky sky, waiting to catch sight of our boat bottoms and our fishing lines, counting our trespassing feet.

They weren't ghosts, she'd assure me when I used to shiver at her story; they were people still alive, having grown gills in place of lungs. They aged slower down at the bottom, where time had gone thick with all that mud. When I was little, she'd rile me up, saying they knew all about me, had noticed me the first time we poached a swim in this very spot. They knew me by my feet, she said, recognized me by the way I kept them kicking, and all they wanted was for me to act up, to throw the last tantrum she could stand, hoping she'd get tired and let them have me.

If she pushed me in, right away their cold, webbed hands would come reaching out for my ankles. But don't worry, she assured me, I'd have everything I needed down at the bottom. Reservoir ice cream was green, which made it mint, my favorite kind. Playing on the swings was way more fun underwater anyway. And having to remember to breathe took up so much time.

That was years ago, when she used to threaten to throw me to Olive, and she never meant it, not really. Sure, when she was fourteen and I was nine she had to take me with her everywhere, and she complained about it sometimes, behind closed doors when she didn't know I was listening. She told our mom that *she* should have been the one to teach me to tie my shoes, boil my boxed macaroni dinners, sign my permission slip to the dinosaur museum. She said all that, but it didn't matter; I knew Ruby didn't actually ever want me gone.

Like now.

She'd sent me out here, but she knew Olive didn't still exist—she'd only been keeping things interesting, telling her stories. Letting me have the whole spotlight for once.

She was on shore watching. I felt eyes keeping track of my movements, her eyes and her friends' eyes, and then more eyes even than that, eyes from below.

I looked back, or tried to, but all the water was in the way.

Everyone probably thought I was still swimming. I wasn't. I'd stopped—though I didn't remember stopping, or even slowing. I was drifting out in the open expanse, my legs feeling their weight.

The water was colder here, no denying it. And something was in my path, as if she'd made it appear there for me. A small rowboat bobbed in the water, unseen from shore in the deep night. I rested a hand on it, leaning my weight into its rusted side so I could catch my breath. The moon up above showed half a face; the stars could be counted till morning.

I waited there, legs loose, hair swirling around me, and listened to her friends on shore. Laughing. Splashing. Dragging a canoe out of the woods. Breaking a bottle against the rocks.

No one called my name.

I wondered if they'd forgotten, if I'd taken too long. Or maybe they knew I never meant to do it. I didn't do everything Ruby said, not every single thing. I did what I wanted. I did things and then looked back to see what she'd say.

Maybe everyone knew this was a joke, a misdirection. Because surely she had to be joking—I did need air to breathe like everyone else; I did have only two legs and no fins. If anyone was a mythical creature here, it was Ruby, the one we all looked to and listened for, the one the boys loved and fought to be with, who couldn't be captured or caged. The stories she told about me didn't matter; the boys just wanted a chance to make up some stories of their own with her.

I could hear Ruby, far off in the distance. Miles away, it seemed, miles and miles. I heard her laugh—I'd know that laugh anywhere—a laugh flat and dry and cut short when others let theirs last far longer. She only really found something funny when she said it herself, or if I did. She'd laugh for me.

My stomach was sloshing with wine, my teeth chattering from the cold, my nose starting to drip and run. Why wasn't she calling for me so I knew to give up and come back?

I couldn't hear her laughing anymore. I couldn't hear her at all. It was as if I'd only imagined the sound of her laughter, imagined her on shore looking after me. Maybe, once I swam back, I'd find she'd shed her clothes, left my twenty folded up inside for safekeeping, and simply . . . vanished.

I was about to let go and push back for shore when my fingers felt something strange. My arm was slung over the side of the rowboat, hanging down inside it. And whatever I felt at the bottom of that boat was far cooler than the water I was drifting in, and cooler than the mountain air. It was cold. Dead cold.

As my hand patted around, trying to get its bearings, to see by touch, the thing took shape. It had a long, mushy stem, a flat soft section. It had five thin pieces spread out in all directions. It had—oh God, it had fingernails.

Then I heard my name at long last. "Chlo!" Ruby was shouting. "Chloe! Chlo!"

Normally my heart would have leaped, hearing her call my name like that, wanting me back so loudly, so badly, so everyone could hear—but my heart wasn't even beating. I couldn't speak, didn't have the sound in me to shout back.

There was an arm in that boat. An arm attached to a cold, dead hand.

That's when the flashlights came. Close enough to reach me — I must have not swam out as far as I thought. Flashlights all over me, beams covering my face and neck and shoulders, showing I was here in the water, hanging on, still alive. But that meant they also lit up what was inside the boat so I could see it. That other pair of shoulders, the long neck, the face that wasn't mine.

A girl, lifeless eyes staring up at the half moon. A girl who left her body here for me to find it. A girl with pale hair, pale cheeks, paler still in a bright white shirt.

Then arms around me — bigger arms than Ruby's arms, she'd sent the boys — holding me too tight at first until they caught sight of the girl in the boat, and then letting go, letting go and shouting, grabbing for the boat and letting me go.

The face in that boat could have been mine; for a split second this thought rattled through me and then, faster than it'd come, it dropped away.

Because it was her face again, the girl's. The last thing I remembered were her two open eyes and her two closed, cracked lips. I recognized her. She was someone I knew.

Her name was London, it came to me. London Hayes. We had seventh-period French together; she was the same age as me.

After that, many more things happened, all too fast to make sense of.

I remember the hard grip on my arm, pulling me back to shore. The shouts. The dragging in of the boat. Light, more light than was possible with even a horde of flashlights, enough light to drown in. I remember the chill that stayed with me, the ice in my gut.

We tried to run, but they caught some of us. They caught me. And once they had me, my sister let herself be caught, too. We were cited for trespassing, held for questioning, since at first—before it was ruled an OD—they suspected foul play.

No one would admit to giving London the drugs. No one would admit to dumping her body in the boat. Not one person had witnessed a thing.

All I knew was how I kept on seeing her face, even after they lifted her out of the boat and carried her away. How I kept hearing the slap of the water, like there were people still swimming in it, even though everyone had been made to get out and stand far, far away.

Then I was turning to my sister, who was there beside me in the back of the cop car, because suddenly we were in a cop car, and my sister, who never found herself in cop cars, wasn't fighting it, or clawing at the cage, or making any attempt to break free.

Her eyes were full of the night's stars and her hair was glowing with the police lights and she acted as if nothing at all was wrong—until she got a closer peek at me.

"What's the matter, Chlo? You look so . . . scared."

I shook my head. I couldn't put it to words. We were sitting in the backseat together, but part of me was wading that cold spot in the reservoir, hanging on to the edge of the boat, shivering like I was there still.

She took my wet hair in her hands and wrung it out on the floor, to leave the cops a good puddle; and she brought my damp head to her lap, and didn't care that I'd soak her skirt, and told me to close my eyes and sleep.

I don't remember much else after that. Or I try not to.

That's the summer I stopped living with Ruby. My dad in Pennsylvania took me, and then my hair grew out, and I lost my virginity in the back of a Subaru, and Ruby wasn't there to tell it to. Ruby wasn't there.

Only sometimes did I call and get her voice mail and hear the sound of her telephone voice — nearly indistinguishable from my telephone voice — saying, "Leave a message if you dare."

I didn't dare.

I thought about other things instead. Like how I could have made it to the other shore, maybe, if I'd kept kicking and didn't stop to catch my breath.

How this could have been the story of that time I crossed the reservoir past midnight on a Thursday the summer I was fourteen. How I would have dove in, traveling underwater the entire way, a submarine in a mismatched bikini, a torpedo of hair and a flurry of kicking feet. Proof, she would have said, that I'm a creature built without need of lungs—inside me a safebox of air and scattered clouds: in case of emergency, break glass and breathe.

In the water, my legs would have formed a tail, my arms fins. Ruby had seen it happen, she'd say, those times all those years ago when she'd been the one to give me a bath when our mother was at the bar. She'd seen the silvery flash under bubbles, the quickly shifting skin, seen it with her own two eyes.

As Ruby wanted, I would have reached the cold spot and then gone deep. I'd touch my hands to the murky floor-boards and abandoned roadways of the town no one could bear to leave, get my prints all over them. Then I'd come up with a piece of Olive in my fist: a rusted fork from a drifting dinner table, an algae-covered comb Ruby could rinse off and use in her hair.

And no one would have believed it, no one would have thought it could even be possible, not till they shined their lights on the other shore and saw me standing there, wav-ing the comb at them like I was someone special, mythical even—just like Ruby said.

CHAPTER TWO

RUBY NEVER SAID

R uby never said, "Stay." Not out loud, not so I could
hear. She came down to the curb as I was leaving for
my dad's and she simply stood there, eyes held back behind
sunglasses, watching me go.

She didn't do much to acknowledge my dad, who'd come
all that way to take me. She spoke only to me, as if he were
a blot on her shiny lens that she'd wipe off when she felt like
it—and until then she'd look right through the speck of him
like he wasn't there.

All she said to me was, "I wish you didn't have to do this,
Chlo." And then her voice got choked up and she backed
away from the car and wouldn't say one more word to me.

Two dark lenses between us, a rolled-up window, a hard
right into the road. Then miles of highway, the phones not
ringing, then years.

The dad I left with wasn't Ruby's dad. We have different fathers, so technically I'm her half-sister, not that we

count in halves. She was there the moment I was born—literally, right there in the room, she'll say and she'll shudder. She saw me born at home on the futon, and though it may have scarred her for life, this means she won't ever forget it. Or me.

"I'll never leave you," Ruby used to promise. She'd cross her heart with me as a witness; she'd hold my hand hard in hers and hope to die. "I'll never leave," she said, "not ever." Not like Mom, she didn't have to say. Not like my dad, who left me, and her dad, who left her. No, she'd promise. Never.

I guess we didn't expect I'd be the one to leave her.

Away from the town where we lived, I tried to forget the details of my life with Ruby. I had a new life now. Wednesdays, I no longer snuggled up on the couch to mock girl movies or laced on old roller skates to ride the ramps behind the Youth Center; I spent my hours alone doing homework. There were no weekend sprees for new sunglasses, no taking turns with the scissors to slice out fashion models' painted lips and eyes from magazines to tape to our walls. After the last bell at school, there was no white car waiting for me—no detour down the old highway alongside the real highway, no windows open wide so the wind could dread my hair. I had to take the bus.

But I thought of Ruby constantly. Of being with her, of what we did.

How at all hours we'd lounge on the hard stone benches on the Village Green, which marked the dead-center point of our town, watching the cars go around, watching them watch us, and only now did I wonder if Ruby sat there just to be seen? Did I know how the universe revolved around the spot wherever Ruby happened to be, be it out on the Green or at home, or did I pretend I didn't know, like a sun that's gone lazy and slips down from the sky to lie out on the rooftop in her favorite white bikini only because she can?

I tried not to think about that.

I thought about our town. The exact blue of our mountains, the certain green of our trees. The Cumberland Farms convenience store where Ruby worked, pumping gas and filling in at the register, her hand dipping in the till, shortchanging tourists. Her apartment by the Millstream, her big, old-lady car. The store where she got her signature shade of wine red lipstick, how they held her color behind the counter so no one else could wear it. The rec field where we took to the swings, the spillway where we had parties. The reservoir, worst of all the reservoir. Every night I walked the unmarked path to Olive's edge and couldn't stop if I tried.

Always, in my dream, it was dark. Always the stars above held the same pattern, because it was the same night, and time had wound back to let me take my place in it, where I belonged.

I had the same aftertaste of wine coating my throat, could hear the same voices echoing from shore. My body made the motions to swim that great distance, even though I knew I'd come to the cold spot soon enough.

Even though I knew I'd reach the boat. And her.

But the cold surprised me each time. The fear felt new.

Because there she was, the girl in the boat, drifting at the exact point in the reservoir where I'd stopped swimming the first night and stopped swimming every night I dreamed it since. Ruby always said she'd protect me, but I couldn't keep myself from thinking the worst thing I could, since she wasn't around to bend my mind her way.

She didn't protect me that night.

The girl who'd been buried could have been me.

The longer I stayed away from town the more I thought about the girl who sat in the last row of my French class, London Hayes. How she'd cut her hair right before the summer, chopped it off like a boy. How I'm pretty sure she had long hair before that, long and without bangs like so many of the girls in town because that's how Ruby wore her hair. But now I remembered how London's ears stuck out after she'd chopped it, like maybe she should have considered her ears before going ahead with that haircut and I guess no one thought to tell her.

London once got called to the front of the classroom because Ms. Blunt, our French teacher, had spied what she was doodling in her notebook. She made London show the entire class: through a crosshatch of shaded scribbles, a naked girl with bloodthirsty eyes and sharp, serrated ribs, nipples dangling like extra fingers, toes black with disease.

It was grotesque, offensive even. Ms. Blunt glared at the lined page, the blue ballpoint put down so hard it left gashes, and in her dramatically accented, overloud French she asked London, *"Qui est-ce?"* Violent pointing motions. Enunciation galore. *"Qui est-ce?"*

And we all racked our brains trying to remember what that meant—this was remedial, not Regents-level French— but London knew the question and knew how to answer. She shook her head sadly and said, *"C'est moi."* It's me.

Something was wrong with the girl—clearly.

Other than that, I didn't know too much about her. There was this rumor that she once took five hits of LSD and went to school on purpose, like a walking biology experiment, which I guess failed because she didn't make it through fourth-period gym. She started drinking in sixth grade, people said, too, but that was mostly a compliment.

I must have seen her outside school sometimes. She knew Ruby's friends, could be spied in the backseats of their cars as they spun their way around the Green. Plus she was friends with Owen—I couldn't help but notice—the boy I tried hard not to hold in my heart as he barely ever looked my way. Also, I'm pretty sure one time she borrowed my pen and never gave it back.

I knew she was at the reservoir that night, even though she wasn't invited.

That's all I knew.

Just weeks into living at my dad and stepmother's house in Pennsylvania, my mom mailed me a package. She was sober again and must have realized she should show a stab at missing me, for, I guess, my sake. But the box was no attempt at amends. It was more a junk drawer than a care package: a spilled cache of feathers and beads from the craft store in town where she worked weekends; a rock from, I figured, the Millstream, dusted in our town's dried mud; some menstrual tea (seriously?); a dog-eared book on power animals (hers was the sparrow, she said, which she'd also taken on as her new name; Ruby said it was actually the vampire bat); and nothing whatsoever from Ruby.

You might say my mom was harmless if you didn't know any better. Hair down past her waist like she was going for some world record, beaded necklaces, gypsy skirts. She really did force people in town to call her Sparrow. But that was only the role she liked to perform for whatever audience hadn't slipped out the back; it was her aria in the shower for whoever needed to pee and got stuck listening.

In reality, my mom had a hard side, made of tin and pounded flat to deflect all emotion, thanks to the poison she poured down her throat. That's why, in the care package, she'd also included one last thing: the obituary. Like she wanted to make sure I didn't forget.

Ruby would have shipped me the severed tip off her own finger before sending that. She would have guessed about my reservoir nightmares: the rowboat bobbing, knowing that at any moment the floating inhabitants of Olive could pull London down to their waterlogged Village Green by her rotting, black toes, and then my toes, and then me. We didn't need to talk about it for her to know the last thing I'd want was a reminder.

My mom barely knew me. If Ruby hadn't witnessed me come out of her body, I would've thought I'd been picked up on the side of Route 28 in the spot where we found that couch.

The obit had been neatly scissored out of a newspaper from the township across the county line. My mom had gone out of her way to get this one for me special, going so far as to cross the Mid-Hudson Bridge to check the papers there. In it was a photo of London with her former long hair and the complete absence of a smile. You couldn't see her ears. The text about her was short and vague: lost too soon, mourned and by who, in lieu of flowers donate to this cause, the usual. No mention of how she died, or where.

It didn't say what kind of drugs she'd been on; that was tacky to tell the world, I guess. It was also tacky for my mom to send it to me.

Ruby, she would have torn the obit to shreds and burned it in the fireplace. She would have cranked up the stereo to forget it, played something vintage, like Rick James or 2 Live Crew, something raunchy and loud and undeniably *alive* to get those words out of our heads. She would have, if I'd stayed.

That was the last I heard of London for a long time. My mom didn't send another care package—she slipped off-radar, as she tends to—and Ruby's sporadic text messages filled me in on other subjects entirely.

dreamed we rode wild horses dwn the mntain. u lost yr hat but i found it don't worry

dreamed we shared a phantom boyfriend & his name was Georgie. cute but made of vapor. smelled like lemons

dreamed we lived in a big blue blimp. the clouds had berries for snacks & u were always hungry

my boots miss your feet

my head misses your hairbrush

my car misses your warm butt

And sometimes, deep in the middle of the night when she had to know I was sleeping, she texted a simple two characters: xo

I missed her, too.

My dad never spoke of what propelled me to move in with him after all these years. Still, he'd look at me sideways sometimes, as if waiting for the first sign of mutation. Like at any moment I could hiccup, have a spasm, pop out an extra head, and then he'd have one more mouth to feed. There was therapy, for a while—the freebie kind with the school guidance counselor—and there were chores. Taking out trash. Cleaning the garage. Dishes, landfills of dishes. Distractions, all.

The physical labor worked for a time, though when I was elbows deep in soapsuds, scrubbing at a stubborn pot, I was reminded of Ruby's way of doing dishes—leaving them piled in the sink and on the stove for a week at a time until there was no other option but to crate them over to the bathtub for a good soaking. Then how, after we gave the dishes a bath, we'd sail them like Frisbees to the couch, and if any dishes broke in the tossing that was just fewer to have to wash next time.

This would have been my life. At my new school, I was nobody special; I wasn't even related to anybody special. I could have stayed there, gotten mostly Bs, the rare B+, studied through study hall, dodged balls through gym, blanked out on my locker combination, passed Algebra I, passed Earth Science, six points away from failing art. Sat on the bleachers and didn't dance at the Halloween dance, stood in the corner and didn't dance at the homecoming dance. No story worth telling past next Tuesday.

And soon enough, as time passed, I let myself forget the details of that night. Why I'd ever been so scared. Even why I'd left town in the first place.

That's when she made a move.

One day, Ruby reached out and shook me. Even from across state lines she could.

The day it happened began like any other (bus stalled on the way to school; pop quiz in first period; ball to the face in gym), but then the stars shifted. The backdrop got picked up and moved offstage for the scene change. That must have been when she decided it was time, the weight of her decision sailing out of our town in the Catskill Mountains, beyond the reach of our river and our roads, finding me in this flat valley of highways and fast-food signs built taller than the treetops, this new town where I'd come to live.

Because this wasn't a day like any other day.

During lunch, a random cheerleader smiled at me. My art teacher called my lump of clay "inspired." My locker popped open on the very first try.

It was late afternoon when I stepped out of Music Appreciation to find the boy in whose Subaru I'd left my underwear, a glimmer of recognition in his eyes.

We hadn't talked for weeks, yet, after all that time, here he was. Waiting for me.

The way he looked at me—it was as if I'd stepped into Ruby's body, slipped on her longer legs, her greener eyes. As if I'd taken possession of her, or she'd taken possession of me.

"Hey, Chloe," he said.

The rest of my classmates streamed out around me, leaving me alone in the music hallway. He moved closer, and I moved away, and soon he had me backed up against the wall. Was this sexy? Was I supposed to go with it, arch my back and part my lips a certain way? I tried to channel Ruby, but I lost her for a second there when his eyes took hold of mine.

"Long time no talk," he was saying.

I was going to say, "I know." Say, "So how've you been?" Dumb things to say, dumb, dumb. I don't know what would have come out of my mouth had the thought of Ruby not turned me. Because what I said instead was, "Really?" Like I hadn't even noticed how long it had been.

It was as if she stood beside me, whispering deep into my ear. *Don't tell him how you waited by the phone for three weeks*, she breathed. *Don't say how you cried.*

I thought of that windy February night up on Cooper

Lake Road when her big white Buick ran out of gas. How we'd never run out of gas before in that car, even when the needle got stuck on *E* for days and we had no clue how much gas was left, so that was strange enough. But stranger still was how Ruby insisted we go on foot to the closest gas station—like she wanted us to really feel the cold. I thought of how our legs under our long coats prickled at first from the biting air, then burned. How, the longer we were outside, trudging through old snow, the sooner our thighs lost all feeling and went perfectly, senselessly numb.

In time, it felt as if we were hiking the road beside the icy lake on two sets of beating wings. We could barely tell we had legs at all.

It felt like we could have made it to the station in seconds, flown there and back with a canister of gasoline, our eyelashes glistening with frost, our bones weightless from cold. But then a truck stopped for us—some guy Ruby knew. And the heat in the cab brought our limbs back to life, stopped our teeth from chattering. We would not have to amputate our fingers due to frostbite; neither one of us would lose the tip off a nose.

We were grateful for the ride, but there was something to be said for the bodiless feeling that came after the cold. Something I would always remember. When you forget how bad it hurts, you feel so free.

This was what I was thinking as I stood there in the

music hallway. I made my heart go numb, listened for the wind, and on it what she'd want me to say.

"You didn't call," he said.

I kept listening.

"You said you'd call," he said. And then—the cinder-block wall at my back slick with its own sweat, or with mine—I remembered. Maybe I did say I'd call. Maybe he said he'd call me, and I said no, no I'll call *you*.

Anyway, that's something Ruby would have done.

He was still here, blocking my exit with a clutter of music stands and an old bassoon.

I surveyed him as Ruby would, had she been there across the corridor, near the cracked viola and crate of dusty sheet music, taking stock. Definite points on the hair: It was cut crooked and fell into his eyes. But his pants were too tight and slung too low. And his shoulders were set too cocky; he thought having me that one time meant he had me still.

He was talking, saying I'd been the one to ignore him, not the other way around. Acting like it's the boy who's supposed to stop talking to the girl after unmentionables are traded in the backseat of a car, not the girl. He'd obviously never met anyone like my sister.

"What's the matter?" he was saying. "Didn't you want to?"

I shrugged one shoulder. (Ruby, should I say I did?)

"You didn't say you didn't want to," he reminded me.

I shrugged the other shoulder. (Ruby, should I say I didn't?)

"So." He took a breath. "What're we doing tonight?"

That's when my phone vibrated from inside my pocket. I was able to slip out from under his arm, through the jumble of music stands, past the bassoon, into the center of the hallway, to freedom. I checked my phone to find a text.

don't get too comfy. im here 2 spring u. ps what's up w yr room? where are the wheels?

It was Ruby—and somehow she'd figured out where I was sleeping at my dad's: a tiny camper without tires set up on the back lawn, bed cavity overtop the steering wheel that looked out onto the flower garden, a net between me and the bees. It was pretty convenient; I'd even strung an extension cord from the garage so I could watch TV.

I wasn't sure how she knew, and wondered if she'd been talking to my dad, or my half-siblings, or my stepmother, to find out that once the weather turned warm I'd vacated my room in the house in favor of the camper.

And what did she mean she was going to spring me? Was she here?

My answer came immediately after, with another text:

my pink glasses! been looking 4 these 4ever chlo!

No one had told her about the camper. She was *inside* the camper, going through my stuff. She must have found the sunglasses I'd swiped the summer I left—the ones with

the pink-tinted lenses that she said made a person happy to
see through, like a drug you could wear on your head.

The boy—his name was Jared—was eyeing my phone
suspiciously, with a protectiveness he didn't deserve. "Who's
that?" he asked.

"I have to go," is all I said, because Ruby was here.

I didn't know how things could be the same for anyone,
how we could still be having this conversation, how anyone
could be having any conversation, didn't know how I could
pretend to be content living my days in this ordinary life, in
this ordinary hallway, with this ordinary boy, now that she
was here.

CHAPTER THREE

RUBY TRIED

Ruby tried to convince my dad. She tried in all the ways she was used to trying: her eyes staring him down until no light could escape and there was nowhere else to look but straight at her.

She tried with misdirection and misleading topics of conversation, with the subterfuge no one ever saw coming until days later, when they went searching for their wallet and thought they remembered it opening wide for one quick moment in Ruby's hand. She tried talking low; she tried talking loud. She tried being sweet; she tried being mean. Behind the closed door, where I couldn't see, I know she tried.

I waited outside his home office with my stepmom. She wasn't anyone special—if Ruby and I ever happened upon her in conversation, we avoided calling her by name.

She had two children who, since we had the same father, carried half my blood in their veins, just like Ruby did, the exact same amount, though I didn't feel connected to them in any real way.

They were like any two people I might pass in the halls at school. One boy, one girl. You see them and wave. Maybe you have on the same color sweater and you're like, "Hey, look. We're wearing the same color sweater." But there's nothing else to be said beyond that, so you each keep moving. You know you'd barely give it a thought if you never saw them again.

This is how I know blood is meaningless; family connections are a lot like old gum—you don't have to keep chewing. You can always spit it out and stick it under the table. You can walk away.

Ruby was my sister, but she was so much more than that. She loved me. She loved me more than anyone else in the whole entire world loved me. More than Mom, more than Dad. More than friends. More than any guy ever had, because no guy had. No matter how far apart we'd been these past two years, there was no question she did.

My stepmom cleared her throat. She did things like that, she had to, or else I'd forget she was there. "Are you sure you want to go away with this Ruby?" she said.

"Ruby is my *sister*," I said. "She practically *raised* me."

"Well, this is the first time I've ever seen her."

I didn't feel like explaining how Ruby never left the state of New York, let alone the confines of our wooded county.

Mostly she stayed in our town, where everyone knew her, where all you had to do was say her name and anyone in hearing distance would snap to attention, wondering if she'd been sighted around the corner and was coming this way.

Not just the boys but the girls, too. Did Ruby like this song? Then everyone had to hear it. Had Ruby worn this jacket? Then everyone wanted to slip arms into its sleeves.

Back at home, I got used to people knowing about Ruby, peppering me with questions about her, saying how this one time they talked to Ruby about really old French movies and did she say anything about it, do you think she likes Godard? How Ruby pumped their gas last Tuesday; how Ruby bummed their smokes, but they didn't mind; how years and years ago Ruby saw them play live at the old Rhinecliff hotel, and how, after the show, they let her bang away at their drums.

Pennsylvania was a strange state. No one knew who Ruby was.

"It's odd that she didn't visit all this time and now here she is," my stepmom said.

"Yeah," I said. "I guess. But that's Ruby."

"We invited her for Christmas and she didn't come."

"She doesn't like Christmas. She says it's too obvious. Plus she hates all the red together with the green."

"Besides the fact that she never calls . . ."

"Ruby has this thing with her ear. Telephones make it buzz. I don't mind if she texts instead of calls. I know all about her ear."

Defending her came naturally. Usually no one asked such questions about Ruby, but I guess I had some answers lying in wait in case they did.

My stepmom, though, wouldn't let it go. "All of a sudden she drives out here, without warning, lands on our doorstep, wearing . . . I'm sorry, but was that a nightie? Did she even bother to get dressed this morning? And then she marches in to tell your father she's taking you with her. Just like that?"

"Yup. Like I said, that's Ruby."

"Did she even ask if you wanted to go?" my stepmom said, pushing.

(She hadn't.)

"Didn't she think there was a reason you came to live with us in the first place?"

(There was . . . but what was it?)

"And why now? Why today?"

(I hadn't asked Ruby that, either.)

"Chloe?"

Ruby wasn't here to tell me what to say or remind me of what I wanted. Maybe she should have coached me before going in to talk to my dad.

All I knew is she'd landed in Pennsylvania so suddenly—appearing in my camper, hoodie sweatshirt on over summer negligee, a new freckle I didn't recognize on her nose, the pink sunglasses I'd stolen and she'd stolen back perched on her forehead, standing there sucking down the bottle of tropical fruit punch she'd found in my minifridge—and I hadn't had a chance to decide how I felt about it.

If I wanted to go with her.

If I was allowed to go, if I even would.

But, before I had a chance to answer, Ruby emerged from my dad's office. This was down in the basement of the house, wood-paneled and lit with dim, dull bulbs so it looked like we were lost in an alien forest, walled in on all sides by flattened trees.

She walked out and stood before me and my stepmom near the jaundice-colored couch. She didn't sit. It wasn't the kind of couch she'd ever sit on.

From the cloudy expression on her face, I knew it hadn't gone well. She seemed . . . there was no other word to call it but surprised. He must have said no, which didn't happen to her often. She probably had no clue what to make of it.

One time, I remember, a boy she was sort of seeing tried to say no when she told him she was craving a slice of cheesecake and he needed to go get her some, like right this minute. "Where's the best cheesecake in the whole state?"

she'd asked him, and when he'd said down in the city, she'd said, well, that's where he needed to go. She was testing him, I knew, doing it only because she could. But he had to work early the next morning, he said. It was late, he said, too late to drive two-and-a-half hours to the city just for cheesecake and two-and-a-half hours back so he could make it to work on time, especially if she wasn't going to ride with him.

She gave him the eyes first: green in the way nothing else in the world is green, green to stun you, venom green.

She moved closer to him on the couch, lowered the volume on the TV. Then she took a single finger, just the one, and traced the line of his chin—accomplishing two things at once: a reminder that he really should do something about that stubble, but also of who he was dealing with, who she was.

"Don't you like cheesecake?" she asked him innocently, and I'm trying to remember if his name was Raf or Ralph or Ray, because then Raf or Ralph or Ray said, "You know I do," and she said, "Do I really?"

She leaned on his shoulder and mumbled something into his ear that I couldn't make out from across the room.

She'd had him at the chin, I could tell, but she'd also made him late to work a few times already and I knew he had that on his mind, too. Being fired was apparently something that normal people concerned themselves with.

Ruby herself was always late for work at Cumby's. She ate M&M's free off the vine in the candy aisle and popped the cap on her gas tank to keep her car full up on unleaded, but she wasn't fired, not even close. Then again, no one else in town lived a life like Ruby's.

Raf or Ralph or Ray was trying to make a decision. Then he saw me looking.

I was thirteen then, maybe twelve. He saw me across the room and smiled. That's how I knew he'd risk getting fired for Ruby; lots of boys in town would.

"You up for some cheesecake, Chloe?" he asked me then, because if a guy wanted a solid shot at Ruby, he had to make an effort with her little sister. And I said yeah sure I wanted some cheesecake, and with cherries, and before you knew it he was heading south for the Mid-Hudson Bridge, trying to beat the 1:00 a.m. weekend closing at Veniero's, some bakery in Manhattan that he assured us made the best cheesecake in the whole state. We didn't even give him gas money, though Ruby donated a nickel for the tolls.

And I honestly don't know—didn't care—if he got fired the next day or not.

How easy it had been to convince him. He could have said no; he'd made a valiant effort. But in the end he didn't. He physically couldn't. And I don't think he even liked cheesecake.

My dad, though, he seemed to have a strength that boy

couldn't muster. Or else Ruby had lost a touch of her magic in the years we'd been apart. My dad came out of his office all beard and big head, like he held all the power, like no one could tell him what to do, and I hated him a little bit then, hated him a lot, for thinking he could deny Ruby what she wanted.

"So it's all settled," my dad said. "I assume Ruby's staying for dinner?"

"Oh no," Ruby said. "I'm staying, but not for dinner. I'm on a liquid diet, you know, a cleanse. Shakes only, the fruit kind or the milk, and I don't want you to go to any trouble with the blender."

She nodded politely at the man who was my father, though he'd skipped out on me before I could walk, and then she nodded politely at the woman who was married to the man who was my father, and pulled me by the sleeve up out of the basement to get the hell away from them both.

I should have known she'd come for me at some point. I should have been waiting. Ruby was impetuous. She did things like head down the driveway to check the mailbox, wearing only rain boots, a hoodie, and a summer slip with a jam stain on the lace hem, and end up across state lines, hours from home, telling my dad she'd come for custody.

I don't know what happened during her walk down the driveway that made her decide she had to have me back immediately—she didn't say. It must have been really important to leave right then, though, because otherwise she totally would have put a dress on over that slip.

Once Ruby decided on a thing, it was like, in her mind, it grew legs and turned real. She could write on a piece of paper the color underwear I'd have on tomorrow and fold it up a dozen times and hide it down deep in the toe of her boot, and even if I searched through my dresser drawers blindfolded, picking out a pair I hadn't worn in weeks, she'd have known, somehow, that I'd pick red. Almost as if she'd willed the color on my body by writing down its name.

"What did my dad say?" I asked. We'd convened in my camper, climbed up to the bed compartment wedged over the wheel, even though it was pretty humid up there, to discuss in private.

"He said you have school," she said, wrinkling her nose.

She pressed her palm to the screen of the porthole window that looked out over my stepmom's garden and, outside, a bumblebee flew up close to it, then flitted away. She tapped the screen, but it didn't come back, not even to be near her.

"I do have school," I said. "For three more weeks."

"He said you have finals and if you don't take them you'll fail out or whatever and have to repeat the tenth grade." She flipped over to study me. "You lost your bangs."

"They grew out like a year ago," I said, but softly, because I wasn't mad. I was thinking that this was the moment she was seeing me after all this time without bangs, and I'd always been thinking about this moment, wondering if she'd like me this way.

"I'll cut them again for you if you want," she said.

She folded up my hair and held it above my forehead to create the illusion of bangs, that curtain over the eyes to hide things you don't want to have to see. The world closer in, less inhibiting, easier to deal—and that was all she had to do to make me miss them.

"When we get you home, that's the first thing we'll do," she said, "cut your bangs, then get veggie lo mein at the Wok 'n' Roll, and I'll give you all the baby corns like always. There's been no one to eat my baby corns. I've had to throw them away."

"I thought you were on a liquid diet. A cleanse."

"I wouldn't need to cleanse anything anymore if I got you back."

She let her hand fall, and my hair was the same length again. My eyes could see all. I made a face. I was thinking of driving into town, where the Wok 'n' Roll was, of who we might see—or not see. "We don't have to get lo mein . . ."

"What, you don't want Chinese? Do you want pancakes at Sweet Sue's?"

"That's a drive," I said. "You mean the place way out past the high school, right?"

She looked at me funny. "You don't remember Sweet

Sue's? The pancakes at Sweet Sue's? The strawberry-banana pancakes?"

I did—I remembered everything about the town and about Ruby. Or I used to. Maybe it was being so close to her now, but I felt like I'd been spun around and around with my head bagged in a mosquito net and then asked to give street directions.

"I remember . . ."

I was going to bring her up. London. That's who we were talking around, not haircuts and what to eat for dinner.

The girl who died.

The reason I was here in the first place.

London.

The girl whose name I couldn't make my mouth say.

So to Ruby, what I said was, "Yeah. Of course I remember Sweet Sue's."

We were talking like I was already coming back, like my dad hadn't said no. Like I had no dad and there was no such thing as no. Like I would be stuffing myself full of pancakes tomorrow.

"Also . . ." she said, eyes on me now, eyes in all my wrinkles and corners, eyes up inside my clothes, "something's different about you, and it's not just the hair."

I let her look, though I wondered what she was seeing.

"What size do you wear now, a B?" she asked.

"Um, yeah," I said, blushing. She was looking at my chest.

She smiled softly. "Well, you *are* only sixteen. Don't worry, that'll change."

I flipped over onto my stomach so she couldn't keep looking. But she was sitting up now, staring deep into me, her body between me and the ladder, the only way down.

"Don't tell me his name," she said. "I don't want to know."

"Whose name?"

"Don't say it. Just thinking about it makes me want to murder him. You cannot let me in the same room with him, Chlo. I can't be responsible for what I'd do."

"Ruby, what are you talking about?"

"I'm talking about the boy you lost your virginity to — don't say his name — who else did you think I meant? Is there someone else I have to kill on your behalf?"

I looked away. She looked away. We looked away together out the porthole and stayed like that for a long while.

"Why didn't you tell me?" she said at last.

"What, like in a text? 'Hi, I just slept with this semihot guy Jared from sixth-period study hall. TTYL'?"

"I told you not to say his name," she said. "I should absolutely not know his name."

"Oops," I said, though she sure knew I'd done it on purpose.

"*Semi*hot?" she said, with some small concern. "How semi?"

"Oh, you know. Cuter in the dark."

"Aren't they all?"

Then, quickly, before she could ask more questions, I added, "It was no big deal. What happened, I mean. I'm glad I got it over with."

She let out a breath. Clearly she was *not* glad, not one bit. And here would be the time to ask the questions big sisters were supposed to ask after a secret like this had been revealed—about protection, for instance, all the slimy stuff no one wants to talk about. Force herself to say the word *condoms*, to make sure we used one. Ask did he treat you all right? Ask how do you feel now, you okay? Say it'll be better next time. Next time it won't burn so much, next time you won't want to sock him in the eye for not going slow.

Big sisters had to do it, when the mothers weren't sober enough to string five words together and say it themselves.

But Ruby told me a story instead.

"My first time," she said, "was right on the edge of the water, on the rocks. I had on these little silver hoop earrings, like three in one ear, and when we were doing it they starting humming and my ear got really hot—like that time with the iron on the bed when you thought you unplugged it first and don't make that face it didn't hurt that bad really—and then the earrings were flying out of my ears, these shiny, silver whirling things high up over the water, they'd come totally alive and, wow, was it something."

"So you lost your earrings?"

"Yeah, they fell out. I guess I wasn't supposed to have them anymore. The whole thing sort of ruined the idea of earrings for me. I mean, you'll only lose them. Why bother wearing them at all?"

I wasn't sure what she was trying to say with this. Ruby's stories didn't have morals. They meant one thing in the light and one thing in the dark and another thing entirely when she was wearing sunglasses. If she was disappointed in me, for what I did in that Subaru, she wasn't showing it.

"This was at the reservoir?" I asked.

She ignored that. "I remember looking up and seeing these silver swirls in the sky, bright like stars, brighter even than the moon, which was full that night . . . well, almost. I bet that was them flying over the mountains—and what's on the other side, the big mall in Poughkeepsie?—and you could see them for miles and miles." She sighed. "That was the best part of the night."

"Who were you with?" I asked. Because she'd never told me.

"Some guy," she said. "So, *anyway*, your dad's all hung up on those final exams you have to take at school, and also, FYI, he called me irresponsible, and I said that's our drunk mother not me, and he said our mom's an alcoholic and it's a disease and we should not make fun of her because she has problems, and I said he's got no idea what kind of problems, and he said only over his dead body could you go back upstate with me, and I told him he didn't own you, and he said actually he did, that's what child custody is, and you're technically still a child until you're eighteen, and then I stuck my tongue out at him like this." She stopped talking, to demonstrate.

"You didn't!"

"Kidding. Well, only about the tongue."

"What else did he say?"

"He said I'm a bad influence and got you mixed up in drugs. I said you don't do drugs because I won't let you, and if he knew me at all he'd know that."

Now I rolled my eyes. She was right, though.

"Because if *anyone* knows how to look out for you, it's me. He has no idea what I'd do for you. No idea."

This was true; then again it wasn't. It was true because I wanted it true, made it so by stowing it in a picture frame on the wall of my mind where I reminded myself of things, the things I knew about Ruby, the things I knew about myself. One and the same, all hung on the selfsame wall. But it also wasn't true because I was here. She let me stay here in Pennsylvania, and it had taken her two years to come.

"If he says I can't go, I can't go . . ." I told her. "He's only remembering what happened to London."

I had finally said the name and I swear, for a second there, she stared blankly back at me as I had when she'd uttered the name Sweet Sue's. She just stared.

"London," I reminded her.

Nothing. Her stare was especially intense, like she was trying to shove a noise signal into my head—but I could think and hear just fine.

I tried again. "What happened . . . with London?"

She blinked, broke the stare, and said, "Oh, yeah. That."

"That's why he doesn't want me to live with you. Even for the summer."

"Hmmmph. What happened to that girl could never ever happen to you. Like I said, I wouldn't let it."

I'd turned away from her here, somehow, on that narrow bed stuffed up over the wheel, the compartment so small our four feet were hanging off the end. But she wasn't letting me stay turned away; she wasn't letting me not face her. She wanted me to look at her, to see her mouth as she spoke. She climbed over me, she rolled into me, she did a series of swift jujitsu moves on me that tangled me up in her arms and locked me to her, elbow-to-elbow, one bare foot held fast in the crook of my neck, and then, calmly, hardly even breathing heavy, she said:

"I wouldn't. Let it happen. To you."

She rolled away. Far enough away that I immediately wanted her back.

"I want to go home with you," I said, the words coming true the moment I said them. I didn't do everything she wanted, not every little thing. But I wanted to do this. "I want to," I repeated.

"I know," she said.

"I'm going."

"Not tonight. You'll have to sneak out. After finals. Whenever you're ready, when they're not looking—that's when you'll go."

"Like how?"

"I dunno," she joked. "Hijack a hot-air balloon?"

Ruby had a thing for heights—being up in them and looking down. She liked imagining herself soaring through the sky higher and higher until she was so high up she'd need a telescope to look back to ground.

Even so, she'd never been on an airplane. And there were no high-rises in our town, so she couldn't dangle out their windows to count the dots of cars and people below. She didn't bother to climb our tall, spindly pine trees, since that was an awkward feat to maneuver while wearing a dress.

The highest Ruby had ever been on this earth was Overlook Mountain, which at its summit showed off a bird's-eye view of our town and not much beyond that, since all the trees got in the way. She once wanted to rent a hot-air balloon to test out our town's clouds, though I told her that I was pretty sure, from science class, she wouldn't be able to poke donut holes through them like she hoped to. She wanted to be able to spy on everyone, she said, from the cloud cover, and shoot them with jets of rain when they misbehaved.

But we could go anywhere, I remember saying. If the hot-air balloon was ours for a whole day, imagine how far we could travel. We could make it to the ocean maybe, or up to sightsee the clouds over some cool northern state like Maine.

But Ruby didn't like to travel far—she needed to be able to see home, she said. She had to stick around, just in case.

She believed this wholeheartedly, which was why it was shocking to see her here, in Pennsylvania, untied and cut loose from her usual haunts upstate. And it also explained why she wanted to get home right away. With me.

"Be serious," I told her. "Please."

"Okay," she said. She took one last look up and I followed her gaze, like together we could cast our eyes skyward and see the way out of here—but mere inches above our heads was the camper's plastic pockmarked ceiling, and the camper itself had legs of cinder blocks, not wheels.

She dropped her eyes back down to me and let her mouth perk up into a smile. "Forget the balloon," she said. "You know . . . you could always take the bus."

"The bus? How much would that cost?"

She let the smile have her whole face. "Don't worry about that. You know the Trailways stops right on the Green."

Maybe she'd lost her grip on everyone all around her, maybe the Ruby I remembered wasn't the Ruby who was here now, but she had enough of an influence on me to make me sure. I would go. Balloon or bus or thumb out on the highway, I'd head home to her.

I didn't know then that she hadn't lost anything. Not me—and certainly not what she could do. It was only the physical distance. The farther she got from her blue mountains, down away from her green trees, the less she was herself. She couldn't do anything she wanted, not like she was used to, not while she was all the way out here.

Back home, though—that would be another story.

That night, my dad wouldn't budge, and my stepmom— not like we cared—backed him. On hearing the definitive decision, Ruby wouldn't set foot in the house again. But she didn't leave the state yet, either. She said she'd go when she was good and ready and how'd my dad like that?

All that happened that night was Ruby and I drove to the Wendy's, then to the KFC, because there isn't much in the way of dining options off Route 80 in Pennsylvania, and then we drove back to the camper to drink our milk shakes—we'd both ordered chocolate—plus spoon each other mouthfuls of mashed potatoes because we figured they were liquid enough to keep Ruby cleansed. We spent the night in the camper with the screens wide open, listening for mosquitoes instead of bees once the dark had fallen, and by morning she was gone: a wrinkle on the sheet and a long strand of hair, like I'd imagined her.

I wouldn't have believed she'd come at all if I didn't get this text:

look under yr pillow xo

And there, under my pillow, like how all those years ago she'd snatch and reward my teeth, she'd left probably every cent she'd had in her purse: six twenties, two fives, eleven singles, seven quarters, ten dimes, one nickel, and twenty-seven pennies, totaling up to $144.07. Not enough to rent a hot-air balloon, but more than enough for a bus ticket home.

CHAPTER FOUR

I WANTED

I wanted to skip the good-byes entirely. Skip all the hours of every night that came after, skip the entire three weeks.

Time sped up, calling me closer to Ruby, but it wouldn't run fast enough. Back in my dad's house, it felt like she'd never been there at all. She was a hazy vision in boots and jam-stained slip, guzzling down my bottle of juice. Only the wad of cash in my pocket let me know she'd come for real.

I wanted school to end so I could go. To skip the math final, the science final, the final count of all our sit-ups and pull-ups in gym.

I would have skipped the fight about my grades in the kitchen, definitely. The half-siblings—one boy, one girl—knocking on the door to my camper, asking why won't I come inside the house to eat. The moment Jared did or didn't call eventually and if I made like Ruby and tried not to care either way.

I'd skip the last night in the camper, propped up on cinder blocks, unable to sleep. Skip sneaking out over the fence the next morning.

Skip the longest bus ride of my life—please.

Skip all thoughts of London, or try to.

I would have, if I could have.

Far easier was avoiding thoughts of my mother, because who knew where she was spending her nights these days, and it's not like I felt like calling to tell her I was coming home.

I landed in the Port Authority terminal in New York City, to change buses. That meant I was less than three hours from Ruby.

I wanted to skip the layover. The woman taking a bath in the sink. The hours spent in the basement level of the bus depot and the pretzel vendor who tried to grope me. The free pretzel when I threatened to scream.

Then the Lincoln Tunnel, which cuts through the Hudson River to escape the city. Skip the worries of being trapped in that tunnel, the gush of relief at seeing the light at the end.

Skip the entirety of New Jersey.

The New York State Thruway at night even though that's the best time to drive it.

The familiar turn to exit 19.

The traffic circle, where Ruby once got pulled over and convinced the cop not to search her and then laughed maniacally when he let her go.

We were getting closer.

The bus turned onto the first highway that led toward town and passed the spot where Ruby blew a tire and got three guys to pull over and offer to fix it, though she ended up fixing it herself, while they watched, and then let them watch her drive away. The bus turned onto the second highway, where Ruby liked to ignore all signs noting speed limits and, sometimes, if there were no trucks coming, jammed the gas and raced with headlights dark, fingertips guiding the wheel.

The bus took the left turn toward town.

There was the tattoo shop where Ruby got her eyebrow pierced, then decided she didn't want her eyebrow pierced and instead got her nose pierced, then decided she really didn't want anything pierced, not even her ears.

Cumby's, open twenty-four hours a day. Even so, there was no point asking the bus to stop there, since Ruby's car wasn't parked out front.

The rows of storefronts, shuttered and dark, and how Ruby could walk into any one and come out with whatever thing she wanted on layaway, which to her meant getting to take it home with her and never bothering to come back and pay.

Soon, the bus was pulling up to the Village Green, the center of the town where I was born and where Ruby still lived. The bus doors were opening and I was climbing down the stairs with my bags and retrieving my suitcase. The bus doors were closing and I was left standing on the Green with my bags at my feet. The bus was pulling away.

It was a Saturday night, late June, and there was absolutely no one here.

I texted Ruby: **guess where i am**

No response.

I texted Ruby the answer anyway: **im here**

almost didnt survive bus ride

bus driver had rly small head. wondered if he cld even see road

drove us off bridge

I waited for some time, then tried again.

kidding abt bridge. u still live @ Millstream?

want me 2 go there? or u pick me up???

My phone was silent, not a beep or a buzz to let me know.

When I last lived in town, our mother had a place back behind WDST, the local radio station, but Ruby said the classic rock the deejays insisted on playing filled her head with near-total boredom, and had on occasion put her to sleep while standing, which was terribly dangerous, like when she was getting the mail at the curb and "Stairway to Heaven" came on *again*. So that's why she rented her own place on the opposite end of town, near the stream—that and the fact that she couldn't stand our mother. My school papers said I lived at my mom's, but all my things were at Ruby's. Or they had been.

The Millstream Apartments weren't far from the Green, but I had my bags and my suitcase and there was that hill.

So I waited for her to pick me up. She'd be here. She knew tonight was the night. It was her idea, after all, that I come home.

I sat on a prime bench in the center of the diamond that made up the Green and took it all in: these trees, that sidewalk, this place imprinted on every surface with thoughts of Ruby as if she'd gotten her greasy hands all over everything and trampled the lawn and dirtied up the benches with her muddy boots.

Only, it was too quiet. I'd never seen the Green empty in warm weather, not once, not in my life. On summer nights, there was always someone out: a random townie tripping too hard to operate a motor vehicle; some tie-dyed tourist who hitched here all the way from burning things up at Burning Man to camp in our shrubs; a few kids from the Catholic high school the next town over who never got invited to our parties but still came here hoping; or that guy Dov Everywhere who lived somewhere out in the woods, no one knew where. He took care of the town's stray dogs, collected sticks to walk with, and always gave fair warning when it was about to rain. He also barked for no reason and threw his sticks at cars, so you had to be careful on what night you caught him.

Not even Dov was there on the Green that night.

I would have thought time had stopped completely, leaving the town untouched since I'd left it—if the wind didn't snatch the stub of the bus ticket out of my hand and shoot it across the Green, plastering it against the window of the empty pizza place, then flip it back down the stairs to flutter and gasp at my feet.

The wind would have stopped, if time had. Time would have had to stop for Ruby not to come meet my bus. So where was she?

My suitcase rolled itself too fast down the hill that led to the Millstream, and I had to run to keep up. I knew where to find Ruby's key, as she tended to use the one hidden on the windowsill more than the one on her key ring, but when I got the door to her apartment open, I saw an empty room with takeout menus for the Wok 'n' Roll and the Indian buffet scattered over the floor. The windows had no curtains and the sink had no dirty dishes. There was a mattress left behind in her bedroom, but it had no sheets.

It was like a home abandoned before the floodgates opened and the water came spilling in. She'd gone away and wasn't coming back. She'd gone away, and she didn't tell me where to find her.

I saw the few things she must have forgotten: an orange zip-up sweater bunched up on a hook behind a door; a toe ring in the sink drain; a book of matches blotted with the dark pressed smudge of her lips, one full row of matches left to burn.

Dusky impressions on the carpet showed where her furniture had been. This here a table, that there a couch. The air was stale, unbreathed. The refrigerator had been pulled from the wall, fat black cord dangling. Inside the fridge was a perfectly preserved plum, petrified around the marks of her teeth to show where she'd taken one small bite, then let the plum be, like it might get sweeter in a day or two. She often sampled fruit this way, even in the supermarket.

"Ruby?" I called out. Her name echoed through the empty apartment, bouncing back at me from the ceiling, and when I looked up, I saw her scrawl:

Ruby

Like anyone could forget she'd once lived here.

That's when I heard the screech of tires outside. A car had come to a sharp stop in the parking lot below. I stepped to the edge of the second-floor walkway outside Ruby's apartment, my heart beating fast, but the car wasn't an old rusted Buick on its last legs; it wasn't even white and she wasn't in it. Then I recognized the person lurching out of the driver's side door bellowing my name.

The guy was one of Ruby's ex-boyfriends, and there

were many. This one, Pete, had shaggy hair, a scraggly chin, and wore a pitted Pixies T-shirt so old I could see through to the sweat shining on his skin. Years ago, Ruby had dumped him as she'd dumped all the others, but he never did seem to get the hint and go away.

"She said to look for you here if you weren't on the Green," he was saying. "She said to drop you at the party and she'll meet you there."

"Ruby sent *you*?" Still, I started down the stairs.

"Thanks," he said once I reached him, "thanks a lot."

"Why didn't she come get me herself?"

He waved that question away as if it were a puzzle he sure couldn't answer, one of those mysteries of the universe that scientists chase after their whole lives, like the Big Bang and if it really happened, or life on Mars.

"You know Ruby," he said. "C'mon, get in the car. The party's way out at the quarry and we'd better get there before the beer runs out."

I did know Ruby. I knew her better than anyone could possibly know her, the way no guy could come close to knowing, no matter how long he was with her and what, behind closed doors, he thought they did.

I'd seen her in ways no one else had. I'd heard the names she called every boy she'd been with, names that would haunt them forever if they knew. I'd seen her happy. I'd seen her sad. I'd seen her when we both hennaed our hair, the mud mixed with paprika and egg yolk that dripped down her scalp and turned her ears orange. I'd seen her laugh so hard she peed a little. I'd seen her so mad, she punched a hole in the wall. And I'd seen her after, her knuckles scratched and swollen, but her eyes clear and wide open, when she said it didn't matter—nothing mattered but her and me.

Yes, I knew Ruby. But even I couldn't understand why she wasn't there to meet me and had sent some random ex in a sweaty nineties T-shirt instead.

It wasn't until I got closer that I realized someone else was inside the car, sitting shotgun in the shadows.

"You remember Owen," Pete said, motioning at his younger brother. "Aren't you guys in the same grade?"

"Not exactly," I said, eyeing his silhouette. "He's a year ahead of me."

"Same difference," Pete said.

I felt it as soon as I piled my bags in the backseat and scooted over to sit behind Owen. That intense craving to be in his orbit, close enough just to see him—even around a corner would do. I felt the hope crawling under my skin. The thrumming pulse. The hot stars crowding my eyes and tightening in a lasso around my head.

Oh, Ruby.

Did she have anything to do with this?

She must have. She'd sent Owen's brother, Pete, to pick me up, figuring there was a good chance Owen would be in the car. Though I'd been careful not to say it out loud, how I felt about him, I'm guessing she'd always known. No secrets could be kept from her, not anymore, is this what she was telling me?

She had to know I'd be inches away from him for however long it took to drive to the quarry. That maybe I'd have to talk to him, that maybe he'd talk back. I could see the shape of her smile hovering in the seat beside me, so very smug and amused.

Only, there was something Ruby didn't know: Not even she could make Owen like me.

"O," Pete said, "you remember Chloe. *Ruby's* sister."

Owen took a second to respond. He let out a breath, which I didn't know how to read—a sigh of annoyance or a grunt of acknowledgment; it could have gone either way—and then with great effort he turned a millimeter in his seat and said a word to me, just one, "Hey."

He didn't turn any more than that, so my only view was a partial profile and the back of his neck. In the time I'd been gone, he must have given up on another mohawk and let it grow in again, because his hair was sticking up, longer in some spots than others. It was too dark to see what color he'd dyed it now.

"Hey," I said back. Then his brother gave the car some gas and pulled out of the parking lot.

Ruby would want a story of the drive to the quarry;

she'd expect it. What she'd want was something fantastic: an action-adventure moment to get our hearts pounding.

I had to imagine one, there in the car. Imagine something worth telling.

First, we'd have to get Pete out of the picture—a given. Ruby wouldn't want Pete in the story, so maybe we could stop for gas and he'd take forever to pump it. Or we'd be driving along like normal, but then we'd hit this patch of road where the sky opens up and this shadowy, flapping thing we wouldn't know what to call would swoop down and pull him out by the throat, and Owen would have no choice but to take the wheel. Something impossible like that, pure fiction. Something to hold Ruby's attention.

Pete would be long gone, who cares how, and I'd slip up into the passenger seat next to Owen, the only things between us the Big Gulp in the cup holder and the stick shift.

It would be when we were speeding down Route 212 that Owen would look at me, like really *look at me*, for the first time since forever. Maybe he'd remember how he ignored me in school, and he'd feel bad about that.

I knew I shouldn't care. I was like my sister, wasn't I? I was made of her snide comments about what all the boys were after and her brick walls built up and up to keep the boys out. I should act the way Ruby did with a boy she no longer wanted, like her heart had crawled up inside her rib cage to die, and you'd never know it was up there, as it had climbed so far in, you couldn't even smell it rotting.

But I didn't want that.

If this were a story I was telling, if it were *my* story and Ruby let me tell it, Owen would turn in his seat and he'd say—

A buzz sounded. I looked down to find my phone blinking.

didnt forget you chlo. just wanted u 2 come see

See what? I was in the backseat and Pete was still driving and all I saw of Owen was the back of his head.

When we reached the quarry, Owen leaped out as soon as we stopped. A jumble of cars crowded the gravel lot out of sight of the main road, but Ruby's big white Buick wasn't among them. Knowing her, she'd volunteered some poor sap for the position of designated driver and secured us a ride.

There was smoke in the air—faint, I could feel it in my throat—and a flicker of warm light filtering out through the woods. A bonfire.

I left my bags in Pete's car. I had to: The party was deep in the quarry and the only way to reach it was down a freshly trampled path through the trees. Pete led the way, with me close behind, and then Owen. I stopped short once, and Owen, who was nearer than I expected, stepped on the back of my shoe.

"Sorry," he mumbled.

"Sorry," I mumbled back.

And in the night beneath oaks and pines and other trees I'd never bothered learning names for, he and I were closer than we'd ever gotten, close for three, four, five countable seconds, until he stepped away and went slipping past and his arm brushed my arm and he smelled like cigarettes and I wished he smelled different and he was gone.

I'd lost Pete, so I walked the rest of the path with my arms out, feeling my way until the trees broke open. My feet found gravel and the noise hit and I started sliding down the declining slope toward the bottom. It was a pit, a cavernous hole filled with people I used to know. Or people who knew Ruby, so they had to at least pretend they knew me because I was her sister. Here, back home, that's the first thing I was.

Ruby was near—somewhere. I could sense her in the dark.

I reached the bottom of the pit and looked up at the other slope, a gleaming red crest in the night to show where the bonfire was burning, and where I'd find her.

Waiting for me.

Waiting to hear about the cold shoulder I gave the state of Pennsylvania. She'd ask, I'd tell, we'd be in sync again, and then the summer would get started, picking up where we left off two years ago, on a warm night like this one, before it all went so wrong.

I was almost up to the top of the other slope when someone stopped me. A hand drawn closed around my ankle. Pulling me down.

"Chloe! I heard you'd be here!" some girl said. She was stretched out on the gravel slope with a few of her friends, and I guess we knew each other, or used to. Then other girls were there, and guys, and remember-this and remember-that, and was I living with Ruby now? and really? and wow and, hey, did I want a beer?

My pocket buzzed. Ruby again. **ur here!**

She was somewhere in the dark—she could see me, but I couldn't see her.

Then another text: **im SO thirsty**

And one more: **meet me up at the keg xo**

Which was strange, because she didn't exactly like beer—it fizzed. And maybe this should have been my first clue that she'd set me up. I should have known meeting her here had nothing to do with some party, because Ruby didn't care about showing her face at parties, even her own.

But all I could focus on was finding that keg in the dark, and, as I did, climbing over the people sprawled out on the slopes, trying not to step on anyone's hand.

It was up at the keg that my eyes finally adjusted to the

low light. I could see where we were: either an old construction site or a place where gravel was stored. There was a crane in the distance, blocked off by stacks of concrete slabs. The air was thick with dust, brushed up by all these trespassing feet. The trees, they were everywhere around us, and the mountains, they were out there in the dark, pale imitations of the ones found in day.

I could see clearly, and then I couldn't.

It felt like I was looking up at the surface from deep below. I was down under, and getting sucked deeper, covered in bubbles from all my thrashing, lungs blowing up tight with unbreathed air. So familiar, like I'd been there before.

Time pooled around me, spun me in a washer, jerked to a stop. And I was back here, as if it hadn't happened. I was here.

And so, it turned out, was *she*.

"Hey, Chloe," she said. "Long time no see."

She was at the nozzle, controlling the flow of beer. I could see her hand holding the plastic cup she was filling, red plastic, the foam rising, white foam, the cup tilting to sift the foam, the hand holding it, the five fingernails on her hand.

"Take it," she said, passing me the red cup. "There's not too much left in the keg anyway, so you may as well or the guys'll hog it."

She wasn't who I expected to find—not now, not here.

But I didn't say that. I took the cup, put the cup to my lips. Opened the lips. Held out the tongue. Tipped the cup back. Took one swallow.

"See you later?" she said.

"Yeah." That's all I said, all I could say. Because the girl who was talking to me wasn't a girl I thought I'd ever be talking to again.

Was I even at this quarry? Standing at the edge of this gravel pit? Holding this cup?

I'd turned away, taken a step in some direction, because I wasn't beside the keg anymore and now two familiar arms were around me, a familiar voice in my ear.

"Chlo! You're here!" Ruby cried. She pulled back to take a look at me.

I must have been making a peculiar face because she laughed and snatched the cup from my hands and poured out the rest of my beer. "What are you doing!" she said. "You *hate* fizz."

Ruby looked just as I remembered, as she had three weeks ago, but she was a stranger to me all of a sudden, red-eyed in the firelight, weird.

"That's—" I choked out. "That's—" I pointed toward the keg. I couldn't get control of my mouth to make it say the name.

"Pabst," she said. "Tastes like puke before you've puked it, I know. Don't worry, you don't have to drink it."

"No, no. Not the beer."

"Oh no, that bus ride was worse than you texted, wasn't it? Did you really almost crash? Did you get lost on the thruway? Did you hit like a whole herd of deer?"

She was distracting me, trying to get me to tell a story about something else when the story was right here.

London.

But that couldn't be London filling another cup of beer from the keg, I was positive. Not London talking to that boy. Not London with the stripes on her sleeves, a hand up to her mouth to keep from laughing. Not her hair chopped more uneven than I remembered, bleached closer to white than before, though still showing off both her ears. No. Not London's laugh, though it sounded like hers, lifting up over the bonfire and echoing through the quarry. The dark night, the party noises were tricking me, the fire was making me see things, I was the one who'd gone all weird.

Then London looked up and met my gaze. She smiled. And it was her — it couldn't have been anyone else.

London, who was buried close to two years ago, was somehow still alive and standing right here.

I looked to Ruby to get her confirmation, but we weren't alone anymore, so we couldn't speak freely. "Petey," she was saying, "watch it with the hand."

Pete was there with us. He was shaking out his hand, like he'd been slapped, saying, "A guy's gotta try, right?"

Ruby glared at him. "No," she said, "not twice. Not with me."

"But, Ruby," I said, and I wasn't talking about Pete and where he put his hands.

She knew. She was looking at the keg, too. Then loudly, for Pete's benefit, she said to me, "You know that girl London from school, right?" Her mouth said those words, but her eyes said something far different. Her eyes had the red lights in them. Her eyes were telling me to not say what I wanted to say.

I had the reins of the story then; I could have turned it in any direction I wanted. Back down to the bottom of the pit, or straight-flash into the bonfire, or up into the tallest of the tall trees. The story you choose to tell isn't always the story you believe. So, out loud, I said, "Yeah, I know her from school."

And Ruby smiled, placated, and closed her eyes. All at once she seemed tired, a little wobbly on her feet like she had to sit down. Pete reached an arm out, even if he'd get slapped for it, as if she might need to lean on him. But she didn't. Quickly she shook her head and opened her eyes to show the green I remembered, the green she was known for, her bright and searing green, and said, "That's what I thought. You had French class together, right?"

"Right," I said, my voice faint.

"So you want a beer?" Pete said.

"Chloe doesn't drink," Ruby snapped, silencing him.

She took a step closer to me. Her arms were around me again, her elbows and wrists and fingers slung tight at my neck to keep me with her. She could have put a hand over my mouth, but she didn't have to; I wouldn't say a thing.

She hugged me close and I swear she breathed these words into my hair as she did, "See, Chlo? It's just like it used to be."

And—suddenly, without any explanation or mystery needing to be unraveled from any undiscovered corner of the universe—it simply was, and I had no idea how.

Because, look: There was London, like things were back the way they'd been before. Like it had never even happened. Just like Ruby said.

CHAPTER FIVE

LONDON DIDN'T KNOW

L ondon didn't know she was supposed to be dead. Anyone who did wouldn't be laughing so loudly, opening
her mouth that wide and letting out those sounds. A girl in
her grave wouldn't knock back that Pabst like she didn't
care how it tasted, then smile so sloppy and let the beer
dribble down her chin.

She looked happy, in a way I didn't remember her. She
was near the fire with three other girls. She glowed, though
I guess it was from the flames, because the girls with her
glowed, too. We all did. She was alive, as alive as me.

"I think I—" I started to say. "I think she—" But Ruby
wouldn't let me finish.

"You thirsty?" she asked me, which meant we would discuss all of this later. "I'll get you some water. Petey, keep an
eye on my baby sister and don't you let her go anywhere
near that fire, all right?"

He nodded, and Ruby slipped away. There she was,

crossing the gravel in boots that skimmed her shins, and then there she wasn't, sundress swallowed by the night.

Just as I remembered her.

"I need to sit down," I said.

Pete hopped to attention and led me over to a slope of gravel. Agreeing to take care of me wasn't entirely selfless. I could see how he was counting on some reward Ruby would never be game to give him, picturing that reward as he helped me to the ground, rewinding and playing it back as he reached out to pat my head, caught in freeze-frame as he missed my head by a mile and clocked me in the chest instead.

There went his reward.

"Crap," he said. "Did I punch you in the tit?"

He had, but I wasn't about to acknowledge that. "Don't worry about it," I heard my mouth say. My eyes were still on the bonfire.

"You okay? You sure? You're not hurt?" His voice was dripping sap and concern like he'd just run over my puppy, but this concern was really only for Ruby.

Ruby, who'd kill him dead if she thought he'd hurt me, no matter what history they shared. Ruby, who'd duct-tape him to a tree with his pants to his ankles and leave him there through the night to let the wood creatures at him. The raccoons and skunks, the black bears that climbed these mountains, the animals that came out only at night with their sharp claws and rabies-soaked teeth.

Pete must have known all that. But I bet he also figured if he could get me on his side, he'd have a real shot with Ruby. That's how it used to be: The way to Ruby's heart, they'd all assumed, was through her little sister—it's how I got my very first iPod. But I never did put in a good word for any of her suitors. It wouldn't have worked. Ruby's heart had room inside for me only.

I realized Pete was watching me. "You look so much like her . . . with your hair like that," he said. This was something he shouldn't say, we both knew it, so he changed the subject, fast. "Jonah doesn't deserve her, y'know? How'd *he* get so lucky?"

This was the first I'd heard of any Jonah. Apparently, my sister had a new boyfriend.

Pete kept talking, all dejected. "He just moves to town and gets my girl and—" He stopped short. "Don't tell her I called her 'my' girl. I know she's not."

I shrugged. "She's not anyone's."

Pete didn't matter. My eyes kept going back to the fire—to the girl beside the fire—to London.

"You see her?" I asked him. Ruby wasn't there to stop me. She'd walked away.

The fire itself was made of tree branches, built up to a pyramid with a hot burning center, arranged for inevitable collapse. A bunch of people hung around watching. I recognized some kids from when I last lived in town, the summer after eighth grade and before the start of high school.

Names came from under water, bobbing up one after the other: Damien something. Asha something. Vanessa something. Allison and Alison; Kate and Cate. And, of course, London Hayes.

My finger went to her, pointing so I didn't have to let her name touch my tongue. "There," I said, "there in the stripes."

Her stripes were black-and-white, horizontal. Prison stripes.

He craned his neck to find them. "That chick London? Yeah . . . what about her?"

"You see her?"

"Uh, yeah."

"You *see* her? Tell me you see her."

"Dude, I said I see her. She's right there."

Pete was still on his feet. High up above me was his talking head. Above that were the mounds of gravel, like mountains of glittering black-eyed coal. And above them the real mountains, the Catskills, unreadable and flickering in the night like static on a busted TV.

This place had been a construction site. People had planned to build something here, in this patch of gravel where I was sitting; blueprints made and rooms measured, roads mapped out. I felt it around me in the night, what could have been. The walls and floors and windows taking shape, the roof closing in, the automatic doors automatically closing.

Maybe this was meant to be a superstore, a Target. Or a hotel, a Radisson.

In some other time line, the one where London kept to her coffin, this place existed. If I concentrated on it, I could feel the crush of feet on me, the people in that other reality walking on this spot where I now sat, never guessing how close they'd come to being nothing. A woman digging her heels into my liver. Kids skating the asphalt, landing tricks off the curbs. A man wheeling his suitcase over my ribs. Their missed lives thrown in the incinerator so I could have mine.

Pete leaned down closer to me. He was going to say something, but I couldn't concentrate on what.

In the distance, laughter. In the distance, music. In the distance, fire and light and everything I'd left behind when I took off for Pennsylvania. I could go toward the light and the laughter and the music—I could find Ruby, and I'd be fine. But if I turned around and saw London still there, what then?

Maybe she was about to disintegrate. Maybe I'd count to ten and look over at the fire and witness the air cyclone her to mist. I'd blink and see tree trunks straight through the solid space that had been her bones.

Because girls can't come back to life. Not here and not anywhere. Any second now we'd see—

Pete was a breath away from me now, his clammy hand grabbing on to my knee. He gave an awkward shake to my knee and said, "Seriously, kid, you all right?"

"You're asking for it, Pete," said a voice. A girl's voice. As she stepped toward us, the light from the fire made more stripes blaze up all over her skin. "You know that's *Ruby's* sister, right?" London said. Then she added, "So how's it going, Chloe?"

I didn't answer. When a dead girl says your name it's shocking. A brick thrown at you, a brick through your bedroom window.

The light was behind her, hiding her face. "You need some help getting up?" she asked. She put an arm out, dangling one of her two hands before my face. The hand was so close, I could see all five fingernails. Even in the dark I could see them.

She locked her eyes on mine. (The whites of her eyes staring up at the half moon.)

She cracked a smile. (Her lips drained of color.)

I looked away. "Don't touch me," I heard myself say. "I'm fine."

"You don't look fine," she said.

And you don't look dead, I didn't say.

"Just let her help you," Pete said. So he could see and hear her, too.

The hand was still there, the fingers waggling. Her nails

were painted a few different colors. Three were black, as they would be if left to rot in the ground. But three were magenta. Others were yellow. It was all so random.

I grabbed the hand. Her warm, living hand. It grabbed mine back. As it did a hiss of vapor didn't pass through my flesh to reveal I'd grabbed on to nothing; I didn't fall facefirst into gravel and lie there spitting up rocks. I was definitely touching something. And this something used its weight to get me up.

She was no ghost. She could be seen by others. She could be touched; she spoke full sentences; her breath reeked, but not with maggots, with plain bad beer. There was no smoke, no mirrors. If Ruby had made this happen, it was really and truly happening, not just to me but to every single person here.

Ruby reappeared once I got to my feet. She was there for me to lean on, there as if she'd been at my side all along and always would be. The wind played with her hair, making it sway over her bare shoulders. Her lips were painted her color—without a smudge. Her eyes borrowed stars from the sky, or seemed to. Even the fireflies came to lend her their glow, blinking sweet nothings all around her.

I wasn't the only one staring.

"Hey there," Pete said.

"Hi, Ruby," London said meekly, eyes flicking to me as if she didn't think she'd be allowed to tell my sister hi.

Ruby ignored them both. "That took forever," she said. "I'm so sorry, Chlo." She held out a water bottle for me and watched carefully as I twisted off the cap and took a long swallow.

When I was done, Ruby grabbed my hand in hers, so everyone could see. Then she asked, projecting as if she were wearing a wire hidden inside her dress, "London, how *are* you? My sister was wondering. Tell her. Tell her how you are."

I was? But I was. Ruby knew I was wondering that and way more.

London gave Ruby an odd look. Then she turned the same look on me, seeing as I could have asked her how she was myself, and said, "I'm fine, thanks." Her words wavered, like she wasn't sure. Like Ruby could say no, she wasn't fine, and then she'd have to change her answer.

"See?" my sister said to me. To London, her voice shifted and she said, "What are you doing over here with Chloe? What happened to the keg?"

"It's empty," London said.

"Damn," Pete could be heard muttering behind us.

London was shifting from foot to foot. "I should go back to the fire," she said, taking a step toward her friends.

"*Should* you?" Ruby asked this question with great concentration. Her gaze needled into two thin points, aimed with precision at London.

I saw the stabs. Saw how London flinched and then in one last-ditch effort to defend herself squeaked out, "I told them I'd be right back."

"You did?" Ruby said. She had control of the conversation, tossing it high, bouncing it back and forth between her palms.

London's forehead creased up. She put a hand to her head, thinking. The fireflies seemed drunk, glowing haphazardly in downward spirals toward the ground.

"I don't know," London said at last, her voice faint. "I don't remember."

Something was going on here, something between this girl who'd come back to life and my sister, who'd maybe possibly had a hand in it, and I couldn't figure out what.

"Hey," Pete called out, dumb to the world as usual, "is everyone high but me?"

Ruby tore her eyes from London. "Yes," she said, "everyone but you."

Pete looked down at his feet, crushed. It was so easy to hurt him.

"Oh, Petey," Ruby said, softening, "c'mere." She pulled him into a hug for a few lingering seconds. When she pushed him away, he seemed placated, so caught up in the moment and in her that I thought he might keel over—and then she did him one better.

"I have one hit left," she told him sweetly. "And I'm

warning you, Pete—Petey, look at me so I can talk to you—
I'm warning you . . . you've never had anything like this.
You might not know where you are when you come out of
it. You might lose your head."

She had him. "You don't want it?" he said. "You sure?"

She nodded.

Pete's eyes widened in anticipation as she slipped a hand
into one of the small pockets sewn at the hips of her sundress. The pockets were triangular, meant for decoration.
They could hold maybe a stick of gum if it was folded in
half, or one key, if it was a small key for a small lock. But
she took her time rummaging through that pocket as if it
sunk deep down the length of her leg.

Then she pulled out her hand, keeping the treasure hidden from sight in a closed fist. "I guess you can have it," she
told Pete.

"Awesome," Pete said, though as far as he knew it was a
pill of lint.

Ruby pulled the fist close to her ribs as if considering
keeping whatever it was for herself. But then she smiled.

"All right, Pete. Here you go."

He opened his mouth and dangled a flabby pink tongue.
Ruby, ever so careful not to touch the tongue, dropped the
pill onto it and told him to close his mouth. He did, and
swallowed. Then he hacked up lung for a minute and swallowed some more.

He was so trusting, so simple when it came to my sister. He'd do whatever she wanted, always had. Pete was the only one here acting like himself.

"Tastes sort of . . . chalky," he said once he got it down. "What was that?"

"You'll see," Ruby chimed out. "Go over there, Petey" — she was pointing at a rusted bulldozer parked away from the fire, so far off that the flickering light barely reached — "put your head back and close your eyes. Wait a while. Think happy thoughts. Open your eyes. Then you'll see."

"Sweet," Pete said, and stumbled off into the dark to follow her instructions.

Ruby sighed. "Sometimes I have to distract him."

I motioned at the bulldozer. "Think he'll be all right?"

"Do we care?" Ruby said.

"No," I admitted. "Not really. But what'd you give him?"

She pulled it out of her tiny pocket: the leftover rind from a roll of foil-wrapped Tums. "For desperate situations," she said, "and dire emergencies."

And we laughed, knowing Pete was exiled at the bulldozer, eyes sealed shut, waiting for a thrill ride he wouldn't get on any antacid. Laughed, seeing the deep night filled with fireflies and fire smoke. Knowing it was our night, and I was back now where I belonged, we laughed and kept laughing.

I didn't know why I was laughing, but I couldn't stop.

We laughed at everyone down in the gravel pit. Laughed that the keg was already empty. Laughed at the whole show Ruby had arranged for my first night home. Laughed the way we used to, for no reason and every possible reason, Ruby and me.

It was here that I realized someone else was still with us, and she wasn't making a sound. London wasn't laughing or even smiling, but she drifted at the edge of our small circle, like she wanted us to make some room so she could come in.

She was the hot center spot in a lightbulb; when looked at directly, she burned. And even when I turned away, I couldn't not-see her. She was etched onto the backs of my eyelids, there undeniably if I could face it or not.

Ruby was talking to her, asking if she was tired, asking if she wanted to go home.

And all at once London was yawning, as if on command, lifting a hand to cover her gaping mouth. "What time is it?" she mumbled.

"Late," Ruby said. "Really, really late." She said this without checking the time on her cell phone. In reality, I think it was only ten o'clock. It was like she wanted London to leave and, simply by wanting it, she was well on the way to making it occur.

London's eyes drooped closed. I wondered what would happen if she went to sleep right here, in the gravel at our feet, if she'd ever wake again. Maybe only one of us was dreaming, and the one who got to wake up would see the truth come morning.

"You should go home then," I told London, my eyes on the toes poking out of her sandals instead of on her face, "if you're so tired, I mean."

"I . . . I will."

The night shut up for a beat. The fire stopped its crackling. The kids beside it stopped talking. The wind stopped spitting up gravel and howling at the trees. You heard ground crunch under your shoes if you couldn't keep your feet from moving, but other than that you heard nothing. Then, breaking up the absolute stillness, you heard a breath in and a breath out. You heard *her*.

London, alive and breathing: Ruby's inexplicable gift to me.

"Lon," Ruby said, "don't worry. We'll drive you home."

My sister cast her eyes out at the rest of the party, as if testing to see if it was still worthy. I did, too, trying to see what she did. But then my gaze went somewhere else. It fell off track of hers and dropped to rest elsewhere.

She wasn't looking across the way at the figure in the dark, but I was. I found him there without searching. She scanned past where he was standing with his friends, so she didn't notice, either, how his head turned in response to mine, how our eyes met, somehow leaping the distance, how for some reason, with the length of two train cars between us, he was acknowledging my existence for real for the first time that night.

At least, that's what it felt like. I was too far away to be sure.

All the guys in the distance, girls, too, had a clear awareness of Ruby, touching her legs and back and mouth and the plunging scoop at her neck with their eyes at random moments, as if they couldn't help it. Wherever they were, whatever they were doing, they checked back on her, to see where she was and what she was doing. Owen, though, treated her like a black censored box over the screen, impossible to see past so he'd just ignore it. She was standing at my side and I swear he was looking at me.

No one showed much interest in London. I couldn't decide what was stranger.

Then Ruby'd had enough and told me so with the purse of her lips and one quick, dismissive shake of her head. This party could last all night and be the talk of the summer. It could have—until Ruby decided she didn't care anymore.

She turned her back on it and as she did I saw how dull it really was. The drained keg. The fire with the black, hissing smoke. The gravel dust. The kids sitting in dirt.

This party was done. We came, we saw and were seen, and now we'd go.

Only, not alone. It seemed we were taking London with us.

CHAPTER SIX

RUBY LED US

Ruby led us away from the party. Her hand was in mine, and she was pulling me toward the trees. Her other hand had taken hold of London's striped elbow, but only to steer her in our direction. Once we reached the path, she let go and had London follow us, handless, away from all her friends.

We didn't say any good-byes. We simply ditched the party and raced through the woods that skirted the quarry, Ruby and I never once losing our grip on the other, not tripping or slamming into gaping branches or getting a shot of firefly to the eye. It was just the two of us again, except for the girl trailing a few feet behind.

We reached the cars in no time. And in as little time, Ruby was opening the driver's side door of Pete's car, since he hadn't bothered to lock it, and telling us to make ourselves comfortable. My bags and suitcase were where I'd left them in the backseat.

"Where's your car?" I asked Ruby.

"I left it at the house." When she said that—the house—
it stuck out at me, as we'd never lived in a whole house
before. This house was simply one more thing, along with
the girl who'd climbed into the seat behind me, that was
different this summer.

I took shotgun, my reserved seat in Ruby's car, no matter who was riding with us or whose car it actually was. In a
flash the engine was on, and I turned to her, shocked. "Did
you hot-wire the car?"

She eyed me oddly, as if I'd chosen the wrong thing to be
so surprised about. "I'm no criminal mastermind," she said.
"I swiped Pete's keys."

She peeled out, punching the gas so we practically skidded sideways through the knot of parked cars. The way out
was downhill, sheets of gravel cascading behind us as the
tires spun, and the way she drove was with abandon, like
it used to be when she steered another car, during another
summer, taking charge of this same road.

Ruby adored night-driving. She loved letting the wind
have our hair, no matter how ratted and tangled it got after,
often breaking off our brush bristles, and she loved running
every red light she could find. Sometimes, back when I was
little and before she'd technically taken the test to secure
her license, she'd wake me in the middle of the night and
carry me to our mother's car to go driving.

The thing is, we never went anywhere special. For all

the hours spent driving, we could have made it down to the city and back—we heard Times Square stays lit up all through the night, unlike our town, which mostly closed up shop by seven o'clock—but Ruby was happy simply driving the rounds of our village. She'd take us as far as the wooded outskirts, loving narrow, twisting roads and steep mountain passes, speeding the bridges across the reservoir, then cutting swift U-turns to speed right back, but that was as far as she'd go. There was a point on the thruway she didn't like passing. There was a line only she knew about that she considered too far.

The road we were on tonight was a road we'd driven often. If I shoved my head face-out into the wind—drinking in the distance as she tested the limits of the speedometer, letting the wind tear up my eyes, those tears drying before they hit my cheeks—I could be nine again. Or eleven. Or even fourteen.

Except I wasn't.

Except something hovered in the car with us, chilled and unspoken. This summer wanted to be like all the others, but it was another thing entirely and no amount of wind in my face could cover that up.

I peeked back at London every mile or so, noticing things about her that I never did the first time she was alive:

How long her arms were, so long she must have been taller than I remembered, or else she grew.

How she twitched in her seat, unable to stay still.

How when she drifted off, resting her cheek on my suit-case, she drooled, and how innocent she looked as she did it.

"Is she, y'know . . . okay?" I asked. There was no word for what she really was. I couldn't fathom a way to ask it.

Ruby clucked her tongue. "She's as can be expected, I guess. I mean, how do you think you'd be if you came back from—" She cut herself off with a tight glance at the rear-view. "She's fine."

"Do you think—"

"Yes, I think we should stop and get lo mein after we drop her off," Ruby said, as much to herself as to me. "A big family-size tub, one set of chopsticks for me and one fork for you. They always used to forget the fork. Only . . . the Wok 'n' Roll won't be open so late, will it?" She glanced at me.

"I don't remember what time it closes."

"We'll talk about lo mein later, Chlo," she said now, as if I was the one who'd brought it up. "I don't want her getting any ideas."

"She's sleeping," I said. "Look at her. She totally passed out."

"You can still hear when you're sleeping. Sleep-walls are thin, so voices seep in, like how before you were born I talked to you up against Mom's stomach, told you who I was so you'd know me. Every day I did that. And then when you came out you loved me more than you loved her."

"But I don't remember any of that."

"Some deep-down part of you does."

London twitched some more as I watched her, like my eyes held little pointy pins and I kept sticking her with them. Then when she sat up and met my gaze I wondered if she'd been listening the whole time.

"Are you feeling okay?" I asked London. "Did you drink too much?"

"She's fine, like I told you," my sister said for her. "Just leave her be."

We were heading, I thought, straight into the center of town, and then to wherever it was that London lived, but Ruby veered a sharp left over the footbridge and headed a way I didn't expect.

"Where do you live, London?" I asked.

"I don't, I . . . It's, um . . ." She trailed off. Was she so drunk she didn't even recall how to find her own house?

"I know where to take her," Ruby said. She was acting so protective of the girl, like we had to tiptoe around her now, though just before this Ruby had been all about taking care of me.

We'd been driving for a short while when Ruby stopped the car, not near any house that I could see but on a darkened stretch of road running alongside a thick embankment of tangled trees. I knew where we were, but I wasn't about to acknowledge it out loud.

London seemed to live not too far from the place where she died. It was the reservoir that would be found if you pushed through that thicket of trees and went running. Did she have an inkling of this? Did she remember?

Ruby had turned in her seat to face London. "Here good?" she asked.

London opened her mouth and then closed it. Maybe she did have an inkling. Maybe she remembered it all and didn't know if I did.

"I said do you want to get out here?" Ruby repeated.

"Yeah, okay," London said. She drew a curtain over her face that showed me nothing. "I can walk from here."

Something unspoken was hovering between them, but before I could ask what was going on, London shuffled out of the backseat and the door behind me was swinging open and then smacking shut. London stood for a moment on the asphalt, wavering there like she wasn't sure which way was home. One of her feet was bare, as if by crawling out so quickly she'd lost a sandal and didn't feel like going back in to scoop it out.

I turned to my sister. "We shouldn't drive her all the way home?"

"Nah," she said. "She wants to walk. It's not far."

London nodded and echoed that. "It's not far. It's just over there." She pointed into the black night and maybe there was a driveway; I couldn't see beyond where she was standing. Maybe she liked being dropped off in the middle of the road so she wouldn't disturb her parents.

"But your shoe," I called to her.

She shrugged. Then she started walking.

I was mystified by her. Part of me was waiting for her to dissipate into a puff of smoke and leave behind a sandal and a striped shirt and whatever coins and junk she had in her pockets and then for my sister to run over her remains in the road.

But Ruby only waved and drove off.

"You wouldn't let me walk home with one shoe," I said.

"You're you," she said. "She's not."

I twisted around in my seat to look after her, but the dark had swallowed her up entirely.

"Forget the lo mein," Ruby said, as if I'd just brought it up. "I have to tell you two things before we get to the house." She was headed away from town now, away from the Millstream Apartments where she used to live, and away from the Wok 'n' Roll where she'd wanted to pick up dinner. She was heading a way we didn't usually go.

"One," she said, "Jonah is perfectly harmless, even if he gets noisy with the buzz saw, and I'm warning you now, in case it ever wakes you."

"The buzz saw?"

She nodded.

"About Jonah . . . he's your new boyfriend?"

"That's what he calls himself."

"So you're like . . . living with him?" Maybe other people moved in with boyfriends or girlfriends, but in all the years I'd known Ruby, which happened to be my whole entire life, she'd never lived in the same physical location with one. That would make a guy think he had a claim on her. It would be harder to string someone along, push him away, pull him back, push him away, if you toasted your toast in the same kitchen.

"Sure, I live with him," she said. "Technically it's his house."

I let this sink in.

"Is that all you wanted to tell me?" I asked.

She was tapping her fingers on the steering wheel now. Her nails were perfect gleaming ovals, not needing a drop of polish to shine brighter than the moonlight.

"No," she said. "There's still that second thing."

She jammed the pedal to the floor like she wanted to bust the engine out of Pete's car and leave us riding on fumes. Over the rush of wind she said, "Do you trust me?"

I trusted her, always, blindly, forever. She used to ask me that question before she'd lift me up and fling me into Cooper Lake by my fingertips, not ever letting go because she promised she wouldn't. I trusted her then, and I trusted her now.

I trusted her, though I'd come all the way from Pennsylvania and she hadn't bothered to meet my bus. I trusted her, though she'd shown me a walking dead girl tonight like it was no big deal. I trusted her; she didn't need to ask.

"You trust me," she said, "like with your life?"

The road ahead was perfectly dark, seeing as she'd cut off the headlights, but she didn't let the car slow.

"Ruby, what are you doing? Put the lights back on!"

"Do you trust me, or do you trust me? Close your eyes."

"Only if you put the lights back on."

"Close your eyes and I will."

I snapped them closed and it felt like we moved over the road as if through time. Centuries draining past so if only I'd looked out I could have seen my own future, my babies' babies' babies' babies forgetting who they came from in their space-age sun-panel tattoo-thin clothes.

The car flew. Trees stepped aside for us. The mountain split open. There were no lanes here, no cars coming, nothing to stand in our way.

And I guess I could have come back to town only to die in a horrible car wreck, like the girl who found herself wrapped around a tree when I was in elementary school, and everyone in town left flowers in the tree roots, and stuffed turtles because I guess she had a thing for turtles, and Ruby and I would have our own tree, and what would people in town leave for us? What stuffed thing would hold our memory for eternity?

I'd never know.

The car had stopped, the engine down, the wind still. I peeled open my eyes.

Ruby wore a grin. *"You do trust me,"* she whispered.

Lights from a house showed me her face. She had even more freckles than I remembered—at least three more.

The house itself was pale wood, unpainted, and set back away from the road. This was the house where she lived now, where I lived now, where we'd live together.

She pushed the wind-warped hair out of my face and tucked it safely behind my ears. Victory in her eyes, speed still pinking her cheeks, she pulled away and said, "The second thing is this. Go ahead, look."

I was looking—at the house. But she didn't mean the house. She meant what was behind the house.

What was seeping into the distance, blotting out trees, erasing mountains, leaking up into the night with no dividing line on the horizon to show where it ended or if it ended ever at all. The shapeless, formless thing that took a breath in as I was watching it, then let out a breath when I looked away. This thing I'd been avoiding. This thing I ran away from. There before her outstretched arm, lit up from the headlights, was the reservoir.

The one I never did swim across.

CHAPTER SEVEN

OLIVE WAS HERE

O live was here, below the hill. Across the two-lane stretch of road and through walls of trees, far enough away to keep their distance, the people of Olive had come up to watch, called to the surface by the car's headlights.

Ruby might have told me this to send a chill up my spine, but I knew they were down there without her having to say. I felt them.

It was simply something I was aware of, like I'd be aware of getting wet if the night turned to rain and I was out with no umbrella. Down deep in the reservoir, under the water where no one would think to look, was the other town, and the people who'd once walked its streets could be found wading through what was left of them still.

My sister didn't have to say so. She didn't have to make up some story; I could make it up myself. I was doing it right now, imagining them, the people of Olive, bobbing up under cover of night.

They waited for the late hour to do their looking. To-night I wondered how many of them were here. Maybe they formed a chain from the rocky bottom, locking webbed fin-gers to slippery wrists, lifting the lightest one to the top, where the water broke open and the air got them gasping and Pete's car could be made out on the hill.

I wondered if they knew who was in the car. If they spot-ted her, and sitting next to her, me.

If the lookout then dipped back under, to let the rest of them know. If they burbled whispers, playing telephone from one waterlogged ear to the next, all down to the end of the line. *She's back. She's come home.*

While I was away, the reservoir had stayed put. Close to a hundred years it had been there, the towns it swallowed far longer even than that. It had been here before I was a thought in this world. Before my sister was a thought, and our mother was a thought, before the mother of our mother's mother, who I never even met, before anyone who looked anything like us had set foot here, this reservoir had existed.

And it wanted us to know. This was apparent in the wind batting up at us from the water below. The wind that rushed in through the windows, cold hands at our throats, colder fingers angling down our shirts.

But when I looked over at Ruby, she let the wind off the reservoir touch her anywhere it wanted and she didn't do a thing. She had her eyes on the water, not the least bit intimidated.

She was an ant before a bear. She was a girl before a speeding eighteen-wheeler truck. And yet she didn't act like it. Here was the second deepest reservoir in the state and she showed none of the awe most people did when they gazed at it. She didn't let out a sigh and say what a beautiful treasure it was. She acted like it was a challenge, like she was waiting to see who would break eye contact first. She looked on as if it would wither up in a dry spell and she'd go down there and celebrate by stomping around in its dirt.

Then, when I felt sure something was about to happen, she turned her face away.

"That's what I wanted to tell you," she said, as if we'd never paused in conversation. "The reservoir. It's so close."

"You could walk to it," I said.

When we lived in the heart of town, the reservoir used to be a ten-minute drive; we'd have to stow the car somewhere secret before going on foot through the trees. But this new house where Ruby lived had been built to be as close to the water as possible without trespassing on city property. The city of New York still owned the water and the land surrounding it, though they weren't here to keep an eye on it. Ruby was.

"It looks closer than it is," she said. "You have to cross the road to get to it—you just can't see. There's a hole in the chain link, and there's this little path I know of over the rocks, but—" How serious she grew here. How cold her hand was, now that it grabbed mine around the wrist, her skin chilled to the same temperature as the wind. "But, Chlo, don't go down there. Just don't."

"Okay," I said.

"Promise?"

I nodded.

"You won't go near it," Ruby announced. "You *won't*. C'mon, let's show you the house."

We left Pete's car where she'd parked it, inches from toppling over the hill. The subject of the reservoir was closed and tucked away, as were other subjects as far-reaching as mothers we were avoiding and girls come back to life. The night was filled with strange things, but what wasn't strange was being together with my sister again. That was the one thing that felt right.

We followed a path of stones to the house, with Ruby leading the way, saying, "Watch where you walk, step only on the stones, that's why they're there, no, don't walk on that one, walk on *that* one, that's right, that stone there," until we reached a series of short, squat steps and then a door. It was unlocked, and unpainted, and had a hole where the knob should be. Even so, she opened it wide and ushered me in.

Indoors, with a few lamps on to see, the house was revealed to not exactly be a whole house yet. It was a house in progress, one being built up around us as we stood inside. The walls and floors were half-completed, formed from scraps and panels of wood, electrical wires for who-knew-what gaping out from above. And yet furniture was arranged in the room—a table and chairs, a love seat on one side, a couch opposite. It looked like someone had insisted on moving in too soon. Or that the furniture was planted here first, and then the walls of the house were put up around it.

Ruby made no comment on the state of the house. She took a practiced step over a hole in the floor, indicating where to put my feet to avoid falling in, and then gave a quick tour of the downstairs: kitchen to the right, living room and den to the left, bathroom through this hall and around that bend. There were more doorways than it seemed there should be, if the only rooms downstairs were the ones she mentioned, but when I asked where the extra doors led, Ruby smiled and said sometimes you need more than one way to reach the outside.

There was no introduction to Jonah, the new boyfriend, whose house Ruby treated as her own. She said he was around somewhere, but she didn't feel like looking. I'd meet him tomorrow, she said. She'd get him to make us breakfast or something.

Up a set of stairs, turning sharp corners without a banister to hold on to, we reached the second floor, where a hole in the floor meant for a ceiling fixture was poked through with a glowing pole of light. I could see wall frames where eventually there'd be walls, but now I could see through the walls—as if I'd grown X-ray eyes. It seemed that if you walked down a hallway, only when you reached the end would you know if it held a room, because we walked down one and there was nothing, and then we walked down another and there was a door.

"This one's yours," Ruby said.

I went to the door, but it didn't swing open. It was propped there, leaning against the frame and not secured by hinges. A single push, and it could topple.

Here, for the first time, she acknowledged the state of the house. Maybe she was getting worried, now that she could see my reaction.

"Jonah's going to build it up to something great," she said. "He is. It takes time, I guess. But I told him. I told him, 'My sister's got to have her own room.' And so he made sure. He should've gotten this door working first though."

"Thanks," I said. But I was thinking how Jonah knew about me, building this room for me before he ever met me, and tonight was the first I'd heard of him.

"I wanted you to have a room that's all yours, Chlo. There's a bathroom up here and everything. And it's bigger than your old room at the Millstream, too. And your old bed's in there, and your furniture."

She picked up the door in both her arms and moved it aside so we could enter. She made a motion that I should go in first and then hovered behind me, close enough to step on my heels if I backed up even one inch.

"I know this room isn't like that little truck-thing you were living in at your dad's, but you weren't thinking of leaving just yet, were you?" she teased. She'd practically whispered this up against the scalp of my head, so I couldn't see if she was smiling as she said it—though I felt sure she was. Smiling.

Then she backed up and continued, cautious now, timid even. "You won't leave because things are just like they were . . . that summer. Before . . . everything. Right, Chlo?"

She meant London was back the way she was, because she sure couldn't mean the mysterious new boyfriend and the slapdash house.

"Is she alive?" I said, bursting out with it. "Can everyone see her?"

"Pete saw her," Ruby said. "You saw her, I saw her, everyone at the party saw her."

"Then she's alive."

Ruby opened her mouth and let it hang for a second too long—but she didn't end up denying it. "She's not a ghost, if that's what you're saying. You know we don't believe in ghosts, silly."

"How?" I said.

"How *what*?" she said.

"*How* is she alive?"

Right then, Ruby held up a hand to stop me from saying more and shot her gaze over my shoulder, to the open doorway behind me. There was a thump coming from out in the hallway. Then another as a heavy weight was dropped.

Was that Jonah?

I stayed very still as she checked outside the room.

But when she returned from the darkened hall she held in her arms a framed mirror that must have slipped down from the wall—and somehow didn't break.

"Maybe we do have a ghost," she teased.

"That wasn't Jonah?"

She shook her head. "It's the house settling, that's all." She held the mirror facing out at me and for a brief moment it caught a bare corner of the room and I didn't see myself in it—like I was the one whose existence we should be questioning. But it was only the angle. When I shifted, I was back in frame and made a reflection as usual. She plunked the mirror on the floor, careful not to get a crack of bad luck in it, and asked me what she'd asked me before.

"So," she said, "you'll stay?"

"Well, yeah," I said. "Of course."

How could I leave? Now back, I couldn't picture anywhere else. Literally—like my mind had been wiped clean of all other towns clear from here to Route 80. Places that weren't this place had lost their names. Here was home, because Ruby was here.

"And didn't you notice?" she said. "I decorated. You like?"

Tacked to the walls in random spots were photos of the two of us. We grinned and pursed our lips and dangled candy-colored tongues over the electrical outlets. We posed with faces mashed together, nose to nose, or cheek on cheek, the flash deviling our eyes, on a windowpane. There was one of me in her lap posted halfway up a wall, but I wasn't a baby, I was twelve years old. There was one of the two of us in her bright white car, sunglasses on and lenses reflecting white-hot sun, above the light switch. There were no boys in any of the photos. And it went without saying that there were none of Mom.

The last of the photos was taken the summer I was fourteen. There we were, cooling ourselves off in the Millstream, Ruby at the edge of the frame with a diamond-shaped fleck of mud on her nose, and me in the center, too many flecks of mud on my body to count, about to splash her.

That was the most recent photo—missing from the walls were the two years we'd spent apart, a time left unphotographed and unrecorded. Neither of us mentioned that.

"It's perfect," I told her. "I love the pictures."

"We'll bring up your suitcase later," she said.

Suddenly I remembered what I'd wanted to check. I was

propelled to the window. The room she'd had built for me was at the front of the house, and the view out the window displayed only the driveway. Nowhere, from any spot in that room, could I see a hint of the reservoir. Which meant it couldn't see me.

That answered my question.

"Are you going to show me *your* room?" I asked her.

She nodded and led the way.

The "hallway" to reach Ruby's room was a set of ply-wood planks running from one side of the house to the other. I could look down and see the first floor a story below. Walking the planks was like performing the tra-peze in a dark circus, only everyone's gone home already and they've taken the net with them, so if you fall, the hard ground is all that's there to catch you.

Ruby balanced on the planks without looking down. She didn't put a hand to the wall to keep steady. Once in her room I could see that her clothes were scattered about, and a chair was set up in the middle of the floor to hold only sunglasses, and her dresser drawers spilled out more than they held, all of which was like her, explosive and full of color and impossible to step over unscathed because she was everywhere.

The room itself was small, but the bed she slept on was grand, with four tall posts and a place to hang a canopy, though it only held a few T-shirts and a gypsy skirt. The bed was high off the ground, as if a stepladder was needed to get up on it, but I didn't see a stepladder, so I imagined Ruby doing running leaps to reach the bed, nosedives and somersaults from off the chair of sunglasses to the mattress beyond. She'd do it, too—it was something we would have done together, had this been our bed.

I went to her side of the bed, where on the tangled sheets was last night's nightgown, skimpy and dotted with bloodred ladybugs, and one white sock.

On the sock, she'd penned a note to herself at the ankle:

cocoa pebbles dish soap
birdseed tampons
string cheese—lots

A shopping list. She always used to write them in the strangest places.

I stepped around to the other side of the bed, the side where I figured this new boyfriend of hers got to sleep.

I could tell he shared this room. His stuff was all over. There on the dresser, a man's wallet and a bulky ring of grime-encrusted keys. Hanging over a chair, a pair of work pants, the kind with pockets running up the legs and you can't imagine how anyone would need all those pockets, but I guess her boyfriend, Jonah, did. Those were his discarded boxers on the floor. Here was his wrinkled half of the sheets.

It bothered me to imagine him sleeping on that tall bed beside my sister. To think of some guy I'd never met peeling off his pants in front of her and putting his head on a pillow beside her head.

I tore my eyes away from the bed and checked the room again, taking it all in.

"You're quiet," she said. "What're you looking for?"

"Nothing. I don't know."

What I was looking for made no sense, not even to me. Something magical had happened, and London was apparent living proof of it, and maybe I thought there'd be some kind of evidence in here. Like Ruby might've dropped a clue out of her pocket. She could be clumsy like that.

Like if I lifted up my foot, all explanations would be right here.

I did notice that Ruby had two huge windows in her room—looking out behind the house in the direction of the reservoir. They were dark for now, since it was night, but when the sun came up, there would be no curtains or shades to keep the water from showing clear.

"You'll sleep here tonight," she announced. "With me. But take that side, the one near the wall, not the windows."

Jonah's side, she meant. She said those words and clapped her hands together and it was done, without informing the boyfriend first, because why would we?

It was decided and, soon, it was happening: my first night under my sister's new roof. Soon, we were on the bed, divvying up the pillows, and she was so close I could feel her elbow in my side and her knee crushing my elbow. We had each other again, and there was nothing and no one that could get between us.

Everything was as it should be—except for the one thing.

The girl at the keg, the one we'd dropped off in the middle of the road.

The dead girl who was no longer dead.

That's the one thing that prickled at me.

Somehow, while I was gone, she'd been reanimated, blown full of air so she could take her breaths again among us. My sister was connected to her now—which meant I was also, if my sister was.

London was back, as I was—and she shouldn't be.

"Comfortable, Chlo?" Ruby's voice rang out from her side of the mattress—as if she knew right then on whose face my mind had been lingering.

"Yes, Ruby," I said from my side.

"G'night then," she said, choking it out almost, like she had a dry, scratchy spot in her throat. Like being here with me again, tonight, was making her feel emotional.

I waited for her to say more, but she didn't. She had her back to me, but after some long moments her arm reached out, and her hand tapped my hand to be sure it was still there. I tapped back.

Then we both went to sleep and let my first night home dissolve into day.

CHAPTER EIGHT

RUBY SLIPPED

Ruby slipped over to my side of the bed and wouldn't budge, though I tried and tried to wake her. The clock showed that it was morning, and far later than I usually slept, but Ruby was still deep under. Her long hair trailed across the tangled sheets and reached down for the shadowy dust bunnies kept beneath the bed. Her arm circled one of my pillows, and her legs had kicked aside my legs.

"Ruby?" I said, removing a lock of hair from her cheek.

"No, don't," she said in response. Then she rolled over onto her stomach so I couldn't see her face. She was only talking in her sleep.

Sometimes, I knew, if I spoke to Ruby while she was dreaming, she'd speak back. We could have entire conversations, ease out her hidden thoughts, the ones she didn't even know she had. I wondered if any boyfriends ever knew about this.

But I didn't want to wake her, though it was long past

breakfast and she must have been starved. I slipped my legs out from under the sheets and that's when I felt it: something cold and crumbly, down near where we had our feet. I peeled back the sheet to see the dirt spilling out all over the bottom of the bed, as much on my half as on hers. Her legs were covered in it, streaks of dried mud almost to her knees. Her feet were crusty and brown and you couldn't even see what color her toenails were painted.

I was positive her feet had been clean when she'd gone to bed.

"Ruby?" I said, poking her hip. "Did you go outside while I was sleeping?"

"You can't go," she mumbled, eyes still closed.

"Not me," I said. "You. Where'd you go?"

She sighed a nonanswer, making it clear she wasn't getting up, not yet.

The house wasn't quiet any longer. There was noise coming from somewhere downstairs, a gasping, choking, whinnying roar . . .

The buzz saw, as promised. Had to be.

But Ruby still didn't get up. She could sleep through smoke alarms and neighbors' house parties. She'd once slept through a storm that almost took out our apartment, using a hundred-year-old oak as a wrecking ball, and she might have stayed sleeping, even while it crushed her, except she woke to make sure I was okay, because being crushed was one thing, but she couldn't live with herself if she let something crush her sister.

Going down to the first floor was difficult to manage even in daylight—there was no banister on the stairs and no walls, and I had to hold on to air. There was no breakfast in the kitchen, and the dishes in the sink had a week-old glow.

I found Jonah in the backyard and watched him for some time. I peeked around the corner of his house, my back flat against his unpainted siding, fingering his splinters.

He had black hair; it curled. And tattoos, all up and down his arms.

He was skinny but strong, in that ropey way Ruby liked on a guy. From behind, you could see his shoulders working as he used the buzz saw, ripping through a block of wood, pushing his weight into it.

I could see why she'd been drawn to him. He was her type, physically. But there had to be something more to him—something I wasn't seeing. If Ruby called a guy her boyfriend it meant she found him interesting enough to spend time with him beyond the stretch of one weekend. It meant Monday mornings, and underthings tangled together in the same washing machine, and spit exchanged on sidewalk corners where every single person in town could see. It meant the guy was worthy.

It was a rare occurrence, practically unseen in our town, like a comet, or that time Pete swore he saw a live lynx sprinting through the rec field and went around telling anyone who would listen, but we knew he'd only been drinking.

I was far away, across the dirt lot that I guess was Jonah's back lawn, shrubs and a spindly tree between us, but when he turned to face the house it was impossible not to get a good view of his eyes with those safety goggles on. They magnified his eyeballs, making them seem far larger than real life. His irises were a watery blue that seemed all wrong, innocent in a way you knew he wasn't. Alarming.

He caught me looking and stopped the saw. The sudden silence was enough to jolt me out from behind his house, losing my footing in the dirt of his lawn.

Slowly, he removed the goggles and let them hang around his neck.

"So it's the famous Chloe," he said. "The one who took my bed."

I didn't deny it, but I did come closer, close enough to see the bright red ovals suctioned around each of his pale eyes. I wondered how long they'd stay there, and if Ruby could kiss him when he was all deformed like that. She probably made him wait for his face to go back to normal before she'd get close.

He straightened his back, cracked it, then wiped sawdust on his pants. Two handprints, fingers splayed wide, were left on his skinny thighs.

"You look like her, you know," he said. "Bet you hear that a lot."

I shrugged. Before last night, I hadn't heard it in a while.

"So how do you like the house?" he said.

"It's fine, I guess."

"Just fine?" he said, seeming amused. "It's not finished, but you could probably tell." He thumped the block of wood he'd been sawing. "This'll be a veranda. Ruby said she wanted a veranda, so I'm out here making her one. Really it's a back porch. She wants it all the way out to the edge of the property, as far out as we're allowed to build."

"You always give her what she wants?" I teased, because of course he did. The guys she spent time with always did. What would be the point of them otherwise?

"Yep."

"And this is what you do all day? Make stuff for my sister?"

"No." He seemed offended. "I *work*. I have a job. This is my job." He indicated the shed, scattered with half-assembled furniture and haphazard stacks of wood.

"You build tables," I said, unimpressed.

"And dressers, armoires . . . other shit. I sell it. I work on the house on the side."

I walked over and pulled open a random drawer in a random dresser. Inside I saw written in wobbly smoke-gray lines likely sketched with an eye pencil:

Ruby says hi.

I closed it before he could look in.

"Nice," I said. "You're not from here, are you?"

"I've been here a couple years . . ."

"So no, then."

"No. I'm from—"

"It doesn't really matter. How'd you meet my sister?"

"She pumped my gas at that convenience store in town. I was driving through, and my tank needed filling, and there she was. And, she's, damn . . . she's something else. I'm sure you hear that enough about your sister, so you don't need me to say it. I've been places. I've been around. But I saw her at the pump, and . . ." He laughed, like this was funny. He laughed like she hadn't reeled in a guy off the road before.

"And?"

"And I couldn't keep my eyes off her. She filled my tank, said she'd knock back the price because she liked me."

I wrinkled my nose. "She does that to everyone, you know. It's not special."

He smiled, faintly, like he was remembering some other part of the story he wasn't about to tell me, one that could prove she did like him.

"Then—what is it, a week later?—and I'm buying this land and moving my whole business out here and starting work on the house and that girl at the pumps, she's my girl now. All because I stopped for gas."

He probably thought that was romantic. "How old are you anyway?"

"Twenty-seven. That all right with you?"

"We'll see. It might be too old." I let out a sigh. "Truth is, Ruby barely told me anything about you," I said—and I said it because I had a feeling he wouldn't like that. He needed to know his place in her world, now that he was living in it. He needed to know what he was here for, and what to expect. "Ruby doesn't talk about you at all."

He looked down and wiped more sawdust on his pants. Then he looked up into my eyes.

"Do you make her breakfast in the morning?" I asked.

"Some mornings."

"And iced coffee the way she likes it?"

"Yeah, sure. Sometimes."

"Do you answer the phone when it rings so she doesn't have to? Do you make her popcorn on Wednesdays? Do you do her laundry and hang out her dresses to dry?"

He stepped away from the buzz saw and a little closer to me. "Do you do this with all her boyfriends? Ask them questions until they crack?"

"You don't look like you've cracked."

He seemed to think I was only teasing.

"It doesn't sound like you take good care of her," I said. "You're not doing any of the things you're supposed to."

"Listen, I'm in love with your sister. That's what you want to hear, right?"

It wasn't, actually. It was sad to hear. It's not like I hadn't heard it hundreds and hundreds of times before, enough times to blur in my mind so all their mouths mushed together and it sounded like they were talking at me with cheeks stuffed full of leaves and fish-tank pebbles and driveway mud.

When Ruby said the words back to one of them, then maybe I'd care.

He tried again. "That make you happy?" he said. "That I love her?"

"I'm happy for you," I said politely.

I checked the windows of his house, hoping to spot her. Her bedroom faced the backyard. Maybe she was there at the glass, observing.

He saw me looking and said, "She still asleep? She sure was up late last night."

"Yeah, I know," I lied, because what I knew was that she'd gone to sleep with me, and there was no way he'd have a clue of how late that was or wasn't. Then I thought of the streaks of dried mud on her legs and I gave myself away by going, "Hey, you didn't see her out last night, did you?"

"You mean when she went for a walk?" He indicated where that walk had taken her.

He pointed into the distance and I noticed the bright green snake wrapped in fat coils around his arm. The tattoo was so faded, he must have gotten it before puberty or done it homemade, jailhouse-style, with ink from ballpoint pens mixed with spit.

Where he was pointing was out toward the edge of the hill, to the view Ruby had showed me the night before. Pete's car was still there, but Jonah didn't mean the car. Between the gap in the shrubs, a path ran down the hill to the road. And across the road, the reservoir waited.

"She went down there?" I asked.

"I think so. Any reason you weren't with her?"

I shrugged. "Didn't feel like it, I guess."

When I turned back I found him staring at me, simply staring. I had on a tank top and a pair of boxers that had belonged to one or another of Ruby's ex-boyfriends. She liked to confiscate them and use them in lieu of underwear after they were gone. We both did. We also occasionally made use of exes' button-down shirts and Visa cards.

Or maybe these were *his* boxers. Maybe that's why he was staring.

"I should go wake my sister," I said. "And get dressed while I'm up there."

"You should," he said. He was in dangerous territory, looking at me like that.

I stalked off, but I didn't get far before a horn was honking from the driveway. Pete leaped out of some random car, looking dazed, as if the Tums he'd swallowed the night before really had been laced with something exciting.

"*There's* my car," he said, pointing at the car Ruby had swiped from the party.

Someone else was getting out of the car, someone Pete must have convinced to drive him here. But there was another person, too—Owen—and, seeing him, it occurred to me that this was not the time to be wearing some other man's boxers out on the lawn.

I was about to sneak back into the house, but Pete was coming straight for me.

"Why'd you have to take my car?" he whined.

"*I* didn't take your car," I said.

"So why'd your sister have to go and take it then? Do you have any idea how I got home last night? You think this is funny, Chloe? It's not funny."

"We got a ride." Owen stepped in, practically defending me. "That's how we got home last night."

Pete glared at him. "I should've called the cops." Then he softened and his eyes went all wonky and he added, quickly, "I would've. If it was anyone other than Ruby."

At the sound of her name, Jonah stepped up, listening. The other guy with them looked out at the house, as if expecting Ruby to appear there, on the crooked front steps, to open the door that didn't have a knob and welcome them in. She didn't. Even if she was awake she wouldn't have bothered.

I turned to Pete, filling up with a kind of confidence I used to have from simply being her sister—because I still was that; more than ever I was. "You *gave* her your keys," I said. "You told her to take your car, remember?"

He froze. "No, I didn't."

"You don't remember?" I tried to give him the eyes like Ruby would, but I wasn't sure if my eyes worked the same way as hers did.

"Yeah, I dunno." He glanced at his brother, then at his friend, then at Jonah, who didn't look pleased by any of this. "Maybe," Pete said at last. "Maybe I did."

"Man, who cares?" his friend broke in. "Just get your keys and let's go."

They all looked at me. "You mean from Ruby?" I said. "She's not up yet."

A beat of silence as everyone waited to see what Pete would do. Jonah, especially, seemed interested in what Pete would do—would he barge into the house, stomp up to the room Ruby slept in, grab her on the bed and shake her awake until she went looking for the keys? Would he go through her pockets? Would he make Jonah do it, or me?

That was when I felt the chill at my back. The sense of her, close by, eavesdropping from behind a tree maybe, idly twirling sausage curls into her hair as we talked about her.

Maybe she was trying to tell me something.

She used to come up behind me and whisper a little missive, then sneak off, leaving the words to drift in my ears like dandelion fluff. *Stick out your tongue,* she'd tell me—and, bam, I'd get in trouble with the bus driver. Or she'd feed me lines: *There wasn't any No Trespassing sign up on the gate. I swear on my mother, Officer.*

She was here somewhere, sending over the words for me to say. I felt them tickle at my earlobe. She and I had been apart for so long that I'd forgotten what it was like to use my mouth to talk for her—how she did it for me, and I did it for her, and no one ever knew the difference.

But I was also aware of Owen, who met my eyes— once—and then, fast, dropped his gaze down to his boots as if he'd gotten stung.

"I'll do it," I told Pete. "I'll go find the keys. But don't move. Wait right here."

Ruby didn't want him in the house. She wanted me to go around the side of the house where the boys couldn't see. She also wanted other things besides, like toaster waffles, but I figured that would have to wait till after we dealt with Pete.

I went around the house, which, like a tree, grew out

from itself, branching off at all angles and teetering up into the sky.

She was inside, through a sliding glass door, wide awake and choosing between waffle flavors, sundress and boots on. Her legs were gleaming and I couldn't see any trace of dirt. The memory of caked mud was so out of place now, I wondered if I'd dreamed it.

"Buttermilk or blueberry?" she asked me. "You get first pick."

"Blueberry," I said without a second thought. "So did you hear? About the keys?"

"I heard." She popped two waffles into the toaster and watched the coils go red. She pushed aside a stack of shoe catalogs and unopened envelopes on the table so I'd have room for a plate. She somehow wrangled up a clean fork, but only one, so one of us would have to eat the waffle with our fingers.

"I *wish* I could give Pete his keys," she said, "since that would get rid of him faster."

"Why can't you?"

"Because." She held out her fists to show me. She opened each one to reveal her palm. On which, in both cases, there was no key.

"They fell," she said. "The keys. They're gone."

"Fell where?"

The toaster gave a sharp *ping*, and at that Ruby turned

to retrieve the waffles. Mine, she put on a plate; hers, she nibbled at from the empty palm of one hand, her mouth soon stuffed so full, she couldn't possibly answer.

I ate my waffle and decided not to push further. I didn't want her to say it, didn't want to know for sure where she went out walking last night.

Finally she stopped chewing and said, "I wonder what he's going to do about those keys." She licked some crumbs off her fingers. "Poor Petey. He was one of my very first boyfriends—you remember. The first of them all, actually. Maybe I should go apologize or something. Make nice."

I nodded, though she didn't move for the door.

"Speaking of boyfriends . . ." she said. "I guess you met Jonah?"

I nodded once more but didn't comment.

"He's good with his hands, huh?"

I made a face.

"He's useful, Chlo. Don't you go and be mean to him yet. So who else is out there? I don't want to let them see me till I know."

"Some guy, Pete's friend, I dunno. And . . . and I guess, uh, yeah, I saw Pete's brother, Owen, out there with them, too."

The heat of my cheeks warmed the kitchen, like she'd left the oven on. I wasn't sure if she noticed.

Ruby never got this kind of heat in her cheeks. She didn't

have to stop short inside a doorway to catch her breath after she'd been standing near someone. Didn't pause longer than she should, wondering if he'd followed her. Pause a long time wondering, until it was clear he wasn't following, because why would he? Boys didn't follow me the way they did my sister. A boy once followed her around town for miles, tailgating her car and trailing her cart in the supermarket, and when she whirled around to ask what he wanted, he said he only wanted to say hi.

Come to think of it, maybe that had been Pete.

Ruby headed for the door and slipped out. She was gone for a while. She was gone long enough for me to shower and get dressed and put on a dab of her lipstick and make myself a second waffle. She was out there for so long that I wondered if maybe she wanted me to join her and I'd missed the signal or something.

But then I looked out the great window in the living room, a window as wide as the room itself and showing the full expanse of the reservoir as if our whole world was made of it. There, in the backyard, were Pete and Pete's friend and Pete's brother and Jonah, and they were all working together, lifting boards of wood in an assembly line, apparently inspired to do some work on the veranda.

My sister had her back to me and was caught standing in the dirt, the wind playing with the hem of her dress, tossing it like wild rapids around her clean, bare legs. She must have felt me looking because she turned then, to give me one of her smiles. A smile for me and me only. No boys had ever seen this smile. They thought they were close enough to my sister to be loved by her, but they couldn't, wouldn't ever get that close—not in the way I already was.

She came in through the sliding glass door and said, "It's Wednesday. We should watch movies." Because on summer Wednesdays that was what we used to do, and the day after, Thursdays, we did laundry, but only if we felt like it, and on Fridays we'd do some shopping and make a pit stop at the town pool.

For now, we sat on pillows beneath the ceiling fan and flipped on the cable.

"I forgot to tell you," Ruby said. "I don't like you going in the backyard when it's still light," she announced randomly. She lifted her face to the ceiling fan, which was on high, and let it cool her cheeks.

"Why?" I said. "Afraid I'll get sunburned?"

"No," she said, "though good point, you do burn easily, your skin is so much fairer than mine—I bet you my dad was Latin, like from Panama or Puerto Rico, didn't Sparrow say he spoke Spanish? I bet he went back to whatever country he came from and it's so gorgeous and sunny down there so that's why we haven't seen him since. And your dad speaks only English and he's as pale as a newborn rat."

"Are rats pale?"

She shuddered. "They live their lives in the dark, don't they? Just don't go in the yard in the daytime. Anyone could see you out there. And you know what? If you go out there at night, do me a favor and stay on the veranda. You could step on a nail. Also, I don't like that boy, why'd he ask if you were coming back out? I told him it's Wednesday and Wednesday's the day we watch movies so, no, you were *not* coming back out. Plus, please don't answer the telephone. Let it ring like I do. And"—here, a glance at the sundress I had on, a short blue one I'd helped myself to from her closet—"you look cute in that dress. It's yours. I want you to have it."

"Thanks," I said.

I was still stuck on the thing about the boy who'd asked for me. But she didn't bring him up again.

She just said, "Got it?"

And I said, "Yeah," though I wasn't sure I understood even half of it.

And then she rested a cold hand on my arm, and the air whipped up by the ceiling fan made it even colder, and she said, "It's *Wednesday*, Chlo. What movie should we watch?"

That was how life returned fully to what it once was, this summer like other summers. The only difference was our vantage point in town. When I got up to make the pop-corn—on Wednesdays, when we watched movies, we also microwaved popcorn—I could see the water, never still, always moving, if faintly, in the near distance. I could see it from every window downstairs, from each room in the house except the room Ruby called my bedroom.

And, who knew? Maybe down at the bottom, where my gaze couldn't reach, the people of Olive were living out their own summer, seeking a breeze on the current, then running to play catch with Pete's lost keys.

CHAPTER NINE

LONDON DIDN'T EXIST

London didn't exist for a couple days. We never left the house, so it was easy to forget her out there, doing whatever she was doing, wherever that was.

Or, no—it was like she existed the way she used to, two years before, when I'd never considered leaving town, especially not without my sister, and when I knew London Hayes as the girl in the back of my French class and not much more. When she was just a girl, one I saw around, on the Green or in the backseats of Ruby's friends' cars, and when I did we didn't even say hello to each other or anything.

Knowing she was around somewhere was enough to keep the memories at bay.

By Friday morning, London was barely a thought drifting through my mind. Instead, Ruby had filled my head with pancakes at Sweet Sue's, as we'd decided that for the rest of the summer we'd eat only breakfast foods, then skip the two courses in between and go straight for dessert. We went all out and ordered the "red monkey" special, pancakes made with strawberries and bananas, since Ruby said twice the fruit was healthier.

On the way back from Sweet Sue's, we drove past the public high school—where she said I'd go for my junior year, once she convinced my dad to give me up for good—and we made sure to take the familiar detour down the old highway alongside the real highway, windows down so the wind could dread our hair.

And everything was the same—except Ruby hadn't cut my bangs yet, so my hair got in my mouth and I had to spit it out to keep from chewing on it and puking it up like cats do. And I noticed, too, how the car was running on empty the whole way there and back, and either her gas gauge was stuck on *E* for good, or she really had been lifted to another plane of existence where she could drive a car with the power of her mind, in the way she could direct a man to build a house for her, staying up all night to hammer and buzz.

In town, Ruby sailed through red lights like they meant go. The other cars let her pass, and no one even honked when she took the wrong way down the road and almost caused a collision. As we drove alongside the Green, we saw kids hanging out on the benches like any summer afternoon, and all eyes went to our car, like we were part of a caravan carrying a celebrity or the president; in Ruby they had that person combined into one. But when anyone saw for sure she was in the car, they looked away fast, like they didn't want to be caught staring. It was a wave of snapped necks, eyes averted to street signs and lampposts. If Ruby noticed, she didn't say.

Ruby cut the brakes near the candy shop where she used to buy me the swirled cherry-mint sticks to suck on. This was our routine: candy first, then shopping for sunglasses. Then we'd lounge on the hard stone bench dead center of the Green, where Ruby would flirt with locals and tourists and curious squirrels. We always made sure to avoid the Village Tavern, a bar across the street that our mother was known to favor, which meant holding our breath when we passed, like the superstitious would beside a graveyard. Then, if we got hot enough, we'd do a few laps in the pool. Well, I would do the laps, and Ruby would stretch out her legs in the shallow end and watch. After that we'd go home.

But now she said we should skip the candy—we weren't ready for "lunch" yet—and, this time, she'd buy me my own pair of sunglasses to keep me from borrowing hers.

We left the Buick with the windows down, as no one would ever dare touch it, and crossed Tinker Street for the boutique that had the best selection of sunglasses in all of town. The store had appeared to be open when we'd driven past, but once we got up close we found the glass door locked, the lights down, and a misspelled hand-scrawled sign that read: Closed for Inventry Sorry!

Ruby was not pleased.

She pounded on the glass and in seconds two salesgirls appeared, all apologies, one glaring at the other as if she was the one responsible for the sign, and the bell on the door was tinkling as it opened for us. We went in and minutes later emerged with our purchases: a dark-tinted pair à la *Breakfast at Tiffany's* for me and a pair of flashy gold aviators that Ruby wore perched on top of her head. The sunglasses cost fifteen each, but Ruby suggested two for five, and so that was what she paid.

Ruby was silent as we returned to the car. She didn't want to lounge on the Green, and she didn't want me to try on her aviators. "Everything is supposed to be perfect," she said. "I don't understand it. What's up with today?"

"It is perfect," I assured her. "Everything is."

"Do you think I'm trying too hard?" she asked, dropping the aviators down over her eyes. "With these?"

They were gold-rimmed, polished up to searing in the sun—and too big for her head. But she was everything and more, even with those glasses marring her face. That was the magic of my sister.

"You can tell me," she said.

"I . . ."

"You hate them," she said, but she kept them on as if to punish herself, and clicked her blinkers, to merge the car into the lane. Then she clicked the blinkers back off, the car staying in park. "Do I look mean with these on? Sorta psychopath?"

I nodded, if reluctantly, since it wasn't exactly the kind of compliment Ruby was used to hearing.

She gave a grin and said, "Then I'm going in."

"In where?" With my new dark glasses on, I could barely see the sign across from the candy store for the Village Tavern. It could be that I was used to not-seeing it, used to imagining instead a sinkhole taking over that spot on the sidewalk.

"Yeah," Ruby said. "In there."

"But what if she's, y'know . . . inside?"

"Oh, but she is," Ruby said. "Don't you recognize the heap of junk over there?" She waved a hand at the brown hatchback parked at the corner. One taillight was busted in, and I knew how it happened: Ruby's foot and a single, well-aimed shot of her pointy black boot.

Inside me, something sunk. I'd been back in town for however many days since the bus ride, and I hadn't run into my mother yet. She hadn't called; it was possible she still assumed I was in Pennsylvania. All this time, Ruby had been shielding me from her. Now she was yanking off the curtain and shoving me in.

"But—" I started.

I didn't have to say it. Ruby knew the patterns my thoughts made before the words left my mouth. She knew even before the first syllable. She shook her head and, softly, told me to stay put. Only one of us was going in.

She crossed the street and stepped inside the tavern, out of sight for a few minutes. I don't know what she told our mother, how she broke the news that I was home, but she must have found some words for it. Maybe she said I was in the car and not coming inside to talk and, ha, how do you like that, woman-who-calls-herself-Sparrow? Ruby must have said something good, though, because when she hopped back into the driver's seat, she had the most delicious smile on her face, like she'd witnessed a thing of beauty and would remember it forever and always. She didn't explain it, though—sometimes a perfect memory can be ruined if put to words. Ruby taught me that.

As we drove away, the door to the tavern opened and a person stepped out. A warm, blinking sign for beer illuminated this person in patches, on and then off again, face aglow and then not. This person watching us go for a few seconds. Then this person giving up and heading inside. I felt so detached from this person who happened to be my mother.

Ruby didn't tell me what she'd said in there. Instead she told a story, as usual.

"Did you know I used to walk around town saying you were *my* baby?"

"Yeah?" I didn't stop her; I liked when she told it.

"What was I, seven? Eight?" she said as she sped the car down the street and made the usual turn toward the rec field, where we'd find the public pool. "All I know is I was small, and I'd wheel you in your stroller and people would stop me on the street. They'd say, 'How cute!' Or, 'You two are soooo adorable!' But then they'd always have to ask, 'But where's your mother, little girl?' And the thing is, I didn't want to say she was doing shots at the bar. Or, last I saw, she was in some-dude-we-never-met's truck. I mean, I *wanted* to say our mother was right there, like in a store buying earrings, right? Our mother was at the library. Our mother was at the Laundromat. Someplace mothers go." She sighed.

"But," she continued, cutting around a slow car, "if I was going to lie, I figured I may as well make it fun. So I'd say, 'What do you mean where's her mother? *I'm* her mother.' I'd tell them different things, depending on who asked. Like I married young and now I'm a widow. Or I got knocked up in Girl Scouts, when I was out selling cookies. Or, you know, if a church person was asking, that Jesus gave you to me. People get all weird when you talk about Jesus. Like unicorns can't exist, but Jesus did—ridiculous." She shook her head. "Anyway, I said you were mine. And sometimes when you say a lie enough times, it's like it's true. Then you're not even lying."

Ruby's stories changed when she told them—the tales grew more impossible physically, and legally, like how she said she picked me up at school in our mom's car while sitting on a *Webster's* unabridged dictionary so she could see the road. Like how she said we lived for a whole summer at sea, barely emerging from the bathtub. But no matter what miraculous way of surviving she chose for us, our mom was always conveniently out of the picture. It was better than the truth, really.

Ruby parked the car in the rec-field lot and removed the gold aviators. I thought we were going to get changed for swimming—we had bathing suits on under our clothes, so all we had to do was pull our dresses over our heads and find the beach towels—but something was holding her attention across the wide, grassy lawn. She couldn't tear her eyes away.

From where we were parked, all I could see was the stretch of the rec field. The swings, the sandbox, the jungle gym, the slides, the great lawn beyond, and past that the softball diamond. A game was going on, but Ruby didn't like sports, so it couldn't be that. Past the softball field was some kid's birthday party, marked by a bouquet of balloons tied to the gazebo and fluttering wildly in the wind.

"What?" I said. "Do you want some birthday cake or something?"

"I wonder . . ." she said, frozen where she sat.

"You wonder what?"

A piece of her expression was unnerving me. Maybe it was the glassy green of her eyes. The hard set of her teeth. Maybe it was her knuckles, gone white on the wheel even though the engine was off and there was no reason to hold it for steering anymore.

"What do you think those people would do," she said, "all the kids there at that birthday party, all the moms, the dads . . . what do you think they'd do if I walked over there and just let them all go?"

"Let who go, the kids?"

She shook her head. What she was staring at was the collection of balloons, watching them fiercely as their long tails whipped against the gazebo post, their brightly colored heads rising as high as they'd reach. It really bothered her to see them tied up like that.

"The red ones first, I think," she said. "If I cut their strings, ripped them off, and let them fly? What do you think?"

"I don't know," I said. "You might make the kids cry."

She didn't seem to care about that; she only looked off

into the distance, absorbed in something I couldn't decipher, as if living out some fantasy rescue mission in her mind.

Or maybe she was trying it right now. Trying to break them free by wishing for it.

But of course the balloons remained where they were, and no matter how hard the wind got—and it did seem to get a bit stronger, somehow; as Ruby held her eyes there, a few paper plates went sailing off the picnic table and some little kids lost their cake—but still, no balloons went free. They were tethered there and would stay put, forced to be guests at that party until someone cut them off after, or popped them and let them die.

"Ruby?" I said.

At the sound of her name, at my voice saying her name, she shook herself out of it.

Before I knew it, she was pulling her dress over her head and slamming the car door shut. "Let's go for a swim. Do your laps. I'll make everyone get out of the pool so you can have the whole place to yourself if you want me to."

"Don't do that," I said. The wind had calmed as we walked the lawn—and as we got closer to the fenced-in outdoor pool, I saw we had company beyond the usual townie kids who came here to cool off on summer afternoons.

She was here, too. Her pale head could be made out in the shallow end, where she stood waist-deep, shivering in the sunlight. She was so thin, I could count her ribs.

"Does she know we go swimming on Fridays?" I asked. "Did you tell her?"

Ruby shrugged. "I may have mentioned it." She called out, "Hey, London. Watch out, my sister's gonna do some laps."

When the townspeople at the pool saw Ruby coming, they cleared away from the stairs in the shallow end to make room for her. They knew she liked to sit there, letting the water pool up to the knobs of her knees, splashing at the surface with her fingers, letting the sun warm her face while she watched me swim. No one seemed surprised that we were here again, after a long absence. No one asked me where I'd been.

Like always, Ruby took to her perch on the descending steps and stretched out her long, bare legs as far as they'd go—which was far. She wore an anklet that glimmered as gold as her aviators in the pool's bright, reflective light. Her bikini was black and white today, the top white and the bottoms black, and her aviators were drawn down over her eyes to keep just anyone from seeing in.

I wore a navy one-piece, and I'd left my new sunglasses in the car.

"Hi, Ruby," London said, wading through the water to reach us. "Hi, Chloe."

I tried not to look at her bare arms and legs; even in daylight her skin had a sickly sheen of blue, as if she couldn't breathe and was standing here drowning and we were made to witness it.

I mumbled something about doing laps. At the deep end, I dove in, the tips of my fingers cutting through the warm water first, then my face, and then my shoulders and the rest of me with a smooth, enveloping splash.

The pool wasn't empty, but I was easily able to avoid people as I went from the deep end to the shallow, then back again into the deep. From underwater I could see their legs kicking as they, too, tried to swim. I could feel it, the motion they made, the wind. If I stayed under, I could hear them screaming from far off in the distance, like from behind walls and locked doors, houses and whole towns away.

I was still under, at the far edge of the deep end, when I decided I didn't feel like doing laps anymore. I took hold of the filter and stayed there, drifting. Seconds passed, though they felt like minutes. Minutes like hours.

And, really, I could have stayed down there till nightfall, couldn't I?

Ruby used to say I could.

I wondered if my sister could make anything happen, if she put her mind to it. Like, right now, here I was skimming my hand along the bottom of this dirty public pool. Maybe I could stay under for the rest of my life, or at least the whole summer, never needing air to breathe. I'd scavenge for supplies to make it through—like if someone dropped a stick of gum, I'd retrieve it and it would be cinnamon-flavored, and it could sustain me for years. It wasn't reservoir ice cream, but it would do. I'd adapt, the way the people of Olive adapted after their town was taken away. Ruby would make it so.

Maybe I really could breathe down here, become whatever she wanted, even some impossible creature long still alive when I shouldn't be . . . like London was.

It was when I let my eyes come open again underwater that I saw her.

London Hayes.

She was down here with me. She'd swum the length of the pool to share the deep end with me, far enough away from Ruby so she couldn't see. London skimmed the bottom of the pool closer to me. There were her thin legs drifting. Her skin so pale as if rubbed in blocks of ice. I noticed that she had a small scar on one knee. I watched the short, bleached strands of her hair reach with electric intensity for the surface. Her eyes blinking and on me.

She stayed still, limbs floating, mouth pressed closed.

Were we seeing who could stay under the longest?

I held my breath, held it till my lungs burned. I kept my hand locked to the filter, not letting myself up though all the rest of me begged me to go. I forced myself to believe in it, in my sister, to stay down at the bottom, to stay.

I didn't want it to be me, but my body wouldn't listen. My lungs were about to burst with the effort—I had to break free to the surface. I needed air.

It was here, before my all-too-human body took over and flung me upward, gasping and spluttering and spitting up chlorine, that London opened her mouth. She breathed without struggle. She stayed under like she could, easily, for years.

She let me see her do it. She wanted me to know.

What is *she?* my mind screamed, needing answers, but then I was up, unable to think anything more, up in the air choking on the edge of the pool, and she was still down at the bottom.

She didn't come up for air for the longest time.

CHAPTER TEN

I COULDN'T FORGET

I couldn't forget what I saw in the pool. Ruby and I were in her car not too much later, driving back to the house, and all I could picture was London opening her mouth underwater and letting me see her breathe. Ruby had misled me when I'd asked if London was alive again.

She was more than alive. She might outlive us all.

Ruby, though, hadn't seen London in the deep end. She'd run over in a panic when I'd emerged, choking, at the edge of the pool, and she was still admonishing me over it.

"Why'd you scare me like that!" she shrieked as she skidded through a red light and narrowly avoided a four-car collision. "How could you do that, Chlo!" She was more frightened by the idea of me holding my breath in the pool than she should be. She was acting like I'd taken a running leap off a cliff.

Then she said the strangest thing. "How do you think I

felt, having them pull you under like that? When I was too far away to get to you? When I couldn't even barely see!"

"Wait," I said. "Them who?"

She shook her head as if shaking herself from a trance. "There were too many people in the pool, Chloe. I couldn't see past them. Don't pull a stunt like that again."

We'd turned onto the road that led to Jonah's house when Ruby slammed the brakes without warning. I lurched forward and was kept from flying through the windshield by the seat belt, which I had absolutely no memory of putting on.

"What the—!" I cried. I checked to make sure she was okay—she was—and checked to make sure I was okay—I was—and checked to see if we'd hit anything, like another car or an animal, and that's when I saw her, standing in the road with her thumb out, having stumbled directly into traffic as if she were begging to be run over.

Ruby threw up her hands and said to the car's ceiling, "Hitchhiking?! Sometimes I wonder if certain people are just *meant* to die."

Before I could ask what that was supposed to mean, she'd leaped from the car and was dragging the girl out of the road. Just in time, too. Ruby moved her out of the way seconds before a truck took the blind turn and barreled straight over the spot she'd been standing in. It was so sudden, I didn't know what to make of it.

All I knew is it looked like my sister had saved London's life.

Again.

London was trying to explain how she ended up out there after her swim at the pool. She was talking fast, saying she'd left the pool and was driving her parents' car home and it got a flat. She was only hitching because there was no spare and no one had stopped to help and her cell was dead and she had to pee—and because she was an idiot, Ruby broke in to say. It was only a coincidence, London swore, that she was on the road not a mile away from Jonah's house, where we happened to live. Just as it was a coincidence that Ruby had leaped out in time to save her from the speeding truck. That Ruby was there whenever London needed her, as she used to be solely for me.

I watched from my window as Ruby talked to Jonah and London out in the driveway—Ruby whispering in London's ear, Ruby plucking off a leaf that had gotten stuck to London's shirt, London letting her—and then I left the window and waited on my bed for Ruby to come upstairs.

"Is she okay?" I made myself ask, once Ruby appeared in my doorway.

Ruby thought some. Then she said, "I don't think she was ever 'okay,' even before, do you?"

I shook my head. I wanted to tell her what I saw. But, more, I wanted to know if she had a direct hand in it.

"Why'd you do it?" I asked, fishing to see how she'd answer that question—if she knew what question was being asked.

If I even did.

"That truck would've flattened her," Ruby said. "She would have had a set of tire tracks permanently etched on her face."

Her expression softened and she stepped inside to come closer to me. She lifted a hand, as if to pick something off my shirt, but then hid the hand behind her back, as if I wouldn't want her doing it. Nothing had changed and yet something had—in the form of that living, breathing bleach-haired girl. "So," Ruby said, "I told Jonah to go out to the highway and fix the flat."

I knew she could have fixed it herself, if she felt like bothering, and I liked that she'd opted not to bother, and stay with me instead.

"London went with him," she continued. "We have the house to ourselves. Wanna go up on the widow's walk? Let your wet hair air-dry? If you want, I could do it up in braids like I used to when you were little? Remember? Then we could stay up there till the sun sets?"

The widow's walk was Ruby's most favorite part of the

house, even if it wasn't a widow's walk, not technically. She'd had Jonah build the tiny platform of a porch as high as he could on the slope of the roof, reachable only through a window at the top of the last set of stairs. She could see everything from up there, she'd told me. She even had a straight view, over the treetops, into the heart of town.

"Sounds good," I said.

She led the way down the hall, moving so fast she'd made the last turn before I reached the first one, and she was all the way up the stairs before I'd even started climbing.

That was when I caught sight of myself in the mirror she'd returned to its spot on the wall. The mirror was hanging crooked in a dark corner, and the face bobbing in the glass startled me. With my hair all one length and down to the middle of my back, and sixteen now to her almost-twenty-two, I resembled her more than ever before.

I stepped away, unable to look anymore, and climbed the stairs. Everything seemed brighter now, drenched in sun. And the brightest point was beyond the three last steps leading up, at the top, on the widow's walk. Out there in the light were two browned feet. The feet, attached to Ruby, wiggled in greeting when I came close, then snapped out of view, indicating that I should crawl through the open window to join her.

She had a lawn chair waiting for me beside hers and beckoned me to sit in it.

"I'm so glad you're here with me, Chloe," she said. "It's how I promised it would be, isn't it? The way it was before? Just like it?"

She wore only her bikini, black on bottom and white on top, and the gold anklet she had on at the pool. Her hair hung down to the curve of her hip, and around her wrist was a single hair elastic. Her face was clean, not a dab of makeup, her nose shiny since she hadn't powdered it. She looked stunning. She looked real. She looked all the more stunning because she was so real.

Somehow, I didn't want to answer her question.

I turned from her and looked out over the railing. We were at the highest point that we could get on the house, short of climbing to the peak of the roof and stretching out our limbs like two weather vanes. And there it was, beyond the dirt patch of the backyard and the half-built wooden deck, past trees and across road, where the land broke open and the water flooded in, exactly where it had been when I saw it my first day home.

Except this time I could see the entire expanse of it, a bird's-eye view of the whole living, breathing thing.

"What are you looking at?" she said, knowing full well what.

"It looks bigger," I said. "Since the last time I saw it."

"That's just from up here. It makes even the mountains seem bigger, see?"

I saw the blue humps of the Catskills, there in the clouds where they'd always been. They didn't seem bigger. They seemed closer from here, not as tall as they appeared from the ground. I turned back to the water.

"No, really," I said. "The reservoir. It looks . . . deeper than it used to. Like, look at those rocks. They used to be way out on shore and now they're almost completely covered in water. Isn't that weird?"

"What rocks?" She shot over to the railing, balancing her weight on the tips of her toes. I heard her take a breath in, surprised by what she saw, I thought, but then she said, "Those are different rocks, Chlo. You've never seen it from this angle. You're confused."

I wanted to argue it—as if I wouldn't remember the rocks on the shore I'd been visiting since I was a baby— but then a small crinkle showed in her forehead, midway between her eyes, and she rubbed at it and rubbed at it and seemed to forget all else.

"I'm getting a migraine," she said. She returned to her reclining lawn chair and moved it into a patch of shade.

"Has there been a lot of rain?" I asked. "Is that why the reservoir looks bigger?"

"Nope," she said, "I can't remember the last time it rained." She swiftly changed the subject. "Hey, Chlo, don't you love this widow's walk? I told Jonah I had to have one, like in the olden days when the husbands went away to sea in pirate ships and the wives kept watch at home. After like a year apart, the wives would see the Jolly Roger out on the horizon and wave the ship into port. Though if I'd been alive back then, I bet I would've been the pirate and made some guy wave for me at home. You think?"

"I don't think widow's walks were built for waving to pirates . . ."

I was noticing how haphazard an addition this so-called widow's walk was to the house. Boards were jutting out where they shouldn't, the platform supported in a way that seemed to have no support at all. I wouldn't have been surprised if the whole thing gave out from our weight and skidded down the side of the house.

Ruby was still talking.

"But you'd wait and wait up on the widow's walk and you wouldn't see any skull and crossbones on the water, not for years. And that's because they weren't coming back, the pirate husbands. They used to drown at sea—which is what happens when you don't take swimming lessons." She shook her head. "In the end, I guess a wife could only hope his ghost would decide to come home and keep her company. She'd go up to the top of her house, and when she saw her husband on the wind, she'd catch him like a firefly and keep him in a jar, on the windowsill, forever. And that's why widow's walks were built on houses."

It was Ruby's favorite kind of story: where the boys lost

and the girls won and got a souvenir in the bargain. It was also factually inaccurate and made no sense if you thought on it too hard.

"I thought you didn't believe in ghosts," I said.

"I didn't say *I'd* catch my husband and keep him in a jar," she said. "If I ever even have a husband."

"Besides," I said, pointing out at the water. "That's not an ocean."

"I know that," she said softly.

The widow's walk had been built, clearly, because she wanted to keep an eye on the water, ocean-size or no. Here, she could watch over what she said lay drowned at the bottom, as this spot was the best view in all of town.

"This patch of land used to be in Olive," Ruby said, jolting me by saying its name aloud. "Before the suits in New York City said there was no such place anymore because they were erasing it. Right up this hill and halfway down the driveway: Olive. Not anymore, of course. Can you believe we're standing in Olive right now, Chlo? Isn't it funny how you'd never even know?"

"I guess," I said. Each time she said its name—Olive—I felt a sharp tug. I had to step away from the railing, sure I'd tip over. Sure I'd fall.

She'd forgotten about doing the braids in my hair like she used to when I was a girl. Instead, she began another one of her stories, telling me again about the people who wouldn't go. How the city bought up their land and forced them to tear down their houses and move someplace else — and some people, they refused. Because who says? Who says they could come up here with their bags of money and make our town their bathtub? She was getting worked up now, saying she understood why they wouldn't leave.

None of this was new and yet, somehow, with the reservoir at my back and the wind spooling out my hair, I felt like I was hearing it for the first time. Really hearing it.

Her eyes glimmered at the idea of the loyal people who refused to abandon the town where they were born and raised. These were Ruby's people. This was practically her town. She wouldn't have been a pirate gone off to pillage vast oceans; she would have been one of those who stayed.

She startled me by telling a part of the story I'd never heard before. Maybe she was making it up, right here, on the spot. Inventing it piece by piece, and girl by girl — for me.

"Back then there were these two girls," she said. "One was the big sister and one was the baby sister, and of course the big sister was the one who took care of them both, because there was no one else to do it, you know?" I did know. She kept going. "The people of Olive didn't understand how close the sisters were. They were jealous. Most people don't have another person who'd do anything for you. *Anything.* Most people, in the end, really are all on their own."

"Didn't the girls have a mother?" I asked.

"I've got no idea," she said dismissively. "Probably she died. Consumption. Fever. Mountain lion. I don't know."

I kept quiet.

"The sisters had the same dad though. That's why they looked so much alike. Their dad . . . guess who he was. Someone important. The mayor of the whole town."

"Really?" I watched her warily. "Who was he?"

"You know Winchell's Corners, on the way to the high school?" That was a lone intersection on Route 28 made up of a pizzeria, an antique store that I was sure had closed, and a traffic light. Ruby tended to ignore all existence of the traffic light, so we always sped right through.

I nodded.

"That was named for him. Mayor Winchell, the last known mayor of Olive. He died before the town got demolished, and no new mayor came after. Once he was gone, the two girls were left all on their own. No one in town would help them—jealous, like I said. The big sister knew she had to take care of her baby sister, because no one else could be trusted to do it."

"And she had to take care of herself," I added.

Ruby waved that away, unconcerned. "All the sisters had to their names was their house in Olive. And when the city came with bulldozers, that house was supposed to get flattened with the rest. The girls were supposed to follow — even though they had nowhere to go and no one left. But the big sister had another idea." She smiled here, waiting for me to say it.

"She didn't go?"

"No, she refused. She and her baby sister — they stayed." She was filled up to glowing at the idea. "Those girls were some of the ones who stayed till the very end, Chlo."

"How do you know all that?" I asked. "Did you read it somewhere?"

"Hmm?" she said, distracted. "We wouldn't've left, either. We would've stayed put until the last day, till they finished building the dam and the machines went quiet and the workers got sent back to wherever they came from. Till it was time."

"Time for what?"

"Time for the flood, Chlo. Time to take away our everything."

"What would we have done?" I was almost whispering, but still she heard me. I wasn't sure anymore who she was talking about — the two Winchell sisters, the older one who knew what to do or the younger one who followed, or us, real or unreal, alive or dead, catalogued in history or completely made up, the four of us confused and washed away on a wave together.

"What do you think we would've done?" Ruby said. "We would've climbed to the highest point of our house. And waited it out, just like those two girls did. The big sister led her baby sister up there, and they perched on their chimney and waited. Because when the dam was opened, they couldn't be sure how high the water would get—it's not like there was a line drawn in a tree trunk to give a heads-up or anything. All the trees had been chopped down.

"But before the water came, there was this sound, so loud you could hear it for miles. That was the only real warning they'd get. Last chance, run while you still can. . . . Know what it sounded like?"

She pursed her lips and let loose a shrieking hiss, like some instrument had its holes plugged and then broke apart, bursting with noise. Awful, painful noise. Ruby—it wasn't known by many, or else they all ignored it—was actually tone-deaf.

"A steam whistle," she explained. "But imagine that it played on and on—for an hour. A whole hour to give everyone time to get out. Then it stopped, and it was so quiet for a few seconds, you could've heard birds chirping in the trees . . . if, you know, they hadn't burned down the forest and killed the birds. The steam whistle stopped. And the water gushed in. And you and I know what happened after that."

"And those girls?" I asked.

She let her eyes go to the water, and I let mine follow. That was her answer.

"So the big sister lost her little sister after all that," I said. "Didn't she?"

"What do you mean?" Ruby said blankly. "Weren't you listening?"

I was. I was trying to hear—and understand.

I returned my gaze to the reservoir, and now a shiver ran through me as I studied the calm, smooth surface. You wouldn't think there was anything living underneath, not even fish. But my sister and I knew better.

When I looked back at Ruby, something had changed in her face. Her skin still glowed, her lips flushed without need of her lipstick, and her eyes taking on the green of the trees, but that was only what she was showing on the surface. Underneath, there were things she wasn't letting me see.

Things involving the reservoir, I felt sure of that. Things involving Olive.

"Why are you telling me this, Ruby?" I asked.

"I only wanted you to know," she said innocently.

"What does all this stuff about Olive have to do with us?"

She opened her mouth. Then she closed it because we could hear voices down below in the yard. Jonah had come back, with London.

Ruby went to the edge of the widow's walk and called

over the railing, "Did you fix the flat?" They spoke some, and then she turned to me.

One thing she'd forgotten to bring up to the widow's walk was a pair of sunglasses, so she covered her eyes with a hand while she looked at me. That way, she could see me, but I couldn't see all of her.

"Lon said she's driving in to town to hang out with her friends, those girls, I can't remember their names," Ruby said. "She wants to know if you'd like to go, too."

"Me?" I said.

"Yes, you. She invited you."

"Did you tell her to?"

She didn't answer that. "Maybe you *should* go. Like I said before"—she tapped at her head—"I do feel a migraine coming."

She lifted the hand from her eyes and gave a faint smile. When the light hit her face, all at once she did look a bit ill, which was odd, as she'd looked close to perfect before.

"You sure?" I said.

"Yeah, yeah," she said.

I doubted her story of the headache. She kept flicking glances at the reservoir, acting like she and it had some business to take care of. But to do so she needed me well out of the way.

Ruby leaned over the railing. "Who'll be there again?" she called to London.

I heard London rattle off some names. Vanessa, Asha, a Cate or a Kate.

"Okay, then, that's all right," Ruby said.

I took a step to go downstairs and join London, but Ruby wasn't done with me yet.

"Chlo," she said, "could you do one thing for me? Keep an eye on her?"

"Why?" I wasn't about to explain what I saw in the pool. She probably wouldn't believe it; no one would.

"Because I asked you to," she said.

"Okay," I said, slipping a leg through the window. "I'll keep an eye on her. Are you sure you want me to go out?" I was hesitating, hovering at the windowsill, knowing I wouldn't argue if she called me back.

"Yeah, I'm sure. Oh wait. I thought of a second thing. Stay in town, you and London both. Don't go anywhere else. Promise me."

"I promise." I put my other leg through. She didn't call me back. "You're not staying out here, are you? Not with your migraine and all?"

She shrugged. "I like it up here. I'll probably be in this same spot when you come home." To prove it, she reclined the lawn chair and stretched out, as though she wouldn't just sit up as soon as I was gone.

Still, I felt her watching me as I balanced along the boards of the hallway and went down the stairs. I felt sure she wanted to call after me, take it back, all of it: telling me to go with London of all people, distracting me with stories about the reservoir of all places, making up that story about that Winchell girl and her little sister . . . But she didn't call for me, and it wasn't until I was in the passenger seat of London's parents' car, window rolled down and my hair ratting up in the rushing wind, that I realized this was my first real moment apart from my sister since I'd come home.

I wasn't sure who I was without her anymore. Now I'd find out.

CHAPTER ELEVEN

WITHOUT RUBY

Without Ruby, I turned quiet next to London and her friends.

It was London's idea to go to the graveyard—to get high. If we smoked up in the car, she said, the cops or someone's parents could drive by and see. This sure wasn't what Ruby had in mind when she sent me off with London, I knew that, and yet I was reluctant to text my sister and fill her in.

I was left standing in the parking lot as they set off in the direction of the old cemetery. I looked across the road back at the newer cemetery, the one with the tall iron gate and the neatly mowed lawns, the one where London herself would have been buried if time had gone another way.

"Chloe! Aren't you coming?" That was London, shouting from across the road.

More of London's friends were there, climbing the hill. Asha and Cate. Vanessa and Damien. Some boy whose name I hadn't caught. And then Owen, here though London hadn't said he would be, here and not having spoken a word to me yet.

"Chloe?" London called, and then she turned and started climbing without me, so I crossed the road and headed up the hill before I lost sight of her.

This old cemetery was the one without a gate to mark its boundaries, with the stones so weathered, they sunk at odd angles back into the earth like they didn't want you remembering them after all. Anyway, making it so you couldn't even try.

Also, it was more private than the newer cemetery across the road. There was a raised mausoleum facing away from the sidewalk, and back there were two stone benches and a long-dead fountain, so you could fit a whole group of kids — five, six, seven, with me there, eight — and do whatever you wanted, having full confidence the town's lackluster cops or occasional lurking perv wouldn't be able to see. It was also a fantastic place to hook up with your boyfriend, or so I'd heard.

The mausoleum was gray stone, pitted and murky like it had been left at the bottom of a pond for a thousand years and then dredged up for some sun. I'd been here before. Ruby used to let me color with crayons over the engraved, locked door.

Before the private perch of the mausoleum there was a rising hill littered with the cracked and withered headstones of the people who didn't matter enough to have their own house in which to spend their eternities. These people were so long gone, none of their relatives even lived in our town anymore. No one left flowers or came to have picnics atop their dirt beds on passing birthdays. No one tended the weeds here, so the hill was really all weeds now, far more weeds than stones.

The gravestones themselves were thin and plain. Many were chipped and blackened with mold, some growing mushrooms. Even now, one of the boys, Laurence—I heard someone call him by that name—did a running leap and knocked over a thin, tall stone under which no one we knew still lies, and he didn't even go back to pick it up.

Laurence and Asha and Cate and the rest of them weren't thinking of dying, not while they were racing up this hill. They didn't know how close one of them had come. The taste in her mouth when it happened, the last sight of the stars overhead seared on the backs of her eyes.

Maybe London herself remembered—though how could she? The mind stops printing new memories once they've been flatlined away.

Before that night at the reservoir, Ruby and I used to talk about dying—about how it might happen, what we'd do if it did. She had a whole plan for her afterlife, which involved haunting certain blood relatives, playing polter-geist on former landlords and schoolteachers, and playing chicken with cars. She'd have a road in town named for her, or better yet a bridge, and leave me every last thing she owned in her will. She acted like she would stay forever the way she was, never marrying and never having kids, and surely never leaving our small mountain town, and that I'd be the only one left to remember her, though really everyone would, I told her, especially if she got her name on a bridge.

Ruby wanted me to know that her headstone should be pink granite, even if it cost extra. Pink or no headstone at all. And she'd already written out the inscription, handed over to me a long time ago for safekeeping:

Ruby
Beloved Sister of Chloe
Gas Station Attendant
Phenomenal Kisser
(ask anyone)
Lies Here

For those leaving flowers, she wanted a small directive added at the bottom, to show her preference:

Poppies Only, Please

She was very specific in letting me know what her headstone should say, but she didn't like it when I tried to figure out what I might want for mine. I couldn't pick a color, and

I couldn't tell her what should be written on it, because she never wanted to read those words, not in this lifetime, and not in our next lifetime, if there were such a thing as multiple lifetimes, which Ruby happened to think there were.

Up at the mausoleum, London's friends were passing around a joint. I accepted it when it came my way for politeness' sake, and took the tiniest puff of a hit before passing it on. I didn't know if Ruby would have let me go if she knew we'd be smoking and sharing spit up on this hill full of headstones like we were, that I'd be coughing out smoke longer than anyone, unable to get that dry tickle out of my throat. Ruby smoked weed, but that didn't mean I could. She did a lot of things I wasn't supposed to imitate. She did them in the room with me, but I guess she expected me to look away.

I was here now, without her, and I wasn't looking away. My eyes were starting to come clear.

That's why I found myself staring at London.

Her friends acted like she was nothing unusual. But, to me, she was a shrill and shrieking fire alarm in a quiet library, and not a single person seemed to hear it. Were they deaf? Was everyone?

"Right, Chloe?" someone was saying—I hadn't been paying attention.

"What?" I said.

"Your sister drew that, right?" Cate asked.

"Yeah, guess so." Only a single glance told me it was one of hers.

Because there it was—a masterpiece à la Ruby—covering an entire side of the mausoleum. She'd used chalk, the kind made to scribble slogans on sidewalks, the kind that washed away to nothing when it rained. She liked to scrawl her name to show she'd been somewhere. Practically our whole town was tagged. But this mural was more of a mark than she usually bothered to leave. In fact, it was enormous.

"I love it," Vanessa breathed.

"It's, like, really beautiful," Asha said.

Cate nodded. "That's you, isn't it?"

And there I was—I mean, anyone would assume it was me—a chalk stick figure in blue, since Ruby said that was my color, and with my hair in bangs, since Ruby had always liked my hair in bangs. I didn't look like that now, so clearly she'd drawn me as she remembered me before I went away.

In the drawing, my stick hand was holding the hand of another, far taller figure. This one was drawn to be the size of a mountain in comparison to me—with a head made of swirls and enormous green orbs meant to be her all-seeing eyes. Her hands alone dwarfed my stick body, dwarfed the yellow smudge of the sun. Her feet in tall boots walked the water, touching only the tips of her toes to the blue squiggles meant to be undulating waves. She carried me above it all, my toes touching only air. Her dark hair made a long, flowing cape behind us both.

The drawing was Ruby by Ruby. And below it, so you could make no mistake who was responsible, etched out in red chalk, it read:

RUBY WAS HERE

For some reason, she wanted her mark there, and she wanted no one to forget it.

I dragged my eyes from the chalk mural to find Owen glaring openly at it. He hated what she'd done to the mausoleum, this showed clear in his face, but maybe his hate went deeper than her drawing ability. Maybe he hated the one person in the world who I loved.

I knew that art wasn't one of Ruby's talents, but no one seemed quite willing to point this out. So I said, "It's sort of"—surprising myself as the word found my mouth— "hideous, isn't it?"

Owen had been leaning on the bench across from me, toking up, but when I said that, he stopped slouching and paid attention.

"Oh no," said Vanessa. "It's not. Not at all."

"It's *not* hideous," Cate said sharply, as if she herself had drawn it.

Did they think I was trying to trick them?

I stepped closer to the mural, touched Ruby's bulbous head. "She looks deformed, don't you think?"

Damien laughed, then choked on the laugh, then pretended he was only coughing. Laurence cracked a grin and didn't bother hiding it. London, who hadn't said a word about the mural yet, had a look of grave concern on her face, as if she were watching me step out too far on a patch of ice. If it cracked, I had no way of knowing if she'd reach out a hand to pull me back in. Ruby wasn't here to see if she didn't.

"I wouldn't say deformed . . ." Cate said.

I watched her, waiting to hear what she *would* say.

"It's like a, like a"—waving her hands now, trying to talk faster than the thoughts would come—"like a Picasso or whatever," she finished.

Most everyone murmured in agreement.

There was a chill in the air, one that couldn't be explained by the wind, because it was summer and we were all sweating. A chill not even explained by the fact that we were in a graveyard where a bunch of dead people were buried and some of us were maybe sitting on them. A chill that, I guess, was explained by me.

Or by London.

She was breathing like she had two working lungs inside her, as any living person would, but that's not what was in there, was it? I couldn't keep my eyes off her chest, the rhythmic rise and fall of her ribs—the simplest thing and yet so wondrous of a thing, too, because it was her, and I didn't totally believe in her yet. There was a time not too long ago when I didn't think I'd ever again see her breathing.

I still questioned if she was really here. I could turn to pass the joint, skipping over myself and giving her the next drag, and there'd be no hand to take it. No fingers reaching for my fingers. I'd hold it out for her, bright and burning, and she'd be gone.

But while I watched her, what she was watching was my sister's picture. She kept her eyes on it like it could come alive at any moment and step off the wall onto the nearest grave, chiding us for what we said. What I said.

Like, somehow, it *knew*.

"What do you think, London?" I said, startling her. "About the picture."

Would she lie to me because I was Ruby's sister and everyone always only told me things they thought Ruby wanted to hear? Acting like my ears were on her head, or my mouth was in her ear? Would London say it was like a Picasso?

Before she could answer for herself, Damien said, "Don't ask *her*, she probably helped draw the thing."

"She did not," I said automatically. Then added, "What do you mean she probably helped?"

"London and your sister were like this," he said, twining his two fingers together to make one twisted lump of a finger. "All spring."

"You were?" I asked London. No matter what she said, there was no way two people could be close the way Ruby and I were close, not if they weren't sisters. It went beyond biology, beyond years spent together, beyond secrets kept. It wasn't possible.

Vanessa spoke up. "It's not like that. It's far more pathetic than that. Right, Lon?"

London looked uncomfortable now. She wouldn't meet my eyes. She coughed, though the joint wasn't even near her.

"London's like her little pawn," Vanessa spilled out. "She does whatever your sister wants, whenever she wants it. Ruby'll text her at two in the morning, and London'll fly out and like get her a lemonade or whatever. She'll drop everything if Ruby wants her. If Ruby says she can't do something or go somewhere, or I dunno who knows, Lon just says okay. Like it's God talking." Vanessa snickered at this and then shut up when no one else joined her.

London only shrugged. She didn't try to deny it.

"People act like that with Ruby," I said, going on the defensive. "It's not her fault. She just . . . inspires it, I guess. I mean, half the people in town are, like, in love with her and she never asked them to be, you know?"

It wasn't out of the ordinary, someone following my sister like a shadow and keeping her in lemonade—it happened to be summer, and my sister happened to get thirsty. Ruby always had followers. Look at Pete, look at Jonah, look at any number of her exes and acquaintances and the Ruby-wannabes with the long hair and short dresses and tall boots who filled our town. London wasn't special.

Except for the fact that she was.

"Yeah, but London's not in love with her," Laurence said. "*I'm* half in love with her—no offense, Chloe, your sister is fine—and even I don't go all zombie-slave in front of her like Lon does."

"It's not like that," London said. "You guys, you just don't know. You don't know, okay? You don't know."

Not one of her friends said a word.

"She's been looking out for me," London said quietly. "Ever since I got home this spring."

"You got home this spring?" I asked. "From where?"

"Rehab," she mumbled. "I was there . . . a while, and when I got out of rehab I guess she, y'know, cares enough to keep an eye on me."

I couldn't tell if she was lying for everyone else's benefit. That's what she thought happened to her . . . rehab? Maybe she didn't know as much as I thought she did.

"She OD'd," Cate shot out helpfully. London glared at her, but Cate kept on going, oblivious. "She totally almost died at some party out at the reservoir. What was it? Two summers ago? It was, like, really awful. I mean, I heard it was awful. I wasn't there or anything, but yeah."

Asha sighed and made a sad face. "I never knew anyone

who had an overdose before," she said randomly. "Did you get to ride in an ambulance to the hospital, Lon?"

"I . . . I don't know," London said. "I don't really remember if I did or not."

She did; at least her body did—only, it didn't end up at the hospital.

Owen was extra quiet during this conversation. He'd been there with London that night—he just wasn't revealing that bit of information.

I thought of what Ruby had asked of me when I'd left her up on the widow's walk to go with London. *Keep an eye on her,* she'd said.

Ruby was acting as if the girl were about to combust. As if this thing that was happening—the breath coming out her mouth, the beat thumping in her chest, whatever bit of science or imagination was keeping her alive—wasn't permanent after all. But none of us had any idea what London was made of now and what she might do.

I was trying not to think of her lying belly-up in the boat, trying not to see her blue and OD'd and dead. I was focusing on her mouth moving, hearing the words come out— and she was undeniably still here.

"I—I'm sorry," I said to London. There wasn't much else I could say.

"Yeah, that's why I was away for so long," she said. "But I'm way better now."

I didn't say a word about the joint she'd been smoking, as, technically, that wasn't something you were supposed to run off and do after rehab, even if you shared it eight ways with friends. I wondered if I should have stopped her, if that was part of keeping an eye on her like Ruby wanted.

What London didn't seem to remember was how Ruby had saved her. How, somehow, my sister had turned back the clocks and grabbed her from the swirling, sinking fate she'd gotten herself caught up in and flipped time another way. Ruby had done this wonderful thing and given her this second chance, and here was London, having no idea of any of it.

But I knew.

I knew that Ruby, my own sister—she'd done this.

When something big happens, you don't immediately point the finger at one person. A bridge collapses, and maybe that's what people call an act of God, not of the little girl in the backseat of a passing car wishing something would happen to keep her from having to stay the weekend with her creepy uncle. A plane loses its propellers and crash-lands on water, and no one blames the guy sitting in 13B who can't get a date and wants to die over it and doesn't care if he takes the whole damn plane with him.

No human being could take credit for changing fate.

Except for Ruby.

CHAPTER TWELVE

I'LL TELL YOU

I'll tell you what happened if you want," London said. She'd taken a few steps from the group and was lying on the ground just outside the stone platform of the mausoleum, playing with the grass surrounding an unvisited grave.

"Okay," I said. I stretched out, too, and let the setting sun warm my face. I kicked off Ruby's boots and put my toes in the cool grass.

"I don't remember any ambulance. But I do remember these really weird things." She hesitated. "I think it's all right to tell you. Ruby said I shouldn't tell anyone, but . . ."

"Ruby said?"

That's when we heard yelling. It had been so slow, the afternoon gone in a haze, but now there was commotion on top of the hill. Stomping. Shrieking. A heady, musty scent billowing out from somewhere up above.

Asha called down an explanation. "Laurence kicked that tomb thing open. There's a whole room inside!"

Soon we were all up there, pushing in to see for ourselves, and just as soon, we were vacating the small, dark
space filled with cobwebs and reeking of mildew, nothing
worth stealing that anyone could find. But it was then, as
I was the last to leave, that I saw the words etched on the
inner wall.

Dust tried to hide them from me, but I could still make
them out.

Beloved Mayor of Olive, the words seemed to say, the
dates below showing 1851–1912. The name itself was partly crumbled out, some letters lost to the years, but when I
carefully dusted it clean, this is what it read:

W lt r Winchell

Rest in Peace

Mayor Winchell, the last mayor of Olive before the town
got itself drowned, according to Ruby. Now his name was
known for marking a streetlight.

I returned to one word, putting my finger to it to wipe
decades of grime away, tracing the *O* and the *live*, the name
of the town I'd never pictured existing above the surface,
though it had, before the reservoir wiped it away. Ruby had
said so, but now I knew for sure: The person in this tomb
had lived in it.

I was rubbing at my eyes, wondering if I'd smoked
too much, how even if I hadn't, it must've seeped into my
brain anyway, that I'd breathed it, that all along I'd been

breathing it, because now I was hallucinating. My mind was carving words into the walls and my eyes were duped into reading meaning into them.

I touched the words once more and noticed London hovering in the tomb's doorway.

She moved slowly through the dusty air like it was thicker than it felt, a plodding, ceaseless bobbing nearer and nearer to me. And once she stood beside me, as near as I let her get, I felt the chill of her, the creeping cold radiating from deep inside her icy bones.

I remembered how she looked at me at the bottom of the pool. How she wanted me to know just what she was made of.

"What's wrong?" she asked, though she had to know, she had to. Now her long, thin finger was tracing the name of the town the way mine had. Her finger was bitter cold, stinging my hand before I moved it away.

She read the word and didn't blink.

"That's the town," I found myself telling her. "The one at the bottom of the reservoir that Ruby always talks about."

"I know," she said.

"You do?"

"I know things," she said. "Ruby tells me stuff."

She slunk back against the wall, and as she did it seemed that the shadows were moving all around her, crouching low as if they had a hold of her by the legs. Maybe we weren't alone in here; maybe we had company who'd come out to listen.

My own legs were getting heavier now. I felt it at my ankles, the familiar tug, and before it could fully bring me back—to that night, the night London remembered differently—one of her friends poked a head in.

"You guys, we're so bored!" Asha shrieked, breathless. "You know what we should do? Go on the swings! In the rec field!"

Vanessa ran up next. "We totally should. What do you think, Lon?"

"Sure," London said, her face expressionless. Maybe what she really wanted was to stay back alone with me, in this darkened tomb, just the two of us, but she ended up giving in and following her friends.

I couldn't get my heart to stop thumping for minutes after.

We left the mausoleum to find that, outside, dark was clearly falling. For a moment, I wasn't sure how long we'd been inside that tomb. It was here when I thought to check my phone, to see if maybe Ruby had texted.

The light was flashing, and Ruby's texts went on for a whole screen:

dreamed we ate mushrooms growing on ceiling & u had only 4 toes

4 toes ON EACH FOOT not only 4 toes! omg what if

u had only 4 toes????

did u hide the good cereal? want frosting chlo

migraine gone away. u should come home

come home now. miss u

starting 2 worry. y not answering? y not home yet?

worried

worried

worried

think i need new boots we shld go shopping

btw could u bring home cereal?

"Wow, are those all from Ruby?" Asha said, leaning over.

"I should call her," I said.

"Please don't," Cate said quickly, then she had her hand over her mouth to show she hadn't meant to say that, not out loud in front of me.

Vanessa started talking for her, trying to ease the damage. "What she means is, maybe you don't want to call her right now? Maybe we should go across the street to the swings first? And you can call her after?"

"I should at least text her," I said, pulling up her number on my phone.

But then Damien had my phone, then Vanessa had it, then Laurence, then Damien again.

Owen wouldn't have anything to do with my phone — or me — and stood at a distance, hands behind his back so no one would make him catch it, but then he opened his mouth, and he said some words in my general direction: "Do you have to tell her every single thing you do? She's not your mother."

"No," I said. "I don't have to."

I never had to. Her hand wasn't at my throat forcing me to open up and spill so she could know all. She never dug around inside me, grabbing secrets to pull out; she didn't have to go digging, since she knew them already.

"Good," Owen said.

Owen had never seemed enamored by Ruby. Sometimes it felt like a typhus epidemic had taken out an entire village but spared one lone person and that was him. Not even I had the immunity. It made me distrust him, but somehow, against my better judgment, which meant against all words of Ruby-wisdom in my head, it made me like him more.

"Okay," I said, and didn't ask for my phone back, and soon I was following everyone down the hill, headed for the rec field across the road. It was night now and I was crossing the dark street, free of traffic, and running across the lawn to reach the swings. I was well aware of the chain-link fence just beside us, on the other side of which was the newer of the two graveyards, the one that maybe, if I'd only known where among the headstones to go searching, would have revealed an empty plot in the grass that should have been London's grave.

Asha, Vanessa, and Cate already had the only three swings, so the rest of us were left standing in the grass.

"This is lame," Owen said. He made a move as if to walk off, but I must have startled him when I saw the light flashing, because he stopped and turned back.

The light was coming from inside Damien's pants pocket—my cell phone. It wasn't a new text message from Ruby, it was an actual phone call from Ruby, an event that was really quite rare.

I grabbed for his pants and answered her call. "Ruby?"

"Chloe!" she shouted. "Did you want me to think you got kidnapped? To call out the dogs? Send an APB? What were you thinking, Chlo!"

"Ruby, I'm okay, I'm fine, really . . . what's an APB?"

"I dunno, something cops do. Whatever, Chlo, it doesn't matter, I was worried!"

"I'm okay, I swear."

I could hear her take a long, deep breath to calm herself. She held it in, then let it out and said, "You have all your legs?"

"Both legs," I said, smiling.

"And toes? All ten?"

"All my toes. How's your head?"

"Fine now. You sure you're okay? No one tried to—"

I stopped her before she said anything we didn't want said. "No one tried anything, Ruby. I'm here with London and, uh, you know, Vanessa and Asha and . . . Cate. We lost track of time, that's all."

"That's not all of who's there," she said, and she said it as if she were watching the scene right now from a hiding spot concealed in the trees.

"And Laurence," I mumbled. "And Damien. And . . ."

"And?"

"And O," I said. "Owen's here, too." His face was unreadable as I confessed him being there; I couldn't tell if he wanted her to know or not.

There was a long beat of silence on the other end of the line as she took this in. She could have yelled, and everyone would have heard, and I would have been mortified. But she saved her true response to that for later.

"I see," she said. "So what're you doing that's so interesting you lost track of time and couldn't text your sister even though I know you have a clock on that cell phone?"

"Nothing," I said.

"Where are you then, doing this nothing?"

"Just"—I eyed London and her friends—"no place really."

"Are you at the reservoir?"

"Why would you think that? No, we're not at the reservoir."

"You sure?"

"I swear."

Everyone was looking at me now. *"We were in the cemetery,"* I whispered. I walked away to the fence.

"Okay," she said. She didn't seem the least bit surprised. *"The* old *cemetery."*

And, here, before I had the question on my tongue, she was saying, "The one that used to be in Olive. My favorite one."

"So you knew about that?"

"Sure. Parts of Olive got moved before the water was flooded in. Roads got rerouted, and some houses were picked up and stuck somewhere else, and then there were the cemeteries and what they did with them . . . I'm sure I told you before. What did you think, all this time we were swimming on people's graves?"

"I—I don't know." The way she'd told it, maybe I had thought that.

"Oh no," she said. "All the graveyards were relocated first. Sometimes people did their own families, and could you imagine? One of us having to dig up our mother?"

"No," I said. I couldn't—didn't want to—imagine that.

"So you were in the graveyard," she said. "I'm glad you two stayed in town like I told you."

"Yeah," I said. "But when I was up there . . . I saw . . . *the mayor."*

"What do you mean you *saw* him?"

I turned and caught everyone still eyeing me. They

couldn't know what we were talking about. Maybe they thought I was inviting Ruby here, or that Ruby was inviting herself. Their eyes said something I couldn't quite decipher because none of them were Ruby and I wasn't used to reading anyone's eyes but Ruby's. Something about . . . about how I should try to keep Ruby from coming if I could.

"Ruby?" I said into the phone.

"Don't worry, Chlo. I know what you're thinking, and stop it. I don't want you scared. Because there's nothing here that could hurt you. I made sure."

Just hearing her say that made me think she'd once thought something here could. Hurt me. That this had been a real and viable worry in her mind and, without warning me first, she went ahead and found a way to be certain it couldn't.

"Is Lon still there with you?" she said.

"Yeah."

"You're keeping an eye on her like I asked?"

"*Yeah,*" I said, immediately annoyed. "I'm looking at her right now. She's fine."

"At least there's that," Ruby said. "As for you, Chlo, we'll talk later, after London drives you home. Your curfew is midnight. I've never believed in curfews for myself—like I would've listened if our mother gave me one." She laughed, sharply, and I held the phone away from my ear as she did.

"But," she went on, and I pulled the phone back, "I've decided I now believe in curfews for you. Midnight." And at that she cut the line.

I turned around to face everyone. "I have to be home by midnight, London."

"No problem," she said. "Ruby knows I'll drive you."

London took a step forward now, like she'd been voted the one to speak.

"So," London said, as I walked closer, "does that mean Ruby's not coming?" She suddenly looked so fragile, as if I could knock her over into the dark, damp grass with the tap of a finger and she wouldn't have the strength to pull herself back up.

"She's not coming," I said.

"Sweet," Laurence said.

"Good," Owen said.

But Asha said, "Know what was weird? Your sister like totally freaked when she thought we were all at the reservoir, didn't she?"

I tried to be nonchalant about that. "She's protective. She worries."

"Was she worried about Lon? 'Cause of what we were talking about before?"

"No, she just doesn't want me swimming there, that's all."

Asha wouldn't let it go. "But why would she worry about

you swimming in the reservoir? That makes, like, no sense."

I didn't get it.

"Yeah," Damien called from a dark spot in the grass, "didn't you swim all the way across back in the day?"

"In the middle of the night," Asha said with awe in her voice, "from one shore to the other and then back again — everyone talks about that night."

"The night I *tried* to swim across," I corrected her.

"Yeah, right," she said, as if I were being modest. "I heard it was amazing. Everyone says so. Ruby said you could swim it, and no one believed her. But Ruby was like, 'Just watch.' And so you dove in. And you went deep under. And you made it to the other shore and everyone saw and you waved and then you came all the way back across with, like, proof or something, and it was amazing, everyone says."

"What proof?" I asked.

Her face went blank. "I dunno. You were there. Don't you remember?"

People in town remembered what they did because that's the story Ruby told them. It's the story she wanted everyone to remember, so she must have recited it again and again, jamming their ears with it till they knew it by heart. Until they thought it true.

"How old were you?" Asha said.

"Fourteen," I said quietly.

"Wow," she said. "You know no one's ever done that, before or since?"

I could say, *It was no big*, act like I could do the butterfly stroke back and forth across the giant expanse of the reservoir if I wanted to—and more. Pretend like I could swim to the end of the Hudson, slip into the bay, circle the Statue of Liberty, cross the ocean, backstroke the English Channel, come home kicking with a Mediterranean tan and an armful of undersea shells for souvenirs.

But I didn't. I shrugged off any more talk of the reservoir and took my turn at the swings. We didn't stay in the rec field for much longer—the guys got bored fast—but I gathered up enough speed on the swings to rise as high as I could before I had to jump down and follow them to the cars.

All I kept thinking was that I was Ruby's sister. In this town, I could do whatever crazy and impossible thing I wanted. Everyone already believed I had, simply because Ruby had made it so.

And if she could do that, she could make them believe anything.

CHAPTER THIRTEEN

WHAT LONDON REMEMBERED

Wwhat London remembered was being asleep for a week. Eyes crusted closed, limbs too heavy to lift, she slept until she couldn't sleep another minute and then she woke up.

The first thing she saw when she opened her eyes were curtains. She remembered those curtains, blue she said, or green sometimes, one day one color, one day the other color, some days both colors at once. The curtains moved, she remembered, always, caught in gust after gust of wind. Besides the curtains, she remembered being cold all the time and that her sneakers squished. She remembered how she had trouble hearing anything anyone said to her. How at first it was only lots of mouths talking at her, and hands with fingers pointing, and then, one day, her ears popped and she could hear fine.

This was rehab.

It was now close to midnight, and London was driving me to the house, back to Ruby.

I'd figured "rehab" would be this blank, cavernous space of time in London's mind, like how when someone overdoses they're not yet dead but the next step to it, and so there's nothing to remember. But London remembered. Did this mean she hadn't ever been dead?

Some things she'd said were sticking with me.

The moving colors.

The ears popping, like water had gotten in them.

And then there was the lack of clocks.

Ruby used to say that time stopped down in Olive— that there was no point in trying to keep track. The poor people of Olive couldn't even wear wristwatches, since the hands got glommed up and the thick, murky water leaked in. There was a clock on the old Village Green, she said, and it always read eleven past two, the exact point in time the flood levels reached the clock face, so forever after in Olive that was the time, day or night, eleven past two for eternity.

Ruby also used to say how cold it was down there. How the people of Olive shivered so, their knees knocking, chattering their algae-gummed teeth. Their liquid sky was too thick to let in more than a hint of sun, so in their underwater village they grew paler, and their hearts grew colder, and the memories of their surface lives drifted up and away.

London was turning the car onto the road that ran

alongside the reservoir—the same road that led to Jonah's house—but she didn't steal a peek through the trees. We drove past the reservoir without a word about it, as if it were any other thing: a garbage dump or a gas station or the guy who sells roses out of a bucket on Route 375.

"Ruby said I shouldn't tell anyone about rehab—it's not good to dwell, she said—but it's okay to tell you, right?" She'd asked me this before, but I hadn't answered.

Now I said, "Right," even though I was lying.

"So I don't know how long I was there," she was saying as we came even closer to the house where Ruby and I now lived. "It was only when I got out that I knew how long. Ruby was there, and she drove me home, and she said everything was back the way it used to be, and—"

"Wait," I said, stopping her from saying more. We were in the driveway now, long and winding and carved out of gravel and dirt, seconds from having to stop this conversation, and I wanted to be sure I had it right. "Ruby was there when you got out? She picked you up?"

London drove slowly, thinking at the same slow pace. "I remember her there," she said. "I think." She shook her head and the car made it around the last curve and we came to a stop. "But it's weird because I also remember going swimming that night, like before I even saw my parents. I must have been really out of it to go swimming first, right?"

The door of the house was coming open. The light inside

showed Ruby, as if she'd waited at the hole where the door-knob should have been, peering out of it like a peephole. She wore a thin, pale dress, her hair down to cover where it was see-through. The headlights were so bright, they about illuminated her insides.

"My parents used to wait up for me like that," London said. Her face had drawn in and closed up, and I could see she regretted telling me about rehab. She must have real-ized that telling me was just like telling my sister, but with a ten-second delay.

"They don't wait up for you anymore, your parents?"

She shrugged. "Everything's different since I got back," was all she said.

Ruby didn't come out to the car. She simply held the door to the house open, knowing I'd be right in. "See you later, London," I said, so casual, as if she were a regular girl and not something entirely other. Something I had no name for.

Ruby hugged me close when I came through the door, and we watched London until she backed out of the drive-way, watched until the car slipped around the bend and there was nothing to see. Ruby sniffed my hair and knew all, at once, without me having to confess to it. Her green eyes had gray in them and her mouth had gone grim.

"Look at the time, Chlo."

I glanced at my cell phone to see that the display read 12:02.

"It's midnight," I told her.

"No," she said, "it's *after* midnight. It's twelve-oh-two."

"But I—" She shook her head, so I stopped talking.

"Did you leave town?" she asked.

"No, I told you where we were."

I stepped into the lamplight of the living room, and when I did she saw what I was wearing, a mistake because she saw my feet.

"Hey, those are my good boots," she said. "You took them from my closet."

I denied it—but only the part about the closet. The boots had been jumbled in with the mess on her bedroom floor, one by a window and one under the bed.

She changed the subject. "Chloe, you should have told me boys were going to be there. You never said anything about any boys being there."

"But I didn't know." I was utterly confused at how she was acting—like she was tallying up all the things I'd done wrong, and I'd only gone out without her this one night, and it had been her idea to send me. Was she being a parent now? What would she do next, ground me?

"Did that boy touch you? Don't look at me like that, you know who I mean."

"Owen? No! He barely even came near me."

"I've never known a boy who didn't at least *try* to touch me."

"But, Ruby, you're *you*."

"And you're you," she said.

She sighed, and I sighed, and we both couldn't fathom what the other was trying to say. Something inside her had come unhinged while I was out, and it was running wild, cornering me near the standing lamp in the living room and blathering ridiculous things.

But then she gathered herself together, gave me space, and said, "It's only that I want what's best for you. Only that I know things you can't know."

"What things?"

She shook her head. Slowly she lifted an arm to point up the stairs.

I started upstairs, but she stayed down at the bottom. "Aren't you coming up?"

"Not yet," she said.

I climbed to the landing and looked down, teetering at the edge where, in a finished house, there'd be a railing so you couldn't fall through and break a leg. She kept to a dark spot in the living room, hovering in a gap of space where I had trouble seeing her. There was also a giant fern, a tall chair, and a love seat in the way.

"Go to bed, Chlo. We'll talk tomorrow."

"Why are you treating me like a child?"

"Because you're acting like one. Getting stoned—you reek, FYI. Not telling me where you were. Not meeting your curfew. Not to mention filching my boots—those ones with the heels are almost my favorite pair, Chlo. Like my second or third favorite."

I tried to protest, but she had a hand raised. A shut-your-trap hand, one like she'd never raised up to me before. Just like we'd never had a fight before. Not ever before this, not even once.

"This isn't why I wanted you home," she said. "You won't turn into her, Chlo. I won't stand here and let it happen."

"You're the one who told me to go!"

"I did," she said, more to herself than to me. "It seems like everything I do has consequences now. I do one thing and something else falls apart. I fix that and"—she heaved a sigh—"never mind. Go to bed, Chlo. Tomorrow we'll have dessert for breakfast and breakfast for dinner. Tomorrow we'll talk. All right?"

I nodded.

I left her then, half hidden behind the love seat and the chair and the towering fern, but I watched from the window in the hallway upstairs as she went outside and walked the section of porch Jonah had been building for her. Watched as she walked it like a runway, the wind billowing up inside her translucent dress and spooling out her dark hair, mak-

ing it seem like she was the one we should really be keeping an eye on. Watched as she walked to the end, studied
the stretch of darkness for some minutes, poised as if she
were about to do something fantastic and I'd be the only
one awake to witness it, then watched as she turned around
and walked all the way back.

CHAPTER FOURTEEN

IT'S TIME

It's time we had the talk," Ruby announced. We were out on the widow's walk again, the sky swollen with clouds and bursting blue, the hammer and tap of Jonah down below traveling up to us as he worked on the latest addition to the porch, and Ruby herself, apparently no longer mad at me, glowing and smiling and patting the lawn chair so I'd come close and sit.

"What talk?"

I took my seat and noticed the batch of helium balloons tied to the far rail. They were big and round and came in a variety of colors, much like the ones we saw at the birthday party in the park, but Ruby's balloons were tied tight with red ribbons, knotted in a bright bunch to the wooden post. She must have had nothing else to use for strings.

Though my sister was smiling, and all the gray had drained from her eyes, she still sounded serious enough.

"*The* talk, the one we didn't have last night. There are things you can and can't do, and we need to talk about them." She counted on her fingers, repeating all the things she'd already told me. The phone, I shouldn't answer it. I shouldn't leave town, I shouldn't eat raisins in front of her (this was new, but I should know that raisins sickened her, and who's to say they don't grow back into grapes once they're swallowed?), I shouldn't go to the reservoir, she didn't want me smoking even if she sometimes did, no drugs and no drinking, obviously, and she didn't think too highly of Owen and if I wanted to like a boy I should make an effort to find another.

This was where I stopped her. "Why? What's wrong with him? He's Pete's brother. You were with Pete."

She shuddered. "Don't remind me."

"Then what?"

"Owen is too pretty," she said. "There's something ugly about a pretty boy who knows he's pretty and assumes everyone else knows it, too."

What a funny thing for her to say.

But she was only getting started. "He can't decide on a hair color," she said. "And then he lets it grow out because he's too lazy to put in a new color. That says something about the state of his heart, Chlo."

I let her go on. "He wakes-and-bakes, he's stoned constantly . . . think of the lost brain cells, Chlo, they don't grow back, so it's worse than the hair. And he won't look me in the eyes. He's always been shifty like that, ever since he was a little kid."

I shook my head; she was being silly now.

"I want you to cut this out today," she said. "That nobody with the bad hair . . . You don't like him anymore."

"I don't?"

"You *don't*. I won't let you."

She was acting like she could forbid me from having an emotion. She could shove a hand down my throat and wiggle her fingers as far as they'd go, plucking out stuff she didn't want in there, like she did when we got up the courage to clean out last season's moldy takeout containers from the fridge. She'd do it fast, and didn't even hold her nose.

"Good," she said. "Now tell me about London. How was she last night?"

There was something in the way she said it, something unsaid more than said, and I looked down to where Jonah was in the backyard to make sure he wouldn't overhear — only to find the backyard empty.

I chose my words carefully. "She told me all about rehab."

"Did she now?" Even though I was her sister, she was playing games with me. We may have played games with everyone in town, including passing tourists, but we shouldn't with each other.

"I know where she was, really." Then I added, "Even if she doesn't."

Ruby waited. She wanted me to say it.

"I thought she was dead. I *saw* her. But she wasn't ever dead, was she?"

"She was," Ruby said softly. "You saw what you saw. But we got her back, didn't we? You wanted everything the way it was before—and that meant getting London out. Even if it took longer than I thought. And the wait was worth it, because you're here."

"All that time . . . she was down there?"

"I wanted her back before you got home, Chlo. So you wouldn't want to go away again."

"I went away two summers ago," I said. "I was at my dad's for *two years*."

She hung her head. "I told you, I tried sooner. I tried last spring."

I couldn't make sense of what she was telling me.

"Chlo, you left and I was brokenhearted. Before I knew it, it was fall, and getting colder. And then winter—and ice covered the whole reservoir, so there was no getting in, and there was no getting out." She eyed me especially here. "But when I came back in spring, they wouldn't let her out then, either."

"So how did you"—I didn't know how to put it—"change their minds?"

"I waited, very, very patiently." Her eyes glimmered. "And then I tricked them."

There was an awkward silence. The weight of the reservoir could be felt at our backs.

"Why?" I asked. A better question was *How?* but that word wouldn't cross my lips.

Ruby kept her eyes shaded from view with a well-placed hand. "Why did I work so hard to get her back? Because she went away and you were sad," she said simply. "Maybe *sad*'s not the right word. Maybe messed-up-in-the-head is a better word, only that's not one word. You left, Chlo. Because of that girl, you left! And I couldn't . . . I couldn't stand it. So I fixed it. Now that London's here again, so are you."

I let that sink in. She'd brought London back from the dead—for me. For us.

Inside my sister was some kind of inexplicable power. She could decide what lived and breathed. Who could stay and who should go. She controlled everything that happened in this town. She really was more than anyone who'd ever said they loved her could have dreamed.

But then she kept talking, trying to explain herself.

"Is it so wrong, Chlo? Can you blame me for taking back what I did to her, for making it right, even if it was a tiny bit selfish?"

What *she* did to London.

A coldness crept into my bones as I realized what she'd admitted. How she needed to make it right. Because what she'd done was so wrong in the first place.

She'd conjured up the girl I found dead. Worse, she'd conjured her into the rowboat in the first place.

It wasn't only that my sister had brought London back— it was that London's body found its way to the boat that night because Ruby put it there. London spent all that time in Olive because she was sent there. By my sister.

It was like she'd given London up for sacrifice—but for what?

What more was Ruby not telling me?

"Chloe!" she snapped. "Why are you staring at me like that?"

"I . . . I just can't believe what you did."

She grinned, openly. "That's nothing. You can't even imagine what else I've done."

And I couldn't—imagine it. Not then, and not for a long time. All I knew was that for the first moment in my life, I felt truly frightened of her. The heavy pull in my legs wasn't a fear anymore of Olive or London or anything I saw in those bad dreams I had in Pennsylvania . . . it was dread.

Were people only allowed to wander our town at the whims of my sister? Could she rub anyone out, and blow the chalk dust away?

If you'd asked me in that moment, standing in the wind

on her widow's walk, I would have put my hand to my heart and swore that, yes, in fact she could.

And, more, I wondered what my sister could possibly do next. Wondered how far she'd go. And if I'd ever need to stop her.

In the house, a few thumps sounded. Someone was coming upstairs—Jonah. She slammed the window closed so he couldn't come out. "I'm glad we can talk about everything now," she said.

She walked to the other end of the widow's walk, the side facing the driveway and the road toward town, the side where, with our backs turned, we could forget the reservoir even existed.

"Chloe, come and look," she said.

The helium balloons on their bright red ribbons reached for the sky, but she'd knotted the ribbons tight enough to the railing so that none could escape, though they tried. It was windy up here, close to the water, windier than anywhere else in town except for the very top of Overlook Mountain.

I followed and sat on her reclined lawn chair. "What are these for?" I said, careful with my words, now that she'd told me what she'd told me and I was suspecting there was still more to tell.

"Guess," she said.

"Are we having a party?"

She feigned a delicate gag into her hand. "And invite

people over? People from town? *Here?* So we'd have to talk to them and feed them our food and wash all their mouth marks off the glasses after?" She looked stricken.

"So no party then?"

"No, thank God. But the balloons are sort of for them in a way . . ."

"Where'd you get the balloons anyway?" I asked.

"The store, where else? You can rent a tank to fill them up and everything. Seeing the ones at the rec field gave me an idea."

When Ruby's hair caught the sun, the henna in it shone through. She blazed up, looking far warmer in day than she did in the dark, wild practically. Her eyes had a fever in them that I wasn't sure could be blamed on the bright light.

She was about to do something impossible again—I could sense it, as if she were at the very edge of something dangerously high and she were about to take a running leap.

"*Look,*" she said, still indicating the balloons.

That's when I noticed that the balloons were tagged already with her neatly penned messages. She'd spelled them out in delicate letters, using a thin-point Sharpie. They weren't little innocent greetings like *Ruby says hi*, the way she'd written inside Jonah's furniture, or even *Ruby was here*, like on the brick wall of the town credit union. They were tiny directives:

bring me a milk shake

bury $8 in your yard and mark it w/ a red ribbon so i can find it

leave a good book on your doorstep for me to take

ask me to dance and let me say no

call me at midnight and tell me you love me

don't wear that dress again, i want it

tattoo me on your body (make it nice)

cook me lasagna

try as hard as you can to make me cry

"What's all this?" I asked, holding up the orange balloon demanding lasagna.

"Do you ever read self-help books, Chlo?"

"Not really."

She grabbed the lasagna balloon from my hands, untied its ribbon, and let it fly. We watched it take to the clouds like a small, runaway sun, a blazing tail of fire spouting out behind as it went.

Next she untied the green balloon wanting eight bucks, about enough for a pack of cigarettes, which she shouldn't be buying anyway because I didn't want her to smoke, and we watched it rise.

"Well, I read in some self-help book that you have to *ask* for what you want, or no one will know to give it to you," she said.

I laughed, but she was serious.

"You know what I want?" she said. "Something fun for a change. I want people to do the work for *me*, instead of me always working so hard for them."

Was she joking?

No. She was absolutely not smiling now.

Her face obstructed my view of the balloons. She was talking very close, so close her nose was a pale, blurred blob. I was struck by how symmetrical the freckle on her cheek was, a true circle, as if her maker had drawn it on with the world's tiniest compass and hadn't messed up even once.

"Right now I want something for me and me only," she continued. "Well, you can have some lasagna, too, Chlo, but you know what I mean."

Did I? As far as I could tell, my sister always got whatever she wanted. And, if she didn't the first time, she went back and she took it and there was no one strong enough to stop her.

That was one piece of her magic, the way everyone melted and let her take and keep taking; it was her charm.

But, for some reason, this was no longer enough for her.

She clapped her hands and made me jump. "I can't wait to let all these balloons go!" she shrieked. "I can't stand to see them tied up. Stuck like they are. It's pitiful."

She quickly untied a red balloon and let it drift.

"Now you," she said. "You let one go, too."

I did what she wanted; I didn't even question it. I held a turquoise one up to the sun. "You want someone to ask you to dance and then you're going to tell them no?"

She nodded, so I unwound its ribbon and set it free.

"I like to be asked," she said. "And I might not say no. Depends on who's asking. But if they assume I'll say no, they'll be surprised if I say yes, and isn't that nice?"

"*If* you say yes."

"You're right, I'll probably say no." She smiled, tucked my hair behind my ears even though it didn't need tucking. She was happy with me now. I was doing what she wanted. "You know me better than anyone knows me in the whole entire world, Chlo. You could write a book about me. If you were standing before the firing squad and they said they wouldn't shoot you in the head only if you could answer one question and it was a question about me, you'd keep your head, Chlo."

Now I smiled at that, couldn't help it. She knew I liked to hear that I was the only one who really knew her. I liked to be reminded.

I watched her let the other balloons go. Watched her unwind their tails to leave them untethered. Watched her step away. Watched her watch each red ribbon take its leave and rise up out of reach even from her.

Soon they were all gone. I looked up into the sky, and her balloons were everywhere, it seemed, the air marred with bloody streaks and littered with demands, and nothing and no one could stop them from coming.

I felt her at my side, bristling with the power of it. The possibility. The rush.

Something in her had come undone just like the balloons did.

Now nothing could contain her.

The sky was hers.

That's when the thumping from inside the house made itself known again. Jonah was knocking on the window. Pounding.

Ruby watched the window idly, as if a bomb could shatter the glass at any moment and she was curious enough to stay and get sliced.

"Are you going to get that or should I?" I said.

"Go ahead. And while you're at it, tell him to go back downstairs, please."

I was already at the window when she said that last bit. In a low voice I said back, "But it's *his* house . . ."

"I don't want him upstairs," she said. "Upstairs is for you and me."

I turned to face the window. The glass wasn't shaded or anything and I could see Jonah right there—my face inches from his face, one thin, translucent sheet between us. He could see us, and he could probably hear us, too.

I undid the latch and pulled up the window. Before I could open my mouth, Ruby called from the railing, "Tell him I didn't put the gate up for nothing. Did he step right over it like it wasn't there? Ask him."

The gate? She put up a gate?

I asked, my voice faltering. "Ruby wants to know . . . Did you, um, step over it?"

He nodded. There were wood shavings in his hair, little flecks, so many he'd have to dunk his head in the shower to get them all out, and some scattered and got on me when he moved.

"She says . . ." I started, trying to find the words, polite words, words that wouldn't make him hate me, seeing as I was his guest, technically, eating his food and sleeping my nights in his bed. But I couldn't finish that sentence. I turned back to let her do it. "You should tell him yourself," I said.

But Jonah said, "No need, I got it."

He slammed the window shut, almost on my fingers. Then he retreated down the stairs and I saw the gate there — a barricade, really, one made from two dresser drawers stacked up and propped across the floor, plus the long handle of a kitchen mop, stretched across, plus a picture frame with no picture in it. It looked like something a child would build, to keep a dog out. But Ruby used it on Jonah.

"How long has that been up?" I asked.

She shrugged and her expression didn't soften. "He has the couch to sleep on."

"He's mad," I said. "I think he's really, really mad." Never before were we in the precarious position of making a boyfriend mad who we still had to face the day after. Previous boyfriends we could kick out. Or drive away from. Previous boyfriends didn't live downstairs.

"He's fine. He can't get mad," she said. "Not at me. Besides, he's not the one we have to worry about."

Her bright, glowing green eyes flicked out at the water in the distance, the water hiding what had once been Olive. But then her eyes weren't on the water at all, they were on the sky, on the clouds, on her red-tailed balloons making their way toward town.

I believed in her. I even believed in those balloons.

I'd seen what she could do, hadn't I?

For barely a flicker of a second I thought otherwise. I thought about how maybe this wasn't happening at all, except in some locked-off part of my mind where sane people retreat only when they're dreaming or doped up on cough syrup.

It could be that somewhere off Route 80 in Pennsylvania you'd find a trailer propped up on cinder blocks and in it a girl who'd lost her mind. She'd be forced to stay out there because her dad wouldn't let her in the house. Her trailer door would be padlocked from the outside. But if you found that trailer and peeked in through the peephole you'd find her eye staring back. An eye darkly circled, sunken. A crazy eye. That girl would call herself Chloe. She'd say her sister was magic. Her sister brought people back to life, made them into more than people, made them something other. Her sister could force you to do things and think things and bend to whatever she said. This Chloe had seen it; she was watching it happen right now. She'd scream this at you and claw at the trailer door and you'd do the smart thing and run away.

Because this was impossible. Ruby was, and London was. And yet, somehow, here we all were, as Ruby decided we would be.

And now the balloons were on their way.

CHAPTER FIFTEEN

RUBY STILL SAID

Ruby still said there was no reason to worry about Jonah. See? There he was down in the yard, building up the railing around the back porch so she wouldn't slip off. Hammering hard at it. Measuring to keep it straight. Sanding it smooth.

There he was ignoring the real, paying work he had in his shed so he could keep remodeling the house for her — because he knew it was what she wanted.

Ruby was dressing for her evening shift at Cumby's while keeping an eye on him out the window. She was dropping a short black vintage slip over her head and dipping bare feet into motorcycle boots, combing out her damp hair and letting it air-dry into loose curls down her back, coating her lips in wine, her favorite lipstick color and her favorite drink, then pressing her lips on the small white square of a store receipt to blot them dry. She looked like she was going out dancing rather than to restock and restyle the candy aisle by color (white, pink, red, orange, yellow, green, blue, purple, brown) and fill a few gas tanks. Every other employee wore a uniform smock to work at Cumby's; Ruby wore the smock once, on her first-ever shift, said it pinched, and never put one on again.

She dropped the receipt in the general direction of the trash can, but it missed, fluttering to the floor, the flower print of her lips captured for always.

"I'm forty minutes late," she said, glancing at the time. Even so, she didn't rush. She took a moment to observe herself in the mirror over the dresser—mostly checking for food in her teeth, as we'd feasted on a tub of roadside-stand blueberries and whippets of whipped cream for dinner. Then, as if in preparation for the harsh fluorescent lights in the store, she perched a pair of sunglasses on top of her head and left the room.

I followed her out into the hallway and climbed after her over the gate. "What if I went with you?" I said.

"What, to *work*? To help me at the pumps and tell people to take-a-penny, leave-a-penny, though all anyone ever does is take? I know you love me, Chlo, but you'd be too bored and I couldn't do that to my baby sister. I'll be back later tonight, with treats."

Ruby didn't go to her job often, and she rarely worked

through the hours of a full shift, but she never seemed to consider quitting. She'd made it clear to me that a girl should always have a job, gainfully employed boyfriend or no. A girl needs her own money, just like she needs her own car. But I was sixteen this summer and still didn't have my learner's permit or my first job. The difference was, I had Ruby. That's what she told me. When she was growing up, she had no big sister. Imagine that.

Downstairs, I could see the full reach of the porch. It ran to the bank of the hill, and if there wasn't a fence and city property in the way, I was sure it would have bunched up into an arching bridge over Route 28, then climbed down, step by step, to the water's edge. Now, it stopped where it stopped. It made it so you could walk from the house to the hill without touching your feet to earth.

"He's been good," she said, eyes out the window. "They've all been so good." She meant the other guys out there helping under the falling sun, as Jonah wasn't the only one. Other guys from town had been coming over, some who were former exes and some who'd maybe become future exes. A couple of guys were way too young to become her exes; they were boys my age, boys I used to know from school. One of these boys was Owen, but she made no comment about that. It's not like she would have noticed any one boy among all the others.

"There's a pitcher of iced tea in the fridge if you want to bring it out to them," she said. "I made it from a can."

I watched her long white car chug out of the driveway, muffler groaning unchecked because she seemed to like the noise it made, and then she was out of sight.

I went out with the pitcher and some glasses just as Jonah decided they were done for the day. No one felt compelled to keep working, now that Ruby had left.

Or maybe it was that she'd taken her influence with her off the property and down the road—as if the radius of her charms had gotten smaller and more concentrated, and she had to give up the guys at the house so she could shine a spotlight on Cumby's, casting her spell over coworkers and regulars and innocent tourists.

I'd assumed the house had cleared when I almost walked into him on the landing. "I thought there was another bathroom up here," Owen said, "but all this junk's in the way."

"That's, you know"—thinking madly of how to explain the gate without making my sister sound cruel—"we haven't gotten around to moving that stuff yet. Just step over it. The bathroom's right there."

He stepped over the gate and leaned against the wall, in the shadows, so I couldn't decipher what he was thinking from his face. And maybe it was better that way. Ruby told me it didn't matter what a boy was thinking about you, so long as you had a good hold on what you were thinking about him. But for some reason I couldn't figure out, he was still here in the house, though his ride must have gone away because there was just one vehicle left in the driveway and it was Jonah's pickup truck.

Owen took a step toward the bathroom and then stopped. Backed up, came close. "Hey, Chloe? Could I ask you something?"

Then I knew. Or thought I knew. I'd gotten caught up in my sister's fog, but all the while Owen had been piecing it together. He'd noticed something off about his friend London, too.

"Yeah, sure," I told him, waiting for it. Maybe all it took was one other person to say it aloud for everything to shatter. The walls would come down first; they were flimsy enough. The ceiling would collapse in and crumble. In the sky the sounds of balloons popping, then a rainbow of brightly colored carcasses and limp red ribbons as they fell.

But all Owen said was: "You mind if I take a shower here?"

I had no ready response for that.

"We were working out there for hours," Owen was saying, "and it's so hot. . . . You don't mind, do you?"

I shook my head. "Use the blue towel," I said. "It's clean."

I went to my room and closed the door—or, really, moved the door to the closed position and let it lean.

I sat on the edge of the bed and thought some as I heard the shower running. I thought how my sister was gone, and wouldn't be back for hours. I thought how, ever since Jonah had come up to talk to us on the widow's walk, he hadn't crossed the barrier. I thought how all the other guys had left. How Owen and I were alone, practically.

I thought about how he wasn't worth liking. No. How he wasn't for me—I knew it as well as if he had those three words *Not for you* eye-penciled across his chest in Ruby's distinctive handwriting. Ruby said no, and I always did what Ruby said.

But Ruby had never asked me what boys *she* could be with. Ruby took for herself the things she wanted, and she didn't wait for anyone's permission. This summer was proof of that.

Then I heard my name. Owen was calling my name from the shower.

The door was cracked when I approached, steam pooling out. It was a hot day for such a hot shower, but I was glad for the steam—it made it next to impossible to see inside. "Yeah?" I said into the white. "Did you call me?"

"There's no soap," he said.

"There is, it's up on the shelf."

Through the fog I saw his hand reaching out from the shower curtain, a blind hand with fingers splayed, totally off-target. I took hold of it, my fingers guiding his fingers, leading them up for the shelf, to the bar of soap. When his hand found it, I let go. He pulled the soap into the shower, but not before I saw inside. Saw a glimpse of him in there, saw him seeing me.

I retreated back to my room, my skin slick with sweat, my lungs brimming with hot steam, forced to catch my breath on the end of my bed.

I was still there, breathing, when he came in. He'd dried off and put his clothes back on, but his chest was still damp—his T-shirt stuck to it—and his hair dripped darkening spots onto his shoulders.

"Thanks," he said.

"No problem." The voice that came out of me wasn't one Ruby would use in front of a boy. Ruby wouldn't offer him her one clean towel and let him use her bar of eucalyptus soap, the same one she'd used on herself that morning. Ruby wouldn't sit on the bed staring at her hands. Ruby wouldn't be turning pink, right there with him watching—to her, that would be like racing him up a mountain and trying with all my might until the very last second, when I slowed to let him win.

I was giving myself away. Boys should be left guessing, Ruby always told me. Boys should never know how their night will turn out, because you—here, she'd tap me in the chest, dead center—you hold the power. It's your night, not his.

But, with Owen, I'd lost control as soon as I let him step over the gate.

His hair hung in his face, mostly brown today. He didn't know how long I'd liked him. Since before he had the mohawk, since before he grew it out into the fauxhawk, before that one time he shaved his head. I liked him when his hair was all brown, plain as could be, and maybe he didn't remember how far back that was, but I did. I liked him when his hair was green. When it was red, then when it faded out to pink. Now the tips of it were blue again, the palest blue, like it had been dyed a long, long time ago but had mostly washed out. Like in the two years since I'd been gone he'd dyed it blue and didn't bother to redye it—like all the time I'd been gone was written right there in his hair.

"Should I call my ride?" he asked. "Or . . ."

I shook my head, meaning he could stay.

"Should I . . . close the door?"

"Yeah," I said. "It doesn't lock, but, yeah."

Soon he was wedging the door into the frame to keep it closed, looking back at me to be sure it was okay. Then he ruined it by sitting beside me on the bed and pulling out a bowl, packed full of weed and ready to light. For a moment, I saw him for who he was—this big nothing, thinking he was something—and then I blinked and saw what the younger me had seen, this beautiful, careless boy who acted like he needed no one and how I'd always been drawn to that for some reason, wondering what could have been.

"You want some?" Owen asked, holding out the bowl and the lighter.

"Nah," I said, all casual, though I felt anything but. I needed my head clear so I could be sure of what was going on. To know what this meant. What he was thinking. What he felt. What he wanted.

When he was done, he turned to me and it wasn't any clearer.

But then he was kissing me, or I was kissing him, and his mouth tasted like a whole bunch of things (iced tea, smoke, a hint of eucalyptus soap, and something sweet past all that, which was maybe just how he tasted), and his hand that snaked up my shirt was still warm from the shower, warmer even than me.

Yet I became aware of something tugging at me, something in the shape of my sister, and her voice, or an exact impression of it, cutting into my thoughts saying, *Get that boy off your bed, Chlo.*

I turned my face and in my other ear she said, *Haven't I taught you anything! Don't you dare let him —*

And, fast, I turned my face again and this made her shut up.

Because then it was quiet. Then we were tangled together, and it was all so fast, all before I could think on what

I was doing, and if I did would it even matter? Because hadn't I been wanting this? Isn't this what my sister did?

I knew I wouldn't be able to tell my sister. We'd have to keep it secret. Owen couldn't tell a soul. Unless he became my boyfriend, all official, in which case we'd go before Ruby and confess. But right now—his mouth moving down where in all my life there'd never been a mouth—she absolutely could not know.

I sat up only once and said, "You sure the door's closed?"

And he said, "*Shh*, stop talking."

I should have known that a closed door was no defense against Ruby. Walls and miles of road between us wouldn't matter in the end. She'd find out. But I wasn't thinking straight. I felt like I had no legs, like there was nothing beneath us, like we were floating somewhere without names or faces together, and I forgot about her because what I felt was everything. Absolutely everything.

All at once.

In a way Ruby never told me.

After, we got ourselves together and I walked him downstairs. He'd called a friend to pick him up and we waited on the front steps. We both watched the driveway, unsure of what to say, until his knee tapped against my knee and he said, "I swear I never thought that would happen."

I admitted, "Me neither."

"Because Ruby would've killed me." He said that, and didn't laugh.

"Not if it's what I wanted, she wouldn't," I said.

"You so sure about that? Who's to say she's not going to jump out from behind that tree and slit my throat right now?"

We both eyed the tree, a large oak that could hide the lean, curvy body of my sister easily behind its trunk, shadowing her movements as she crept out under the dark leaves, legs gleaming bare, a sharp kitchen knife secured in her grip.

Even though I could picture it, and vividly, I said, "Don't be ridiculous. Who do you think she is?"

He mumbled something under his breath that sounded like, "More like *what* she is," but then he covered it up by raising his voice and going, "So if she wanted to kill me for—you know, upstairs—she'd have to ask you first?"

"Yeah," I said. "We always ask before killing off each other's boyfriends." I quickly snapped my mouth closed after that last word, mortified, but he didn't even chuckle and play it off like a joke. He stayed completely silent, for a long time.

Then he said, as if I wasn't there to hear, "I don't know what I did. Hooking up with *Ruby's* sister. Damn." He put his head in his hands and stared at the gravel at his feet.

What I needed was Ruby here to coach me, show me

how to lure him in, and keep him dangling. Make him want to stay and let him think he can, then be the one to shove him out the door and say go. I had a feeling I'd maybe done things backward.

Owen cleared his throat. "Your sister . . ."

Perfect. She was all he was thinking of, too.

Knowing that felt like falling full-tilt off the old fire tower on top of Overlook Mountain to the sharp crags of rocks below. Guts to my knees, just like that. He'd come up to my room because he liked my sister. I'd always assumed the opposite, but I should have known.

". . . you look nothing like her, you know?" he finished.

I wasn't sure what to make of that comment, except to take it as an insult—obviously. "Thanks," I said dully.

"I meant that's a *good* thing," Owen said. "Everyone says you look like her, but I don't think you do. I kinda like that."

What a terrible thing for him to say. I wanted to go back inside, leave him to wait out in the driveway all by his lonesome, even if it took an hour for his friend to show.

He stood up. "There's my ride."

The car stopped halfway down the driveway, at the wheel one of his boys, one too lazy to even pull all the way up to the house. Owen waved and went for the car, and I wasn't sure how long I sat out on the steps. I knew he wouldn't be back. And it was only just getting dark—Ruby wouldn't be home from work for hours. But I sat, very still, my knees pressed together, my chin balanced on them, my eyes open for as long as I could stand it and then my eyes closed.

In time, I became aware of it behind me. How it held there in the distance, heavy, breathing over my shoulder. How it had been there all along, keeping track of everything I did.

I was walking around the back of the house when I heard it. The voices carrying. Somehow, from the edge of the reservoir and across the road, then up the hill and into the yard of the house, I could hear the voices.

Jonah came out of the shed when I started walking down toward the water.

"Owen left?" He stood in front of me so I'd have to circle around him to get past.

"We were just talking," I said. I took a step to the side and he took a step to the other side and then I was free and clear to take the hill.

"I thought you couldn't go down there," he called after me. "Ruby told me that."

"I can do whatever I want."

"Clearly," I thought I heard him say.

I spun, searing my eyes at him, or where I thought he was, but he must have slipped back into his shed, out of sight, and I ended up glaring at a tree.

I crossed Route 28. Down at the reservoir, I found the path without anyone having to tell me where to look. There was a flap hanging loose from the chain-link fence and I crawled in easily. The voices carried through the trees; the bright orange No Trespassing signs practically lit the way. I followed the voices as they trickled out from down the shore, getting farther and farther away from the house. When I was close enough, I crept behind a large rock at the edge, ducked down, and listened.

I heard Ruby before I could see her. I heard a whisper in the wind, then a splash.

"Who cares if you're naked? No one can see you, Lon. *God*."

Another splash.

"Hear anyone down there, Lon? See anything?"

"It's . . . cold here, Ruby. This spot right here is really cold. Why's it so cold?"

My sister sighed, showing her impatience. "What do you see?"

I peeked up over the rock and caught sight of Ruby. Her arm was stretched out into the growing night, one finger pointing. The middle of the reservoir hovered, glimmering faintly under a sliver of moon, completely still though it was fluid and should have been moving in the wind. My sister was on the very edge of the waterline, on a pile of rocks that had once been an old town wall before the reservoir was flooded, keeping careful not to dip her boots in. London was down in the water, in up to her waist, her pale hair a daub of light in the deepening darkness, her arms crossed to hide her bare breasts.

Afraid she'd see me, I ducked back down.

"Aren't you gonna come with me?"

"Not me, just you tonight."

"But I'm cold. Can you throw my shirt back? I—Okay. Okay. Okay, I'm going."

The splashing became even then, in strokes, as London made her way into the deep. She went so far, I couldn't hear her. Not at all. She was out there for way too long without any sound and I was starting to get worried, so I peeked back over the rock again and there was a moment—long and drawn out, as my sister stretched on shore, arching her back and reaching her arms, as if this could take a while and she was getting comfortable—where I couldn't see London in the water at all. Where I thought she'd vanished, got herself sucked down to the deep crater of the bottom and wouldn't emerge again in this lifetime.

I was about to stand up, to call out, when I caught a pale flash in the water and realized it was London's bleached head.

She came swimming out, dripping and shivering once she reached the shore, looking paler and skinnier than ever before, and my sister quickly threw her clothes at her to cover up.

They left soon after, following a different trail lacing through the trees. Two red lights—the brake lights on Ruby's white Buick—pulsed and then snapped off as the car pulled away.

I wasn't sure what I'd seen. Had London just gone down to pay a visit to Olive while my sister sat there watching?

The phone in my pocket buzzed then, as if her eyes hung like stars in the night to record my every move through her town.

Her text said: wrk sucks. home soon. hope u want ice pops! bringing some for dinner

My fingers went to the keys of my phone to text her back. But what could I say—i saw u. i know ur not at work? Lie and make pretend and just go, ice pops for dinner yum?

I slipped the phone back in my pocket without a reply.

I crept out from behind the rock, fully intending to head back up to the house and wait for her to return home from "work," thinking how I'd love an ice pop, hoping she brought back cherry, when there was a splash at my back. I turned to find the water settling, as if someone had shot up and plunged down before I could catch them.

I stepped closer to the water, until I was too close, until I was right there, the soles of my sandals up against its mouth. It was breathing.

Ruby had been clear when she said she didn't want me swimming; I wasn't going to defy her and dive in. I sure wasn't going to come back up to the house all wet and have to explain how that happened, in case she got home before I could dry off.

All I did was slip one foot out of my sandal and dip in a single toe.

I let it touch the surface. I let it hold there, and I didn't take it away.

The water was cold, as I'd heard London say, colder than you'd expect on a hot summer night. I let my foot dangle, the chill creeping up the length of me. Then, quick, I pulled my toe back and slipped on my sandal and stepped off the rocks.

Nothing happened tonight. Nothing I needed to tell Ruby about. Nothing with Owen. Nothing having to do with the reservoir. Nothing.

I was waiting to cross the road, letting a truck pass, when I heard the sound coasting through the trees. A low, creeping whistle choking and hissing and coughing out from the darkness.

I turned around to face the trees, and it decided to take that moment to stop.

But when I crossed the road, it started up again—growing fainter, the more distance I put between me and the reservoir, but still wanting to be heard. It reminded me of the shrieking hiss my sister had made when she was trying to imitate the old steam whistle. It sounded almost like that.

If it was a trick of my ears, it lasted all the way back up the hill, down the long length of porch the guys had been hammering at all day, and into the house, ever so faintly there even when I closed the door behind it, the sound seeping in through the window screens along with the chirps of the crickets.

I was still listening for it in the living room when my sister came in.

When she found me, her eyes narrowed. London wasn't with her—maybe Ruby drove her home first. Her motorcycle boots were dripping with mud and her hair was partly wet and so was the hem of her slip and she smelled of it, the reservoir, she smelled of deep, dark things and untold secrets and all of what she was keeping from me, the first being that she never had a shift at Cumby's. But she was the one to look at me all suspicious and say, "What are you doing, Chlo?"

"Nothing," I said. I watched her carefully to see if she could hear it, too, but she made no mention of it, the wheezing, whining hiss seeping in through the window. It was growing fainter now, letting the crickets drown it out.

"Did something happen while I was at work?" she said. "You look different."

"No, of course not." I immediately thought of my room

upstairs. If any evidence of what happened was in there . . . if she'd been upstairs, if she'd seen. "Did you just get home?" I asked, thinking fast.

"Yeah, did you?"

"No, I mean, yeah, I mean I was only outside and I only just came in."

She circled the love seat, coming closer.

"I think I'm ready for bed," I said, going the other way and heading for the stairs. "I'm tired."

"But the ice pops. They're in the freezer."

"It's okay. I'll make sure to have one for breakfast."

She eyed me as I walked the stairs to the landing. She eyed my legs as they climbed. She eyed my back and, through it, my beating heart. I turned at the landing before the next set of stairs, before I'd leap the gate and slip back into my room to check my sheets. I said, as casually as I could, "I think I'm gonna sleep in my room tonight."

All week, we'd been sharing the big bed in the master bedroom, lounging up on the high mattress like royalty, if overheated royalty, since there was no air-conditioning and we had to use electric fans. Sleeping in that room was one of the perks of having the gate up and making Jonah stay downstairs.

Ruby lifted her eyes to mine and said, "Okay, if that's what you want. I got you cherry. And there's tropical fruit, too. Ice pops, I mean."

"Thanks."

I turned away. I couldn't hear the whistling anymore, but I could still smell Olive. It was in the house now, in the air, rising up to the top floor, trapped inside with the rest of the thick summer heat.

"Are you sure nothing happened, Chlo?" Ruby called. "Nothing I should know about?"

"Nothing, really," I called down.

"I'll find out, you know . . . if something did."

I kept walking, all the while knowing she would. She was Ruby, after all. She'd dig you up and spread you open and see what she wanted to see. In this town, she was the only one who thought she could have secrets. Everything was hers. Most of all, me.

CHAPTER SIXTEEN

I WOKE UP

I woke up past midnight to a ringing phone, one I felt sure had been ringing for a while.

It wasn't my cell. I moved the door aside and peeked into the hall. The phone was close, out there somewhere, its bleating ring bouncing off the unfinished walls and wire-exposed ceiling. Ruby's door at the end of the hall was closed, and a phone cord was wound up the stairs, over the gate, past my door and past the bathroom door and past the closet that didn't have a door to within inches of her room. It was the kitchen phone, so archaic it wasn't even a cordless, and that was as far as it reached.

It rang and rang. If Ruby was in her room, she wasn't coming out to answer it.

I guess I could blame the fact that I was half asleep for why I answered it. I picked up the phone and said, "Hello?"

There was a gush of breath, and a voice said, "Finally. Took long enough."

"Excuse me?" The person on the other end must have thought I was Ruby; not too many people could tell us apart, even still.

"You need to get voice mail. Or an answering machine. Or something."

"Who is this?"

Another sigh. Then the voice mumbled, "I, uh . . . really love you." And the next I heard was *click*, as whoever it was hung up.

That was the first.

The other requests Ruby had penned on the helium balloons filtered in, sometimes more than once, as if a balloon had landed in one spot only to blow away to somewhere else. By afternoon we had two large pans of foil-covered lasagna in the fridge, though it was too hot to run the oven and my sister said she wasn't in the mood for lasagna after all and what she really should have asked for was a homemade cake.

The balloons were answered, one by one, and Ruby didn't seem at all surprised. In her universe—which encompassed the fuzzy, far-reaching boundaries of our town, skirting up mountains and dredging the lowest point in the valley, dipping into the reservoir and running off on the rapids of the Esopus to other small towns that looked much like this one—she'd gone and asked for what she wanted and every single person here would try to give it to her. As if it was their duty.

Toward the end of the day, when I found a dress folded up on the steps—white eyelet to show bits of skin—I carried it up to our floor.

I found her at the mirror in an odd pose. She'd spotted a gray hair and was stretching out the strand to take a closer look in the light.

"I think this is for you," I said, leaving the dress on the bed. "There's no card."

She glanced at the dress. "Nice," she said absently. "It looked better in the dark, I think." She returned her attention to the mirror, crinkling up her brows in concentration. "Look at me carefully, Chlo, and then please tell me you don't see it."

"I don't see it."

"But you do see it. You're looking right at it."

"You told me to say—"

"Do you see it?"

I nodded solemnly. The gray strand stood out against the rest of her dark hair. I also saw what may have been a second strand behind her ear, but I didn't point it out.

"Get the tweezers. We'll have to pull it out at the root."

We performed the operation together and then carefully

wrapped the long strand—up close I saw it wasn't gray but perfectly white from root to tip, and glimmering at all angles, like a hair pulled from a royal Persian cat—in tissue to discard in the toilet. She flushed and watched to make sure it went down, then she flushed again to be safe, as if we were getting rid of evidence of a crime before the FBI stormed in.

After it went down, she sat on the floor and spoke.

"Something's wrong," she said.

"It's just a gray hair," I said.

"I feel like I'm fading. Like I'm so very tired from all this effort and that"—she pointed at the toilet, where we'd flushed the long strand—"that's just the start. And what's next? Sunspots?"

"What effort?"

She glanced at the dress. "Everything takes at least an ounce of effort," she said cryptically. "I'm not *magic*, you know."

I couldn't tell if that last part was a joke.

She continued. "I'm exhausted. It's like we just climbed up to the very top of Overlook Mountain—we used to skip school and do that, remember?"

"Yeah."

"Remember how we'd get to the top, finally after climbing forever, and catch our breath and look down and we could see the whole entire town from up there?"

I nodded.

"I feel like that. Like we're up at the top and I should be able to see everything. Only, the clouds have come in, and now it's raining or whatever, and I'm not seeing town like I should. So we climbed all the way up there for nothing. And I'm too tired to climb back down. That's what I feel like. Something's in my way and I don't know what it is."

She met my eyes, and this propelled me from the room and away from her, afraid of what she'd see. Maybe the words revealing what I'd done were written on me from the inside out, like a phantom finger pressed to a fogged-up car window.

Anything was possible around my sister, I was guessing, if balloons could summon her clothes to wear and food to eat.

I went downstairs; she followed. We bypassed Jonah in the living room, didn't waste a word on him, and wound our way into the kitchen.

I went to the fridge; she drifted to the table and played with the salt shaker. The dirty cereal bowls in the sink towered to great heights. There were no clean spoons anywhere in the world, it felt like, and there never would be, so we'd have to learn to slurp cereal without.

Knowing she was hiding things from me—while I was hiding things from her—made us dance around each other.

It was almost time for dinner, so I took a cherry ice pop and she took a tropical fruit ice pop, which was blue, though we didn't know why, and she unwrapped hers and I unwrapped mine, and we each took a lick off each other's out of habit, and left the room through separate exits.

It wasn't long before she was knocking on my door. Ruby never knocked and waited for an answer; she just knocked and went right in, which defied the logic of knocking. She knocked, and then moved the door aside.

"Hey," she said, and perched on the end of my bed. I had a chunk of ice pop in my mouth and couldn't talk back until I swallowed. When I looked up, I saw her lips were blue from hers. "Are you going to tell me?" she said. "Or am I going to have to wrestle it out of you with my bare hands? I'm strong, you know. And extremely flexible."

She was joking, and stuck out a dyed tongue to prove it, but I couldn't know anymore what my sister could accomplish once she set her mind to it.

And I did want to tell her about Owen. Or maybe she was the one making me want to reveal it, and it wasn't what *I* wanted at all. Getting the words to climb up my throat by command, jostling into position behind my closed teeth— she was doing that. I kept my teeth mashed together. My cherry-red tongue intact.

Normally she didn't have to force a thing from me. Sisters told each other every last thing; especially the younger sister. The youngest sister couldn't have secrets. She was who she was because of who came first.

She waited for me to say it. She knew there was something.

And if that was all that stood between us—some boy—maybe I would. But someone else was blocking the way. I could see her in the room even if she wasn't here in the flesh. I couldn't help but picture her skinny legs, one long arm bent at the hip. Her veins showing through, blue as Ruby's ice pop. Her hair with the bleach left in too long and her ears sticking out.

So I said only half the truth: "I'm worried about London."

"Why?"

"She seemed so out of it last time I saw her . . ."

Ruby took a long lick, considering. "Really? How so?"

I shrugged. "I don't know. I keep wondering"—Ruby's interest was piqued—"what if she goes away?"

"She's not going to go away."

A cool hand slithering its fingers around her knobby ankle, pulling her down and in, making it forever this time. It was a nightmare come to life this summer, and my sister was the one wearing the ski mask.

Ruby made fast work of her ice pop, digesting what I'd said. "Sometimes I do wonder about that girl," she said.

"The drugs, you know. The trouble she gets herself into . . . things I'd never let you do. I wonder if some people are meant to hang on and others, y'know, *aren't*."

"She's sixteen," I said quietly. "Like me."

"Exactly," Ruby said. "Exactly like you."

There was a threat in there, somewhere.

"She won't go, okay?" she said. "I told you I played a little trick to get her out—I said it was just for a visit, a day trip. But she goes back all the time to say hi. So much so that they barely know she's even away. And, besides, she spends her nights—*Oh my God*, Chlo, your lips are bright red! It's like that time you lost a tooth and I thought some-one punched you and that I'd have to beat up a first-grader! I about got out my brass knuckles and everything."

I wiped at my mouth, but the cherry stain wasn't coming off. She kept telling me little bits of things and then dis-tracting me with others. Where was London spending her nights?

It was here that my phone began blinking. "Someone's texting you," Ruby said. There was a slow-motion moment, extended to thick liquid, when I wanted to reach out and get the phone before she did, but she got to it before me.

Owen, I thought. *Please don't say anything my sister shouldn't see.*

She read the message without expression. Then she hummed to herself and clicked off the phone.

"Who was it?" I wanted to take my phone from her, but she had it in her lap.

"Someone's thinking about you, *too*, if you were wondering," she said.

I'd have to explain, reveal what I'd let happen while she was out, which would open up the floodgates and show she couldn't trust me. I'd have to—

"Don't look so freaked, it's only London. Who'd you think it was?"

She smiled and tossed the phone to me. "I thought it was your dad, too. But he's old. He probably doesn't know how to text."

The message read: **Come to town. On Green. Can u get ride?**

"What do you suppose they're doing on the Green in town?" she said.

"Hanging out, like usual."

"I'm thinking you should go. For a bit. Just don't stay out too late tonight."

That wasn't what I expected her to say.

"It might be a good idea for you to get scarce for a few hours tonight. Have you noticed Jonah loafing around doing the mopey eyes? I get the sense he wants to talk to me. Do you get that sense, too?"

I nodded.

"Text her back. Tell her I'll drive you over soon." She

wandered to the window. "Chlo, look! Outside . . . Is that a balloon?"

She pointed out there, where in the thicket a bright pink helium balloon was perched in an outstretched bouquet of thorns. It had landed there so delicately it hadn't even popped.

"Think it's one of mine?" she asked.

I could see a peek of her handwriting. "Definitely."

"I guess the wind decided to shift in a different direction. Stupid wind. Who said it could do that? *I* didn't give it permission."

She must have seen the look on my face, the one that revealed how, inside, where I loved her unconditionally no matter what she did, where in fact she could do whatever she wanted and I'd never hate her for it, I believed everything she said. I'd just taken her statement quite literally. I thought she really could control the wind.

She started giggling.

"That balloon's for you," she said. "Go out and get it."

"What . . . now?"

"Yes, now. I'll drive you after you go get the balloon, Chlo."

Before I knew it, I was leaving the room, as if on command, heading downstairs, past Jonah, who really did seem to be moping, and outside to the pricker bushes to rescue the balloon. The farther I got from her, the more clear my head became. She was a field of static, but I'd reached the edge. I was stepping onto smooth, flat ground beneath a clear blue sky. I couldn't see her at the window anymore.

Not even Ruby could control all the elements of the world we lived in. Something had to slip. Someone had to get punched in the mouth.

I pulled the pink balloon from the thorns, careful not to pop it. In faded permanent marker, the command said:

try as hard as you can to make me cry

This balloon was for me, she'd said, as if she knew already what I'd do.

CHAPTER SEVENTEEN

RUBY DIDN'T HESITATE

R uby didn't hesitate to drop me off on the Green. She kept checking her hair for white strands as she drove and looking out for red ribbons on the lawns we passed, in case anyone had happened upon that particular balloon and saw fit to leave her money.

She let me out, reminding me that London and I should stay in town, saying she'd be right back here later, and I wondered what she'd do without me, with Jonah stewing in the house, wanting whatever he wanted from her. I wondered if she'd let him upstairs when I wasn't home. Into her room, onto our bed. I wondered and then I forcibly stopped myself from wondering.

London and her friends were nowhere in sight, so I took a perch on Ruby's favorite stone bench—the one dead center on the Green, there for the looking and to be looked at. If you were sitting in this spot, you were near impossible to miss.

Town was filled with tourists and locals hawking their rainbow-painted garbage to tourists, and the sidewalks were crowded enough for me to miss her at first.

But the next time I looked up, there she was, my mother, across the street outside the jewelry store, a few doors down from the tavern. She called herself Sparrow now, I reminded myself; I didn't even have to think of her as Mom.

She was pretending to look into the display window, but when I caught her there, her head turned and I had a full view of her face. Her hair wrapped down around her shoulders like a shawl made of hair and not hair itself. She never used to wear makeup—Ruby once tried, and failed, to teach her how to put it on—and I guess she still hadn't learned, so her lips were paler than her cheeks, her eyelashes nonexistent from this distance. She made up for the washed-out face by being all color everywhere else. Her long skirt was woven in shiny, multicolored threads and the summer tank top she had on was bright pink and way too tight, like something a girl my age would wear.

It was impossible to not see her there; I couldn't pretend I hadn't.

She lifted a hand and gave a tight-lipped smile. She motioned to indicate something down the street. My eyes drifted, following the path, and landed on the glowing light advertising beer. She wanted me to meet her in the bar.

Then I heard, "Hey, Chlo!" And London was rescuing me by sidling up and collapsing on the bench. "What're you looking at?"

She scratched at her lanky arms and followed my eyes to . . . the spot of sidewalk in front of the jewelry store. There was nothing blocking the glass case; no one was there.

"That place sucks," London said. "They jack up prices for the tourists. But I bet Ruby'd get you something from there if you asked her. . . ."

"Nah," I said.

I knew I should be feeling some kind of emotion—that flurry of color and hair retreating down the sidewalk was my mother, biological and all else. I wanted nothing to do with my dad, so if I didn't have Ruby, she was really all I'd have.

She wanted to see me; I should want to see her.

"So everyone's at the rec field now, c'mon," London said.

She had me by the hand, and I realized how my hand turned colder just by being in hers, the joints in my fingers locking up. She led me away from the Green, and from my mother, who I didn't want to talk to anyway, and we'd already reached the rec field before I got up the guts to ask who "everyone" was.

Then there was my answer: Owen, who stood huddled with his friends.

I remembered then that the rec field was where kids often went to hook up. Ruby said you could come here on any summer night, walk up the softball field to the dark tiers of the bleachers, and hear the sounds of sucking face in tune with the crickets.

Maybe that's what Owen was thinking; maybe he'd asked London to get me here for this reason. With his back to his friends, he flashed a grin, like he assumed I'd be up for it, like even though it wasn't dark out yet he expected to slip with me under the bleachers and not talk about what it meant and what would happen tomorrow.

Maybe he thought I was someone other than me. Maybe I'd given him the wrong impression.

Ruby wouldn't have suggested I come to town if she'd known about this. I was treading on dangerous territory — the kind Ruby wouldn't want me stepping on. But she didn't know how far I'd gone already.

"Hey," he said, walking over and getting me at some distance from everyone else. "I wanted to talk to you."

"About what?" We were near the gazebo now, a favorite place of my sister's. I thought of how she'd talk to boys, how she'd barely have to utter a word and how they'd follow. Any boy would do. Sometimes she'd pick the ones she shouldn't. She'd swoop in, pluck them from their girlfriends, and then set them back down after, heads full of fog.

But Owen didn't go inside the gazebo. He stopped, and

glanced back at the guys, then said, "What I wanted to say is, we shouldn't tell anyone what happened."

"I . . . I wasn't going to."

"Like you shouldn't tell London and you shouldn't tell your sister, or you know, anyone else."

"Your friends, you mean."

He nodded. "Mostly your sister." For a second, he looked scared. Then he hid his eyes with his hair so I couldn't see.

"What do you think she'd do?" I asked.

He wouldn't answer. "We should get back. Before they think something's up."

I had this image of him—gone before I blinked—him, belly-up under a night moon, broken and not breathing. Or better yet, the same moon and him, but this time he's sinking into deep water and there's no boat to hold on to. Then I shook it away and I wasn't thinking anything violent that involved him, nothing that would get me sent to prison.

"What?" he said. He saw I wasn't moving.

That's when we heard a horn honking and spotted the red car at the edge of the field. There was London, leaning out of the window, arms out. The car she was in was filled with boys and smoke; their sound and smell leaked out to us from across the grass.

"O! Chloe!" she yelled, trying to get our attention. "You guys coming or what?"

Owen didn't need more than that. He was in the car, taking shotgun without anyone fighting him for it, and I was soon crammed in the backseat beside London. We took up one seat, with two other guys in with us. It happened fast, that's what I'd have to tell my sister, it happened so fast that I didn't realize we were headed out of town until we made the turn onto Route 28, and the car veered away from the reservoir, not toward it. I didn't realize until I looked up and saw us speed under the traffic lights. We were leaving town and I'd promised my sister I wouldn't—I'd promised her London wouldn't leave, either.

"Where are we going?" I asked London.

"That party," she said, like I knew.

"What party?"

"You know. The one at the cliffs in High Falls. Why'd you think I texted? We may as well drive out there now and start drinking early."

Everyone in the car seemed to know where we were headed. The guy driving was someone I didn't know but who seemed to know me by the way he asked after my sister. I'd call her when we got there, I told myself. I'd tell her then.

I had London's elbow in my side, could feel her hip bone cutting into mine. When I touched her, she was hard ice, and even skinnier than she looked, as if her one layer of skin was her only cushion.

Our town had a small center, but the township itself stretched up the mountain and down into the valleys that touched the mountain's edges. It spread out along the reservoir, which had once held the town of Olive, and also other towns, though I'd never bothered to know their names because Ruby never bothered to tell me.

This party we were headed to was beyond the town limits. The town of High Falls was in a whole other school district. It wasn't a place Ruby went to often, if at all.

As we drove, London whispered: "What's going on with you and O? Are you hooking up?"

I averted my eyes.

"*Are* you?" she said, loud enough to be heard over the music.

I shushed her, but Owen hadn't turned around. He hadn't turned around in his seat up front even once.

It wasn't something I wanted to talk about right there, with Owen close by, but before I could think up a good answer, I realized the conversation in the car had turned when we weren't paying attention. Even with the music up and the wind rushing in the open windows, I could hear the guys talking about her, my sister.

"—saw her the other day," the guy driving was saying, "it was sweet."

"—swear she was naked—" said the guy squeezed in beside me.

The wind kept clipping their words; I couldn't catch it all.

"—told her to come out of the water—" the guy near the far window said, adding a few recognizable hand motions.

Owen's voice was noticeably absent; he stared out his window at the passing trees. He wasn't defending her, but at least he wasn't talking about how he wanted to get in her pants. The others, though—they showed no signs of stopping.

The wind tossed their laughter around the car, shoving it in my face.

"Are you talking about my sister?" I yelled over the wind.

They didn't deny it. "You can't blame us," one of the guys in the backseat said, "she's smokin' hot."

"I heard she's a freak in bed," another said.

I covered my ears, hummed out the nasty words and the nastier pictures drummed up at the sound of them. The lies. The lies and lies and lies.

I was used to guys saying they loved her, confessing how they wanted her to marry them and have their babies, mushy things you didn't expect guys to admit to, but this was only physical. They made her sound like an ordinary slut, nothing special about it. And Ruby was many things, more than any of them could know, but she wasn't that.

"Shut up!" I yelled. "Stop it!"

The boys stopped, but when London saw how upset I was, she came alive in a way I'd never seen her. Her eyes had a whole new light in them, and a cruel smirk touched her lips. She spoke in a low voice right up against my ear. "Haven't you ever heard anyone say that? They say that kind of stuff about her. They say it all the time."

As she admitted this, some of Ruby's own words entered my mind, slithering inside me as I felt London's cold lips at my ear. "Stay in town," Ruby had said, me and London both. "Don't go anywhere else."

Was this why? Outside my sister's influence, did London turn into someone else, someone closer to who she was inside? Someone mean?

And the boys, too? Did everyone, absolutely everyone, turn against her?

I couldn't get away from London's mouth if I tried; the car was too small.

"Why does it bother you so much, what they say about Ruby?" London was saying, getting louder now over the wind. "Everybody in town hates her, don't you know that?"

"Not true."

"It is true." I barely recognized her, lit up with lies about my sister, spouting them out of her skinny face. "She's all up in my shit constantly," she said. "You have no idea what she makes me do. She's ruining my life. Sometimes I hate her, too."

That's when I said what I shouldn't have said.

"She could have sent you back," I said. "You don't want that, do you?"

"Back where?"

"Back to . . ."

She held herself very still, waiting for it.

". . . rehab," I finished.

She laughed. "She couldn't do that."

But I kept going. "You can't hate her. Without her, you wouldn't even be here."

"What's that supposed to mean?"

"You're not supposed to be here, London!" I shouted at her. "You should be kissing Ruby's feet right now. You should be *thanking* her and calling her a saint. You're not even supposed to be *alive*."

London didn't get it because all she said was, "Thanks, bitch," and then she was laughing, like this was a huge joke the whole car was in on, and then she was saying what a ho I was for hooking up with Owen, and how everyone knew, and everyone said so, and I was just like Ruby except barely half as pretty, and then I lunged at her and grabbed her by the mouth and told her to shut up, not because she said I was half as pretty but because of what she said about my sister, and I thought she was going to bite me, but she just started screaming.

The guys yelled beside us, egging us on. The wind was rushing through the open windows, throwing my hair in my face. The guys in the back were telling us to stop fighting and go ahead and make out already. Even Owen was involved, looking at me for the first time since we'd gotten in the car, asking what the hell was going on.

I couldn't be sure myself. I happened to look out at the road we were speeding down and I recognized the sign for the old turnpike. It had a weirdly bent squiggle on it to warn drivers how the road curved, but in the quick flash that I saw it and lost it, it showed me how far we were from anything I knew, so far I worried I'd never find my way to Ruby.

And maybe it happened then, maybe it was in that instant of passing the sign and entering the next town when her screams went quiet and her cold, bony face was no longer smashed against the palm of my hand, this moment when I couldn't feel her anymore and I fell back onto the seat and found it empty beside me.

I wasn't clutching her mouth any longer; there was no mouth to clutch. There was no one in the seat but me.

When I turned, the boys in the car were arguing over what CD to slip into the stereo. Owen had his back to me, his eyes out the window. High Falls was maybe ten, fifteen minutes away.

I patted at the seat. I sat up and stared at my reflection in the rearview.

All I knew is that we'd crossed town limits and the girl crammed into the backseat with me, the girl whose mouth I'd just been squeezing shut, whose name I'd been cursing, London—was gone.

CHAPTER EIGHTEEN

STOP

S top!" I shrieked at the top of my lungs. "Stop the car!"

The guy at the wheel swerved to the right and we landed on the shoulder with a jolt. I felt my arms still attached to my hands, my head on my shoulders, my body intact as it should be. I looked around the car wildly—she wasn't in the seat beside me, not in the front, and not in the back, which was jammed full of the enormous speakers. I twisted in circles, looking at the empty expanse of road behind us. Had she . . . leaped out the window when I wasn't looking?

Because there was no other place she could have gone.

The music had been shut off and all four boys were staring at me. Over the silence you could hear the wind rustling the leaves of the trees, a calm yet hair-raising hush of a noise, and every once in a while this low whimper, this terrified and truly awful sound, and it took me forever to realize it was coming from down in my own throat.

"What the hell!" the guy driving shouted.

"What's she on? What'd you give her, O?"

"I didn't give her shit. Maybe she took something, how am I supposed to know?"

They talked about me as if I wasn't there.

"Why'd she scream? I think she busted my eardrum."

"Dude, what's wrong with her?"

I finally spoke up. "Where are we?"

"Outside Rosendale, I think," the driver said, eyeing me warily. "Stone Ridge maybe."

We'd driven a few feet over some arbitrary line outside town, and London had vanished. And not one of them was acknowledging it.

Why wasn't anyone else shocked into a stupor over this? Wondering where she'd gone? Wondering if she was hurt and bleeding on the road? Wondering how a girl could disappear right before your eyes? Why weren't we all screaming?

I had to ask it. "Where'd *she* go?"

"What? Who?"

"London!"

The driver threw up his hands. "Where's the closest psych ward is a better question."

I turned to Owen. I reached out, whispered it. "She was sitting right here." I indicated the empty sliver of seat next to me.

He wouldn't even meet my eyes. He was looking north and to the left of my forehead when he said, "This is a joke, right?" He hesitated. "Right?"

I looked them all in the face. No one had seen her vanish; no one had a clue.

"Yes," I said. "Sorry. It wasn't funny."

One of the guys in the backseat laughed awkwardly, and the other guys went along with it. Except for Owen.

"No," he said, his eyes dull. "Not so funny."

So much of it made sense to me, right there in the back of the red car, perfect sense. If she wasn't lying in the two-lane road, then I'd know for sure. If she hadn't jumped out the open window, she'd disappeared instead. Almost as if she'd ceased to exist once we left the confines of our town.

Exactly if.

I opened my door and stepped out onto the asphalt. I looked for a body, but there was no body. Of course there wouldn't be a body—because here, outside town, London wasn't alive. Here, where the car was splayed crooked across the road, where my door was gaping open and I was looking for any trace of her, she lived only in my imagination. She died two years ago, out here.

I couldn't get back in the car. Who knew what would happen if we kept driving and made it to High Falls. How far was too far? The farther we got, I couldn't be sure what else would start to crumble. Flashing through my mind were images from a zombie flick, fingers and ears and noses and other bits of protruding flesh rotting off when we moved, hair shedding in clumps, arms and eyes coming loose from sockets, tongues fish-flopping on the ground. Would that happen to me, to my tongue? I couldn't risk it.

"I don't want to go anymore," I called back at the car.

The driver leaned out his window, all fed up, like now I'd gone and done it. "You can't be serious," he called to me.

"I'm going to walk home," I yelled back. "Or call my sister to come get me."

The car went in reverse and pulled up beside me. "Get in the car, Chloe," the guy driving said. I looked past him at Owen, but Owen wasn't the one saying it.

"I don't think so," I said.

I waited. Owen was about to open his door. He was about to step out onto the road with me, help me figure out how to get home. To at least make sure I was okay.

The driver turned to Owen, as if expecting the same thing. But Owen was staring out the windshield at the road ahead. "Fuck her," he said. "Just go."

I watched the car speed away, watched it as long as I could, until it went around the bend of trees and I didn't see it anymore.

It would be a long walk back, but I was thinking I might have to do it. Ruby didn't know where I was. She'd dropped me off on the Green; I hadn't told her I was leaving town. And worse—how would I explain what happened to London?

I paused in the road, there for the flattening if any cars sped my way.

Darkness was falling. It had been evening when we'd left, but now it was undeniably becoming night. At some point a car would drive past, heading north. Maybe in it would be someone I knew, someone who knew Ruby. At some point or another, hopefully before Ruby texted to check in, someone would have to drive this road and give me a ride back to town.

For now, I was outside town limits, by myself, in the growing dark.

But then a light flashed. My phone was blinking—and the small screen on it was bursting with a series of missed calls. The notices kept coming: calls and texts and voice mails, scrolling fast across the screen. My cell phone was acting like it had been jammed for days and was now spitting out every piece of communication in a breathless rush before final detonation.

Clearly the thing was broken.

I was about to pull out the battery, to see if that would help, when my phone lit up once more—this time with an incoming call. I answered immediately—expecting Ruby. But I hadn't checked the caller ID. If I had, I would have seen it was a call from Pennsylvania.

"Chloe! I can't believe it, Chloe, is that you?"

It was a woman's voice. She seemed distantly familiar, like a television character from some long-canceled show, someone I swore I knew but couldn't come up with a name and place to fit to her. My mind searched for recognition.

Then the woman said, "Your father's been worried sick! You've given him an ulcer. What were you thinking, Chloe!"

Then it came to me: my stepmother. That's who was on the phone.

"Sorry," I said. "I —"

"Your father's been trying to reach you. We thought something happened! You never answer your phone!"

"I didn't get any messages . . ." As far as I knew, I never even heard the phone ringing. But had all those missed calls eating up the memory of my phone just now been for real?

"We've been calling this number, Chloe. *This* number. Your father called. And I've called. Your voice-mail box ran out of space. We would have contacted the police if your mother hadn't been in touch with us to tell us where you were."

"You talked to Sparrow?"

"Yes. *She* called us. You know I don't enjoy talking to that woman, but at least she could pick up a phone."

Ruby must have forced our mother to call and be my alibi, that was all I could figure.

"Sorry," I said again.

"There must be something very wrong with your phone, Chloe," my stepmother said. "Your father was terribly worried."

"Really," I said. For sure I didn't believe it. Even though my phone was being difficult now, it had worked fine in town—there were no problems with the service, at least before tonight. Clearly he was only pretending to call me. He must have been relieved to have me off his hands all summer, not cluttering up his lawn with my life.

"Yes, *really*," my stepmother said. "Don't be so sarcastic. Stay right where you are; I'm running to go get your father. Do not hang up, Chloe. He wants to talk to you."

As I waited, I sucked it up and decided to start walking. Eventually this road would hit a more trafficked road, like a highway, and I'd come upon a car willing to take me the rest of the way into town.

Town. Where girls didn't disappear, at least for forever, and where no one could die, maybe ever, unless my sister wanted them to. Even if it was all in my head and I'd erased London permanently by letting her leave our borders, I wanted to be back inside. Where my sister had control over what was happening. Where things made sense.

My dad came on the phone and jumped straight into it: "You are *not* staying in New York. Your sister does *not* have the authority to enroll you in school, and I don't know what imbeciles are running that high school, but they can't . . .

when you come home . . . don't even know this Jonah . . . called that house . . . don't even have an answering machine . . . tell your sister I said . . . not allowed to . . . sorry excuse for a mother . . . listening to me, young lady?"

"I can't hear you," I said, which was true, partly. I just liked knowing that Ruby wanted to keep me here. She wasn't ever going to let me go again, and I was glad of it.

Also, the signal was cutting in and out. I checked my phone and I had all the bars; it must have been his phone that was losing service. His signal faltering, not mine.

"You're breaking up," I said loudly.

". . . sister put you up to this . . . don't . . . can't . . . how dare she . . ." is what I heard and then I heard only quiet with the occasional chirping, which wasn't my phone but the bugs and the birds in the night.

I ended the call; it didn't ring back. And I felt relieved, as if my phone sensed that I didn't want to talk to my dad and made it so. It wasn't even my choice, let alone my fault.

My phone must have sensed even more than that—like how I wouldn't want to hear his messages or read any of his texts—because right before my eyes I watched the count of missed messages spool down from 43 to 30 to 11 to 8 to 0.

The last thing I saw before the message light stopped blinking was a view of what was right in front of me in the street: the traffic sign for the old turnpike. The weird squiggle on the sign's face showed me how the road was about to curve, but I didn't see the curve itself, because all light cut out.

A voice sounded out in the darkness. "Hello?"

"Hello?" I took a few steps toward it. "Is someone out there?"

No cars had come down the road in either direction since I'd started walking. I'd walked as far as the edge of town, that sign we'd sped past, without realizing.

"Hello?"

I was hearing things, had to be. Though it sure did sound like someone was out there. It didn't sound like a hooting owl; it was human.

It seemed like the voice had been thrown from the patch of darkness I'd been walking into, darker now the more I got into it. The only light I had on me was my phone, and it still worked enough to allow its light to show my way. The road a foot or so ahead of me became visible, given a pale blue halo from the cell phone's weak glow. I followed the double yellow line, gone sallow green in the light, and took a few more steps forward.

Then something lunged right for me.

My first thought was a car, but there were no headlights. Then I assumed it had to be an animal, something big that would maul me and leave me flayed on the road. A bear, as it was upright and moving fast. But then I heard it say hello again, in English, and I realized the thing was as human as

I was, that it was a person, probably a murderer or a rapist, or both. I was about to regret every decision that had brought me to this moment. Only too late did I think how maybe I should turn tail and run.

But the murderer knew me by name. It also had a cell phone and was aiming an orange-tinted light straight at my face.

"Chloe!"

"L-London?" She was blue in my light, and I was golden in hers.

If I didn't physically feel her arms around me as she hugged me, I would have been sure she was an apparition, come back to haunt me on this vacant road. Then again, in the car she'd been about to bite my hand off—and now she was embracing me as if it hadn't happened. Had time wound back on itself and brought us both together to start over? Did she forget what she'd said about my sister? Were we friends again? Was she back, alive?

"I thought you were a ghost!" she was saying. "I thought, *That's it, I've gone certifiable, I'm like totally seeing ghosts now.* You scared the pants off me, Chloe! I almost peed right here in the road!"

I had to ask: "What are you doing in the middle of the road anyway?"

She was shaking her head in the blue halo, her tired eyes enormous, the circles under them deeper and darker than ever. Her bleached hair caught my light and had gone the color of the ocean. "I really don't know what happened or how I got here or what. I totally blacked out again."

"Again?"

"It happens sometimes. Sometimes I'm like doing something and then I look around and I'm in a whole other place doing something else. Or I think I'm heading somewhere and I forget ever getting there and I'm back home, like maybe I didn't go at all, I just thought I did. Lots of times I wake up at night in the dirt, like I forgot to go to bed, so weird." She shook her head again, her tinted hair poking out behind her ears. "It's seriously screwed up."

"So you don't remember . . . driving to a party?"

"Did I say I was going to a party?"

I nodded.

"See? I must've blacked out. Do you think I have narcolepsy or something?"

"I don't know," I lied, "maybe."

She stepped out of the road and onto a section of grass on the shoulder. She leaned on a mailbox, and in the light of my phone I could see that it said the name of our town's local newspaper, which meant we were back inside, back where London was still walking around and talking, where I wouldn't have to explain how she died all over again, where my sister's illusion was in place. Where I was home.

But this was London's home, too. And in her home, she

was walked on a leash by my sister. And even if she wanted to get away, she never could.

I wondered what would happen if I pushed her over the line. If she'd disappear, like last time. And when she did, if she'd pop up on our side. I wondered what it would look like—a shock of light and smoke? Would the air ripple as if we were underwater? Would I blink and there she'd be, as if she'd been standing here all along?

If she yelled, could they hear in the next town? If she threw her shoe over, would it ever land? The questions were endless.

"But what are *you* doing in the road?" London said. "Did you black out, too?"

"I was in a car I didn't want to be in anymore, so I got out. And they drove away."

"Where's Ruby?"

"Home."

She didn't ask me who was in the car, and I was glad she didn't. It would have hurt to say it out loud. His name.

"This is so freakishly bizarre that you're out here, too," she said. "This is like the weirdest thing that's ever happened to me, except for that time I tried to go to the Galleria mall in Poughkeepsie and I blacked out and all of a sudden I'm like standing on the bridge, you know that big giant bridge over the river . . . Man, that sucked! But . . . oh shit, Chloe, did you just feel that? We're gonna get soaked."

As she said it, I felt the first drops. A scattering of rain at first, touching down one small splash at a time in my hair and on my bare shoulders. Then the rain thickened and fell in drips down to my toes. We made a run for it, huddling under the closest tree. Our clothes stuck fast to our bodies, raindrops pooled in our eyelashes and suspended from the tips of our noses. The sound around us was a rushing flood, but one come from above.

"I should try Ruby," I said, thinking of how to explain this. I lifted my phone and already the water was pooling into it; I was waiting for it to short out and go dark in my hand. I pressed a key and nothing happened. I pressed the same key again, and again.

"It's okay," London said. "I called before I saw you."

"You called my sister? You told her where you . . . *we* are?"

She shook her head. "I called someone else."

She perked up then when a pair of headlights appeared, coming our way through the rain. She leaped out from under the tree and lifted her skinny arms in the air, attempting to flag down the car but more like almost running herself into the fender before it skidded on the slick road to get out of her way.

"It's Pete!" she yelled to me. "Ruby always said you could call him and he'd do anything. I even woke him up, and look—he came anyway. Just like she said."

This was something Ruby had told me. Pete being willing to do anything for my sister, and by extension me, and how I could call him at any hour with any unreasonable request and his deep loyalty to her would make sure he'd get it done.

I guess she'd given London that little tip, too.

When the car came to a stop and I left the tree's shelter to stand with London, the both of us drenched, he got a lopsided grin on his face. "A threesome?" he said, leaning over to open the car door. "Hells yeah. Get in."

"Don't be disgusting," I said, expecting London to also tell him to shut it, but she slid into the backseat, shaking out her short wet hair all over the leather, and let me take the front seat beside Pete. Which meant I had to be the one to talk to him.

"You're soaked," he said, only half-approvingly. "If you two go and mess up my car, I'll . . ." He tapered off before any threat came out, distracted by what happens to a girl's shirt when rain soaks it through.

I crossed my arms in front of my chest so he'd have to look me in the eyes. As I did, the rain enveloped the car for a moment, one thick sheet swirled around us to keep us from seeing out, and then it opened, and lightened, and stopped its pounding, and though it was still raining, at least we could see.

"How'd you find your car keys, anyway?" I asked. I

remembered how, it seemed so long ago, Ruby had lost them.

"You knew where my keys were?"

I shrugged.

He let out a sigh and played with the ugly protruding tuft of his goatee, which he should have shaved, and stat, because Ruby hated unruly goatees or any kind of attempt at a beard, and you'd think he'd know that. He just said, "I looked. I looked everywhere. I had to order a whole new set of keys—for my car, for the garage, my house, everything. But that's Ruby."

He said all that, and he didn't even seem mad. He hacked up a cough, scratched at his old, wrinkly concert T-shirt for a band I'd never heard of, and swung the car around to drive us toward town.

I kept peeking in the rearview at London, like she'd get more substantial the closer we got to town. Fleshier, harder to break. More real.

But she was only herself. She was here, in another car, and this time she wasn't trying to scratch my eyes out. She was leaning over the front seat, reaching for the stereo. She was rolling down the back windows even though it hadn't stopped raining, letting the wind blow-dry her hair and the rain make it wet again. She was asking Pete if he had any smokes on him. She wasn't any more real than she'd been before—the same girl, nothing different about her that I could make out, except that her anger at Ruby had disappeared and her memory had been erased.

Pete went to drop off London first. He got us close to town and made the turn around the bend, coming up on the thicket of trees near where I remembered Ruby said London lived. Only, just the same as last time, we didn't end up taking her all the way to her house. London thumped Pete on the shoulder and said she wanted to get out here.

"What for?" Pete said. "I'll drive you home."

"Nah, here's fine," she said. She whipped the door open into crushing rain and stepped out onto the road. She flicked a hand at me, barely an attempt at a wave, and then she took off for what looked like a patch of trees, disappearing into the storm the way she'd vanished from sight in my hands.

Pete didn't seem to care. He spun the car around to take me to Jonah's and didn't even suggest we go after her.

But I eyed the dark thicket of trees, the shadows growing blacker as the rain came down. "Pete. She's going into the woods." I realized then how close we were to the flap in the fence that Ruby used as her own private entrance-way. It was around that bend a little ways, wasn't it? Maybe London had her own private way in, too.

"Do you know what's through those woods, Pete?" He'd been here before, tons of times. He knew the only thing out there was the reservoir.

"She's not going in the woods," Pete said. "She's walking home. Her house is just over there." He pointed, but at nothing. It was too dark to point at much of anything.

"She's going in. Look."

He stopped the car on the slick road and looked back. We both did, though there was no light on anywhere to catch her.

"It's a shortcut," he said at last.

"Wait here," I said, before he could stop me.

I was running then, running through the rain and skidding in the mud in my sandals and scrambling over the gulley and into the trees. I was pushing through branches and stumbling over rocks, and there wasn't a piece of me that wasn't sopping wet and dripping.

The waterfall of rain from my forehead to my chin kept me from seeing all I could. Even so, I was able to make out London slipping into the dark pocket of a sagging fence, her feet the last two pieces of her to vanish. I watched her go in and not come out.

I went to the fence and saw what I knew would be there, glistening as black as oil on the horizon. The reservoir, which London had come out of just this spring. The reservoir, where I should have known she'd been spending her nights.

CHAPTER NINETEEN

I CAME BACK

I came back out of the woods after a while. When I returned to Pete's car, he didn't comment on how drenched
I was. He opened the door for me and said, "Find her?"

I shook my head.

"Women," he said. "Tell them not to do something, they
do it anyway." When I glared at him, too soaked to respond,
he added, "Ruby used to wander off doing crap like that all
the time. I'm used to it."

He jammed the gas and took us back the way we'd
come. "You think she'll be home when we get there?" he
asked.

"Yeah. But you know what, Pete? Maybe I shouldn't
go there yet. Maybe we should go into town for a while. I
should call her first, or wait for her to call me." I was thinking how she hadn't texted. She'd told me to spend time out
of the house but hadn't yet said it was okay to return.

"Can't chicks ever make up their minds?" Pete mumbled.

But he still coasted us on into the center of town, following my instructions without too much more protest.

I pulled out my phone to make sure it still worked. It seemed perfectly fine—and no longer overloaded with messages—so I texted Ruby.

u ok?

I didn't wait for a response before sending another: **ok i come home?**

Nothing.

Near the Green, Pete turned off the engine and muttered to himself, but he was still doing what I said. Then he opened his mouth and I thought he'd shoot out something perverted, but he kept his eyes up in the vicinity of my face and said simply, "Anything for Ruby's sister."

It was all very heavy and hypnotic, like I'd been the one to bewitch him, but I couldn't take credit, and, fact was, Pete never needed any bewitching. He'd follow my sister anyway, always had. It was thanks to whatever she'd done to him all those years ago, and ever since he'd walked around barely able to dress himself, caught up in the idea of her, even when she told him for the hundredth time to please go away.

"Pete, why? Why are you like this? What'd she do to you?"

"Who do you mean, Ruby?"

I nodded.

She'd broken his heart, that was a given. Maybe she'd done it with one hand, crushed it into a tight little ball. Maybe she'd done it fast, while it thumped in her palm, then ripped it out to keep in the back of her dresser and all this time he had no idea.

He shrugged. "She was my first girlfriend," he said. "My first"—you could see the gears turning opposite-wise in his head, like only with great effort could he keep this from being vulgar—"my first, uh, everything."

I nodded. No special effort needed. No bolts of lightning or hot sizzles of smoke. It was all so ordinary, and that was enough.

"Thanks, Pete. Thanks for driving."

"Don't thank me, I'm just the taxi service."

I tried to think of something to say to make that seem less pitiful, but he spoke again before I could.

"I don't mind. Really. Besides, you remind me so much of her, so if you need something, it's like she needs something. And I kinda like that, y' know?"

"I know, Pete."

Now he was tilting his head, a hand over his eyes, squinting. People did that when they were making an effort to see a hint of her in me. Boys did. Boys did it all the time.

"I see what my bro sees in you. *Saw* in you, I mean. His loss."

I blushed when he used the past tense.

"You shouldn't tell your sister," he said.

"I wasn't planning to."

"Just, yeah. Just be careful what you tell her."

That's the moment we were both startled by the pounding on the hood of the car. I looked out through the rain-spattered windshield, expecting to find the town crazy, Dov Everywhere, who'd been known to thump his sticks on cars if they parked in places he didn't approve of. But the eyes searing through the glass didn't belong to Dov. They were the pale, distant eyes of a woman. She was knocking on the hood with her bare hand.

I turned to Pete. "What do you think she wants?"

"You, obviously. She's not my mother."

I wanted to deny Sparrow, say Ruby was more a mother to me than she ever was, that the word was meaningless, that the word shouldn't be legally binding, and biology didn't mean I had to be civil, but I also felt a tad sorry for her and wanted to get her off the car and out of the rain. I hadn't noticed until now that Pete had skidded to a stop just outside the Village Tavern. We were practically on her doorstep.

"Uh, I think she wants to talk to you," he said, as she wasn't showing any signs of going away. "Just go in with her. I'll keep watch while I have a beer at the bar."

Soon after that, I found myself sitting across from the woman Ruby and I begrudgingly called our mother.

Seeing her up close brought back patches of my childhood:

Standing over her in a sheetless bed while she slept thirteen hours straight. Poking her in a recliner upon finding her passed out bright and early on a school morning. Pelting her with raisins from the packet of trail mix, since Ruby and I didn't eat raisins even if they'd been dipped in chocolate first. Watching her conk out in a car, while she was at the wheel and the car was still moving.

Most of my memories of our mom didn't involve her being conscious.

She looked frailer than ever. Her hair must have weighed more than the rest of her. She took in a ragged breath and said, "She know you're here?"

I shook my head. "No, but she's going to text me back any minute and then I'll have to go."

"I just wanted to see you. Without *her*."

"What for?"

"Because you're my daughter," she said, but she said it so robotically, I didn't believe her. I looked around at the place instead of at her—the Village Tavern was as dark inside as I'd always pictured it, a low-lit room with sunken ceilings, lopsided wooden tables filling up the space and a long bar against one wall where Pete sat with his back to us, slurping a pint. I was far below twenty-one and shouldn't have been allowed inside, but no one from behind the bar was coming over to kick me out. The only person who'd stop this reunion in its tracks was Ruby—and she wasn't here.

This tavern was where our mother spent her time. Maybe the whole of the past two years Sparrow lived in this dark hole, forgetting what sunlight looked like and letting herself be forgotten. This was what happened when Ruby stopped paying attention. You may as well cease to exist.

"Did you want to tell me something?" I said.

She nodded. She was looking down at her hands. She wore numerous rings, eight at least, cheap flea market silver with grimy birthstones from months she wasn't born in, the bands gone tight beneath her swollen knuckles. This was why Ruby said you should never wear a ring long enough to grow old with it—some people shriveled and some people swelled, and you couldn't be sure which way your body would go.

"She told me not to see you," my mom confessed. "She said no visits. Not to call. Said she'd let me know when—" She looked up, and there was a flicker of fright in her watery eyes, and then she stopped talking.

I didn't believe her excuses. The idea of my mom wanting to see me all this time, all while living in the same town, was absurd.

"Ruby didn't tell you not to see me," I said. "She would've said something."

The expression on her face made me think she was more sober than she let on, that if I said the right thing, asked the right question, she'd know exactly how to respond.

"There was something not right with her from the beginning," she said. "A mother knows when her child's not right, she can sense it."

She must have been remembering a different Ruby, not the one I knew. Whatever she saw in my sister wasn't what I could see. And wouldn't want to.

"What do you even mean by that?" I said. "There's nothing wrong with Ruby."

"She has a way about her, ever notice that? Always did, since she was small. A way of getting you to do things for her. To get what she wants. Say what she wants you to say."

I shrugged. This was true, but what of it?

"You couldn't stop her. You couldn't stop her if you tried."

I glanced up at Pete, wanting to mouth *Help!* and have him rescue me, but his attention was too caught up in his beer.

"I should've been there for you, Chloe," my mom was saying. "To leave you alone like that with her. I'm so sorry."

She'd said things like this to me before, about being sorry, about leaving me alone, always after she'd sobered up and had her meetings. It didn't matter what I said back. I could hum with thumbs in my ears, or use an onion to cry. It was all so temporary. Only the things Ruby said to me could be counted on forever.

Still, I realized in this moment that I wasn't mad at her. Maybe another girl would be, to have this kind of mother, but what Sparrow didn't know is that I didn't need a mom, not when I had Ruby. My heart was already full.

"How drunk are you?" I asked. "Will you even remember this tomorrow? That we talked?"

"I remember everything," she said. She enunciated very carefully, as if she wanted to make sure it sunk in. "*Everything*, Chloe. Every single thing."

The dark of the room felt dimmer as she said that. Here, I felt sure, this here was what she wanted to communicate to me. It wasn't about regret or love or how bossy Ruby was—it was this. She saw what I could see, and she wanted me to know that.

Out of everyone in town—even London—she was the only one who did.

"Do you remember . . ." I started, expecting at any moment for a text from Ruby to come through to keep me from talking, expecting someone to ask for my ID, expecting Pete to run out of beer, expecting a blockade that didn't come, "do you remember sending that box to me in Pennsylvania, when I first moved in with Dad?"

She nodded gravely.

"The feathers made a big mess on the floor," I said.

She waited. She knew what I was going to say next.

"And the obituary," I said. "From that newspaper across the river. Do you remember sending that?"

The film over her pale eyes was impenetrable, stuck in place no matter how many times she blinked. A windshield so fogged, the wipers couldn't clear the way to see. When I looked into those eyes, I had to assume she had no idea what I was talking about. There was no way she could know.

Only, her mouth opened and these were the words it said: "That poor girl. Her poor parents." She knew exactly what I meant.

"I told you," she continued. "I remember everything, even the things I don't want to. I remember before, and I remember after, and I remember when it all changed. And now you're home."

My spine was on fire. My fingers prickled with heat, hot static fizzing through my body from end to end. "But . . . how?" I asked. I lowered my voice. "No one else does."

"She lets me," she said. "She's always let me."

Our mother saw more than I'd ever guessed, because Ruby wanted her to. But imagine being a drunk, known in town for passing out in the supermarket and sleeping off benders in the town jail—no one would believe a thing you said then. Imagine how mad you'd think you were, to be cursed to remember. It was a cruel, bitter thing Ruby had done. I happened to think our mother deserved it.

"You know what?" she said suddenly. "You shouldn't've come in here. I shouldn't have asked you. I shouldn't've gone out to the car . . ." She stood. "You should go now."

And it was right then, on cue, that a buzzing sounded. It felt like a moth had found its way in from the rain and climbed my leg, beating its wings inside my jeans so I would let it out. My phone, set on vibrate. This was a text from Ruby—and she'd sent it now, at this moment, to show she knew where I was. And who I was with.

The text itself said nothing about that, though.

ok come home. u need to pack. can't stay in this house. we're out

We were leaving Jonah's? I guessed her talk with him hadn't gone so well.

I eyed our mother, the first person we'd ever picked up and moved out on, when Ruby was seventeen and I was eleven-and-a-half and we decided to live in our own filth instead of having to share filth with our mother.

I texted back: **r u picking me up? bc i'm not on green**

My breath was held when I got her reply:

call Petey. u know he's always good for a ride

CHAPTER TWENTY

I'M THE ONE

I'm the one who made it happen, but I wasn't certain until then.

It was when I slipped my toe in. When I did what Ruby said I shouldn't—and more where that came from, with boys and rides out of town, with our mother, the last person Ruby wanted me talking to, all of what I'd done radiating from my skin like fever sweat once I stepped out of Pete's car and into her arms. She knew something was wrong without me having to tell her. She'd sensed it before, and now for sure she knew.

She wasn't the only one who'd become aware.

Something else knew now, too.

I looked down to find it pooling up over my ankles, murky and thick, more brown than green, churning with sticks and bits of leaves and scattered trash, its surface crawling with thick patches of slow-traveling mud. The reservoir had somehow made its way up here. The water was spreading its fingers over the gravel driveway and the dirt yard, no higher than ten inches in places, but risen up enough to hide all trace of ground and swallow shoes. The back porch was even with the water now, coasting at the same level across the whole yard.

Ruby pulled me out of the floodwater to a high-standing stone, one of the few left visible from the walkway that had once led from the driveway to the front steps of the house. We stood together on the tall stone, teetering, our four feet and four legs locked together to become one conjoined person, except she was taller and tanner and had wading boots on, and I was only me.

"It's coming up," she said. "I don't know how it's coming up from all the way over there, but it is."

"Yeah, but it's stopped raining," I said. "Maybe it'll go down now."

"Maybe. Or maybe we'll need to build ourselves a boat."

I looked back toward the driveway Pete had just coasted down—the one that had been slick with mud but still manageable—and I saw that already it was taken up by large stretches of water. You could see the water seep down to the end, wanting road. You could see Pete cursing and kicking at his swallowed tires. You could see how far the water had gotten, when it shouldn't have—not with a hill and a highway and fences and concrete barricades in the way.

The logistics of it were unexplainable, like so much of what had gone on since I'd been home.

This flood of water was from more than the rainstorm, I realized—and being elevated on a hill hadn't helped any, though it should have spared us. From our view on the tall rock, with all the lights from the house on, I could see how the hill where the house was built now connected straight across to the large expanse of the reservoir in the near distance. The water was a flat sheen, seeming the same height all across. There used to be a road—the two-lane stretch of Route 28—between us. No longer. Now there was no differentiating where the reservoir ended and the house began. Now it looked like we lived at the edge of a great, thrashing ocean.

The reservoir water had crept in to wrap its cold fingers around us, expanding past its own walls and making it up here. It had gotten out.

Because of me.

Ruby balanced with me on the tall stone, trying to figure out what we should do. I was silent, and not helping by staying silent, but she kept a hold of me and made sure I didn't slip. I thought of London down there, and hoped she'd gotten out. Then I remembered she wasn't in any peril. She could breathe in the deep just fine.

Pete would need a tow if he wanted to ever leave, and Ruby's own low-riding Buick wouldn't make it out of the drive tonight, either. Jonah emerged from the house saying water had gotten into the basement and he'd have to rent some kind of pump to flush it, but other than that the house was all right and we should go inside and get dry.

"Are you telling me what to do?" Ruby snapped at him, her wit's end having already been reached long ago and now whipping and snapping in the wind.

"But it's stopped raining," he said. "The water'll go down. Just get in the house."

Ruby shook her head defiantly. But when she looked around the shallow lake of the backyard, her veranda an island drifting in the midst of it, she changed her mind.

"We're going upstairs," she announced. "Jonah, we'll be out of here tomorrow. Make sure my car can get down the driveway."

Jonah squelched closer, his hair wet and dripping tears on his tattoos. He had no idea what he looked like to us, or what he sounded like when he opened his mouth. "Baby, you can't be serious. You're leaving, just 'cause of a flooded basement?"

Here's something I knew: My sister was not his baby. In fact, my sister didn't allow herself to be anyone's baby; she never had, not even when she was one. Anytime a guy called her a word like that, I knew it meant he'd lost her for good.

"Oh, the basement's just one reason," Ruby said. "You

know all the other reasons. Don't make me say them out loud in front of my little sister."

Pete and I had clearly interrupted an argument. I tried to peel my eyes away, to be polite. But he looked on, to be rude. Then he spoke, to make it worse. "Hey, what about me? What about saying all this in front of me?"

"What *about* you?" she said. "If you can't get down the driveway, you can sleep in your car, can't you?"

She took her first step off the stone and into the shallows. The water couldn't have been that deep, but it had gone opaque as the stone itself, hiding everything in its grasp, even her boot toes. She tried to bypass Jonah, but he wasn't letting her through. He grabbed her by the arm and held her still.

It was like seeing a daring, darting bug's glistening, shimmery wing get wedged flat and stuck in place by a pin. She wiggled, he held fast, and then she stopped wiggling, and he kept holding fast, and I couldn't watch anymore. I had to look away.

"Ow," I heard her say. "That'll be a bruise."

"It will not," he said.

"Will so. Give it an hour, I'll have an eggplant on my elbow. And I have two witnesses here to show how it got there."

Jonah was mumbling—groveling probably, apologizing up and down and sideways—and then there was some fumbling around, and wet slurping sounds, like Ruby was making full use of the slimy muck at her feet. I peeked back and saw them standing together in front of the house. His hands were on her arm, lightly now, like he was afraid to keep touching her and equally afraid to let go. There was mud on his shirt.

"You can't treat me like this, Ruby," he said in a low voice. But I could hear. I had Ruby's ears—the same shape and size, the same recessive earlobes. And Ruby could hear you chewing your fingernails from a floor away and would yell for you to cut it out, right now. She could hear the things you think if you thought them loud enough while resting your head on her shoulder. She could hear from across town.

I could hear Jonah plainly, and what he said next was the most pathetic thing a grown man could say to my sister, the four dreaded words: "But I love you." And worse was how he paused after saying it, then added, "Don't you love me?"

She didn't answer right away. She didn't answer for so long, I wondered if she'd forgotten they were having a conversation and that Pete and I were standing here witnessing. It was cruel how long she took to answer, awful and terrible and so very cool of her, something to aspire to.

She removed his fingers from her arm and rubbed her elbow. She had his hand in her hand and took the whole lot and placed it on his heart. Then she let go, so all he had was his hand all by itself on his heart. Her own hand was far away.

"What ever made you think I did?" she said.

She began splashing for the house, signaling to me that I should hold still a moment. That moment was long, with me trying not to fall off the stone, with Jonah withered by what she'd told him, and Pete buoyed up wondering if he had another shot now — but she splashed back to my side as quickly as she could. She carried a pair of galoshes and slipped them on my feet one by one. Then she gave a last glance at the dark and stormy sea behind the house, like they'd won this one, but she'd for sure win the next, and we sloshed up to the front door, opened it by the hole where the knob should be, and tracked mud inside, leaving a trail for someone else to clean up later.

I didn't much care that she'd broken up with Jonah. Over the years, I'd witnessed many breakups, some quick and quickly forgotten, some slow and agonizing and needing restraining orders. Some breakups featured flying food products — or harder, more controllable objects like boots — lots had tears, and most, if not all, included the sight of Ruby being the one to walk away. Her turned back, her long, lingering trail of dark hair . . . That was her flourish of a signature, to remember her by, always.

But this time, she seemed all sniffly about it. She wiped

at her eye, and I wasn't sure if what she wiped off was a tear or a speck of muck. Maybe it was the house, as this was the closest we'd ever come to having one of our own. Maybe she was grieving her veranda.

Now that we were alone, I wanted to tell her what I'd seen: London vanishing and reappearing in the road, then sneaking in to go sleep at the reservoir. But, if I went and told Ruby that, I'd also have to explain how we got ourselves past the town line. Plus I'd have to tell her I knew what happened when London crossed over. How it meant that everything my sister had done could only be found in here, in our small town.

Which meant, if we left, it would crumble to nothing.

"We need supplies," Ruby said to me now, muddying up the kitchen. "We'll stay upstairs all night, no coming down till tomorrow. Just in case."

She filled her arms with anything not yet past expiration. She grabbed bags of nuts, a heel of cinnamon bread, some slightly overripe bananas, a sprig of grapes, and somehow managed to wrangle up a clean bowl to hold it all. We were abandoning our diet due to a state of emergency. Then she swept me up the stairs with her, leading the way over the gate.

I knew how her mind worked. Once, years ago, when our mother had company, Ruby led the two of us out a window onto the rooftop, then a tree branch, then over to the neighbors' trellis and onto their porch, where we sought refuge till morning. This was because if she didn't like a thing that was happening, she wouldn't stand by to watch. Sometimes she'd leave before there was even a chance at a thing happening—she'd slip out of a car just before the kiss, anticipating the moment of denial before having to deny it. If there were still some visible parts of the road out there, we'd be speeding down Route 28 right now. As things stood, we'd wait and hope for morning.

Upstairs, Ruby closed her bedroom door and turned on me. Now we'd talk. Now I'd tell her.

But she said, "They know you're back, Chlo. Explain to me how they know. You went swimming when I told you not to, didn't you? You snuck in."

I denied it. Barely tapping the water was not the same as plunging into it. One touch of a toe wouldn't, couldn't cause all this. *Could it?*

The more I said my denials, the more I felt something in the house with us. It had followed us upstairs. Its smell had seeped into the furniture, the wood now sweating with it, drips of condensation running down. The air in the room was growing cold, too cold for summer, and too cold for the surface. It felt like we were deep under with the rest of Olive, their telltale chill seizing hold of my bones.

I thought of what she'd said. She'd said *they*. So she felt them here, too.

I brought the question to my lips. "Do you think they got in the house?"

Her face chilled, and the temperature of my skin dropped even more degrees, and I took a step back, and was up against the big canopied bed, and then I was crawling into the bed to make sure my feet didn't touch the floor.

The walls looked down on us, knowing who we were talking about, yet not calling them out by name. Shadows in the paint made grave faces at us, eyes as large and serious as my sister's, but without lashes, and without the mechanism to close. Toes curled and went black; nipples dangled to the floor like extra fingers. The lamplight turned murky, the shadows green and strangled around a taut, drowned neck.

You'd think that the people of Olive torpedoed up to the surface to wait for us to start talking. That they broke free and choked out their first earthbound breaths in a near century all so they could hear what she said about them. They crawled the hill, slithered down the porch, suctioned sticky hands to the walls. They braved splinters. They found the widow's walk. They pressed damp ears to the window screen and listened in.

Maybe they did. Maybe they were.

"Have you seen them?" I asked.

She nodded faintly.

"Has London?"

"Of course."

I confessed the way the girl had turned to air in my hands, but Ruby barely blinked at that admission. I said I saw where she sleeps.

She didn't say a word about it.

"You could have drowned, and it would have been all my fault," she said instead. "You've never had a baby sister, so you can't know how it felt. How it still feels. How every morning I wake up and think of what I almost let happen."

"*Almost,*" I whispered.

"Almost," she agreed. "I'd do anything for you—anything. I have. Want to know what happens when you let your baby sister get hurt? What that feels like?"

"What?"

"You want to die. You want to curl up under the wheels of a truck and let it run you over as many times as it takes to flatten you flat. You want to throw a hair dryer in the bathtub when you're in it. You want to do anything to take it back."

And here she smiled. And the eyes in the walls and the eyes looking through the window witnessed this and could do nothing to stop it.

"So," she said, "I did."

A shiver ran through me.

"I did," she repeated. "I kept you from drowning. I gave them her instead."

When she said that, the truth of it all came tumbling

down on me like a waterfall that falls and falls and keeps falling long after you've been swept up in it. I was beginning to remember. Swimming—and not making it—across. The body in the boat hadn't always been there to keep me from sinking in.

Ruby didn't realize I was remembering it, though. She said, "And now I'm tired. Look at the bags under my eyes." She lifted her eyes, and I did see bags beneath them, two purple and puffy foreign objects on her face. I saw how her hair frizzed out. How her elbows had dry spots and how a crinkle had set in deep above her brow. I saw how it had taken its toll, all of it. The effort of keeping this up was leaving physical strain on her body.

"We should sleep now," she said. It wasn't long before she fell deep in, drifting so far that I couldn't rouse her.

In sleep, her face darkened. She didn't sleep-talk at all.

We spent our last night in that house together, Ruby clinging to me like we were afloat on a raft in the boundless ocean— but we'd long run out of food and one of us would have to let go soon; one of us would have to go under before we ate the other.

I didn't dream that night. What I did was remember. I remembered a night two years ago, on the rocks at the edge of the reservoir, a night I'd stuffed up in a paper bag crumpled up inside a sock that I'd balled up and shoved far in the back drawer of my mind, where the worst things go.

It was illegal to swim the reservoir, but we did it anyway. And it was impossible to swim across in the middle of the night, but I started to try. My sister would have propelled me all the way to the other shore—like she held a hand under my stomach, propping me up where no one could see she was doing it—except she thought too much of herself sometimes. She thought she didn't have to help. She began to think I really could swim down to the bottom and grab hold of a souvenir.

Then I felt the water turn cold and, as the chilled spot enveloped me, the downward tugging pull.

A thought bubbled up about Olive. Had they sent an emissary for me—a cold pair of arms to put me in a sleeper hold and drag me down? Is that what was happening? Is that why I was choking on water and couldn't get air?

Ruby is right, I was thinking. Because I felt their eyes on me, the eyes of Olive, heard them calling me, heard how they already knew my name.

And she was right about me, too. I didn't need to breathe, the closer I got to Olive; there was enough air in my lungs to last me years.

That would have been the moment I drowned.

Because then there was dark.

Then there was nothing.

Not because I died, but because I didn't. I didn't die because my sister had a way to bend the world to her bidding, a talent of hers since she was small. In a panic, she did the first thing she thought to do: save me, even if it meant sacrificing someone else.

In a heartbeat, she lifted me up out of that cold, deep water. She'd sent something for me to hold on to, that rowboat drifting there at just the moment I needed to catch my breath.

I didn't sink down to Olive, I remembered this for sure now. Someone else took my place so I could be here.

CHAPTER TWENTY-ONE

DON'T GO

Don't go," I would have said, if she'd only woken me up first. But what I woke to was the sun on my face and bright, shadow-free walls and an enormous expanse of bed, rumpled sheets tossed about like a windstorm, the room empty except for me.

It was morning, and she was gone.

On the pillow beside mine was a glistening strand of hair. Ruby and I shared a hair color, no thanks to having two different fathers: the same exact shade of deep dark brown, enhanced with equal parts henna used to bring out the red. But this strand of hair didn't match our color. It was white, like all pigment had been stripped out in one suck. And when stretched out to flatten its curl, it reached, end to end, as long as my arm.

The unread text on my phone — I could picture her there in the room, messaging me from inches away instead of shaking me awake to tell me in person — said simply:

brb xo

Wherever she'd gone was yet another secret she was keeping from me.

I checked the windows first, to see if we were still flooded in, but all that was left in the yard were scattered puddles and shallow slicks of mud. The reservoir wore an innocent face across the way, waterline still high, but not near enough to engulf the road.

Down in the kitchen, I could hear both Jonah and Pete being all perplexed about where she was, too. When I peeked in, I saw how they kept eyeing each other like they'd kick the table aside and scrap with their bare hands if she came back and said she'd pick only one of them.

"Her car's gone," Pete said.

"I saw," Jonah said. "She took all her shit from the living room. And who knows what she got from upstairs."

"The water's down," Pete said. "Guess she didn't need any help getting out."

"Guess not," Jonah said.

They both stared as I stepped all the way in but didn't utter a good morning.

"She left Chloe here," Pete said, as if I wasn't digging out some sugar cereal from the cabinet two feet away.

"All I know is she's not taking off and sticking me with a fifteen-year-old kid," Jonah said.

"Sixteen," I said, eating cereal out of the box.

"*Sixteen*-year-old kid," Jonah corrected himself.

"Don't look at me, dude," Pete said. "She can't stay at my place. I live with my parents."

"Well, she can't stay here," Jonah said.

"Stop it," I said. "She'll be back for me. She told me."

And she would; it was only that I didn't know when.

The day deepened and she didn't answer her texts. The night swept closer and she didn't pick up when I called. The white Buick didn't roar back down the driveway. When Pete got his car out of the mud and said I could get a ride with him, I went into town looking for her. No one had seen her all day.

Coincidentally, no one had seen London, either.

It was on the Green, standing there with some of London's friends, that I realized I needed to go back. I needed someone to drive me. Now.

I made an excuse. "It's so hot out," I said, sounding so innocent. "I feel like swimming. Let's go to the reservoir."

Cate, Damien, Asha, and Vanessa liked the idea and said sure.

"So, you gonna swim across this time? Like you did that one summer?" Cate said to me, oblivious or stoned or both.

"I thought you asked if she was going to swim across *time*," Asha said.

"Wow," Cate said. "That would be impossible."

"Yeah like completely impossible."

And they didn't wait for an answer—if I'd swim it this time, if I ever even had. We went for the car, but everyone had stops to make first, and at each stop someone new was told and the group got larger. Soon there were snacks and smokes gathered and flashlights and cheap beer from the place in town that didn't card. Word had gotten out and the handful of kids wanting to swim had expanded. There were more kids going than I could count. Some, I didn't even know. I'd accidentally instigated a party.

When we hit the rocks on shore, I could barely look at first—at the water. I kept my back to it, took the first beer handed to me, though it was warm and shook-up from the walk in the woods, tried to go for a sip, and sprayed myself with foam instead. Behind me, voices in the water seemed to whisper imperceptible mumbles of things, hardly words at all. I saw how the water was edging closer to the trees than I'd ever seen it, and it seemed somehow darker in the night, if that were possible, and so deep there wouldn't be just a lost town down at the bottom but a long highway leading down and down, until someone who didn't need lungs to breathe could find herself emerging with a splash in another lake on the other side of the world.

I didn't go in. The last time I'd stepped all the way into this reservoir, I'd found a dead girl floating in it.

Tonight, so far, there was no trace of her. Or of my sister.

"Don't!" Cate shrieked from a pool of darkness, startling me. But she was only goofing off with her friends, saving herself from being thrown in at the last second. She was talking to her friend, not me.

Damien dove in first. Asha made a splash like she weighed three hundred pounds, though she weighed a third of that and no one could figure out how such a big splash had come from her. Vanessa fussed with her bra strap. Some girl I'd never seen before stepped out of her clothes and jumped, and then I couldn't see her anymore. There was a boat being pushed in; there was a jumble of shoes on shore.

So many people were there—too many.

I got caught up in it. My shoes came off, then my shorts and my shirt. I could cannonball down from the high rocks into the water below; the plunge would have more force that way—I'd hit and sink fast toward bottom. Once under, I'd stay down as long as I could stand it. I'd hold my mouth closed and hope the air lasted. I'd open my eyes and hope to see someone. Maybe a person from Olive would tell me where my sister was.

I was at the edge when a voice rang out, echoing off the water and the rocks and the mountains framing the stars and moon above. Coming from everywhere and from one place only. From one person.

"Chloe!"

Everyone froze. The night slipped to mute, the sounds of splashing wiped clean away, so all that could be heard was the hush of the reservoir as it breathed in and then out again, in and then out. I realized that everyone was looking up at me. Then we heard her slosh as she waded out from a blind spot veiled by rocks and trees, and now everyone was looking at her.

She had her flashlight on high, one of those industrial-strength models that investigators use when fishing through a crime scene. The light found Asha and Cate, Damien and Vanessa. It showed them without clothes, dripping wet and covering what they could. It held tight, revealing them shivering in the suddenly harsh and bitter night.

I spoke up. "Hi, Ruby. I'm up here."

The beam of her flashlight cast its way across London's friends one last time. Then it trickled across the other kids who'd joined us, some I knew and some I didn't, some in the water and some on the rocks, more faces to count when you could see them. It was like everyone from town had come, only because I'd suggested it.

Ruby lit up each face until she reached mine, then she lowered the beam to show everyone my black bra and blue-flowered panties, mismatched and cotton on the bottom, like a little girl.

"You forgot a bathing suit, Chlo," she called out. She

stepped onto shore and waved at the spot beside her, to show I should take my place in it. "I have one for you, in my pocket. Just come down here and get it."

I could see her smile. I wished I hadn't, because it was the kind of smile she never gave to me. It was a smile for a boy who wanted to know her and never would. A smile for a girl who wanted to be like her and never could be. A smile for a perfect stranger.

I climbed off the rock and went to her. I felt everyone watch me go. Then I felt everyone look away before I reached her, as if they weren't allowed to keep looking anymore. I patted her pocket, right side first. She wore jeans with the cuffs folded up to her knees; it was strange to see her in jeans. And only the bottom half of her legs were wet. She'd been in the water, but she hadn't been swimming.

In her right pocket was a rusty nail, a quarter, a nickel, a penny, her naked hula-lady lighter, a loose strawberry candy, and a smashed pack of cigarettes with one left inside. I confiscated that; she knew I wanted her to quit.

She shrugged, kept smiling.

I tried her left pocket, and in it I found a bottle of violet nail polish, a tube of wine lipstick, and her car key. Really, I don't know how she kept so much in her pockets. Her jeans were pretty snug already. Still, I didn't find any bathing suit.

"Where were you?" I whispered. *"Where'd you go?"*

"Keep checking," she answered without whispering.

She turned, and poking out the back pocket of her jeans was a bathing suit. It wasn't one of mine though; it was hers. It was her favorite white bikini, the one she'd never before let me wear.

"I said I'd be back," she said, her voice low. "You should have stayed at the house." Then, once I'd pulled the bathing suit from her pocket, she spun around to face me. "But, since you're here, that'll look cute on you. Sorry it took me forever to get here, I got pulled over."

"But how'd you know we were here?"

"You can't do anything in this town without me hearing about it. You should know better than that, Chlo." She shook her head, disappointed. "But it's adorable. I mean, look at all the kids who showed up."

"I didn't . . ." I hadn't meant for all these people to show. But I realized what she'd said before. "Ruby, did you say you got *pulled over*? Like by cops?"

She sighed. "No, polar bears. Yes, cops. One cop. A mustachioed state trooper who told me I was driving too fast. He untucked his uniform and pulled up his shirt to show me his tattoo — I don't like that I was naked in it, but I did like the colors and I liked my hair — so I thought he'd let me go. But then he was all business and took his time writing up this little piece of paper for me and it wasn't a love note or anything."

"So it was a ticket."

She shrugged.

"A cop with a tattoo of you gave you a ticket and you . . . *let him*?"

She saw where I was going with this, how in the world where Ruby lived, where I thought we still lived, she didn't get speeding tickets, or, for that matter, white hairs. She didn't have problems the way normal people did. She lived the way a dream might, if it grew legs.

"It wasn't a very nice tattoo," she said, and sighed. "Just go put that bathing suit on, Chlo. I almost got arrested driving it over here."

She pointed into a thatch of trees, where I'd have some privacy. Then she smiled, the wide and dazzling kind that was all teeth. Something was very wrong and she wasn't telling me what. Instead she was showing teeth. When I looked up beyond the dazzle of the smile, she moved the beam of flashlight away so I couldn't see her eyes.

All everyone else had noticed was that smile. I sensed how they responded to it, visibly relaxing and going back to the party. As if they now had her permission.

I went to go get changed. It didn't matter to me, swimming in my underwear, but for some reason she wanted me to wear this bikini. It took a long time to get the suit untied from the knots that held it together and longer to get it on my body. It wasn't until I had the white bottoms on and was tying the strings that held together the white top that I thought about it. I'd expected her to tell me to go up to the house, and instead she was dressing me in her clothes and letting me stay.

When I got back, she wasn't where I could see. Then I spotted London. She came out from behind the same trees that had hidden my sister, her legs and feet muddied, her clothes as soaked through as when we'd stood together under the falling rain.

Had she gone off again with my sister when I was conveniently out of the way?

She had. I could tell by how she was looking at me. All her friends were there asking where she'd come from and how long she'd been out there and yet she looked only at me. She said to me, "Thank you," like I was doing something for her now. It sunk into me only as she thanked me for it.

She'd taken my place once, and it was my turn now to take hers. My turn originally and my turn once again.

She'd gone off with my sister when I wasn't looking and something had changed.

Then she pattered across the rocks toward her friends, and they enveloped her and left me there to gaze out at the water alone.

Soon, Ruby walked out of the water, from the same shadowed spot that London had come from. She was motioning me backward with her hand, like I should stay where I was on the rocks and she'd come to me. There was ten feet of water between us—dark and dank and seeming deeper than it was, if it only came up to her knees—and then there were a few inches between us and then she was on dry land.

"I don't know how to say it," she started.

She pointed at London, who'd plunged in already with her friends, unafraid of the water. London, who splashed and screamed in delight, naked and drenched to the bone and dipping her whole head in, and she didn't even care.

Ruby's eyes were brackish black without a hint of color in them. The night had swallowed all color up.

"They don't want her anymore, Chlo," she said. "They want what they had before, Chlo. They want what I wouldn't give them." I could tell she was helpless now, more helpless than I'd ever seen her. "Chlo, don't you understand? I tried to give her back, but it didn't work. They knew I'd been tricking them all this time. What they want is *you.*"

CHAPTER TWENTY-TWO

RUBY KNEW

Ruby knew what to do. She told me to go, now. Go to the house, pack whatever stuff I wanted from our rooms. Or, better yet, head straight to her car, since it was parked in the brush over the fence, sit on the hood and wait for her there. Never mind my clothes scattered on the ground and wherever I left my shoes, just go.

But we couldn't leave, I protested. We couldn't leave town.

She ignored me and pulled off her shirt, and I saw the bathing suit she had on underneath, a plain navy one-piece I recognized as mine.

"Aren't you coming?" I asked.

"I can't," she said. She said no more, but I felt sure she was staying because Olive wouldn't let her leave—as if they'd reached up and tied a rope around her ankle to keep her at bay. It was a thick rope, heavy and wet from lying for ages in coils at the bottom of the reservoir, and not even my sister could free herself from its knots tonight. She was barely even trying.

She was letting go of my hand and I was stepping away from her toward the trees—away from the body of water at our backs, the one that plunged deeper than usual due to the rain, leaking far from its normal shoreline, covering rocks and rock walls the way it never had in other summers, even bigger than I remembered, too big—when I grabbed back and got hold of her arm and said, "I think I should stay."

She had this way about her, my sister, this innate talent at getting people to do what she wanted—to leave cash-register drawers gaping open, to tattoo her likeness like a Madonna across their ribs. How many times had I been witness? So I should have known how it felt to have her do it to me.

She locked my eyes up in her eyes and secured the deadbolt. She caressed my arm, her touch softer than air. "Chloe," she said, my name music on her tongue. "You don't want to stay, do you? No. No, you don't. That's right, Chlo. I know. I know, I know, I know"—her hands in my hair here, her whisper in my ear—"you want to go."

I did as I was told. I must have. Because, before I knew it, I'd found the white Buick parked beneath the tree cover and I was sitting on the slope of its hood, waiting for her to come out and say it was time to go. Then two things happened that brought me back. The first was when Owen stumbled through the trees.

He slowed and let his friends go ahead. "What are you doing?" he called to me, not getting close. "I thought there was a party."

"There is," I said, and we heard it sounding out in the night, and he wanted to run to it, I knew, but still he stayed because maybe I had some magic in me, too.

I was about to get him to do something terrible to himself, like stab a stick in his eye, or bash his head with a rock, to see if I could, the way Ruby could, just to see, when he said, "Don't look at me like that."

"Like what?"

"Like I did something to you. Like you cared. Like I'm the asshole."

"But you're the one who—"

"Guess what?" he said, cutting me off. "I did. Like you. I used to. But you're not who I thought. I imagined you were . . . someone else."

"Who am I really, then?" I said. Because I was sitting on the hood of my sister's car in her favorite white bikini, the night stars peppering my skin, and though I had no idea where we'd be living tomorrow, I knew that the one thing I did have in the universe was Ruby, and that Ruby had me.

"You're just like her." He spat it out like an insult. "Guess I'll see you out there."

He pushed through the trees and was gone, and I had no influence over him, none whatsoever. I hadn't even had the chance to tell him I once liked him, too. I used to. But now I never would—not him, and not anyone—not again. For the first time, I felt truly like my sister. My heart had grown and twisted into the exact same shape as hers. We were mirror matches, on the inside.

That's when the second thing happened.

I heard the whistle blow.

The sound of it was faint at first, hard to discern from the wind. Then when I turned my ear to it, when I concentrated and sought it out, I heard it clear. The hiss of a steam whistle. A faint, faraway, years-buried scream.

It was coming from the direction of the water. Where my sister was.

When I reached the rocks, I found her where I'd left her. The air had quieted, no whistles carried here on the wind, and something in Ruby had turned calmer, colder.

I noticed Owen catch sight of me, stop, then walk straight for the rock where London was perched, as if he'd been heading for that rock the whole time and hadn't at any point in history been heading for me.

Ruby spoke up. "So London told me something I refused to believe. A rumor. A lie. You and Owen. Do you know the one I mean?"

I nodded.

"Is it a lie?"

I was careful not to make any sudden movements. "I guess that depends on what she told you."

Her neck snapped to where Owen was with London and this was how, with my sister's hand now lightly circling my wrist, the hush of water at our feet, I happened to see what he looked like kissing someone who wasn't me. How his mouth got on hers and then ran down to her neck, and how his hand pushed through her pale scratchy hair, and how he didn't want me at all, even if he said he once did for like two seconds.

I turned around, physically, to face the water. And I guess that said to my sister all she needed to know.

I didn't realize then how this changed everything. Her attention was diverted now, the spotlight wobbling over to center on me.

"I'll be right back," she said from behind me. She didn't tell me to go sit on the hood of her car and wait for her there, not again. This time, she let me stay.

After she left, I felt it. How something was slipping. The moon pulsed in a perfect half, begging to be punctured if you only had fingernails that were sharp enough and long arms to reach.

I sat on a log, away from the water, near where some boys tried unsuccessfully to build a fire. While they rubbed sticks in the dirt, grumbling about a pack of wet matches,

Pete took a seat on the log beside me and slung an arm around my shoulders. It was too dark to see him, but I knew what I'd see if I could. A guy Ruby had and didn't want anymore. A guy who loved someone who'd never love him back.

"What do you want, Pete?"

"Just saying hi," he said. "Chill."

"Hi."

"Guess your sister's back."

"She was always coming back."

We sat there in awkward silence until he said, "Hey now, I saw that before. Sorry about my brother. He's a dick, what can I say. Here, have some of my beer."

I grabbed it, though Ruby could have been out there watching, and I took a swig, downing more than I should. Not even Pete's spit on the mouth of the bottle stopped me.

"Thanks, Pete."

He patted my leg.

"Listen, you don't really like my brother. Between you and me, he's a loser. He wet the bed till he was nine. The kid's selfish as shit. Take, for example, tonight. He's got a stash in his bedroom like you wouldn't believe, and he won't share a little with me?"

I shrugged and still he kept talking.

"Not to mention that he left you on the side of the road. I heard about that."

His hand, as he said this, kept patting its way far up above my knee.

"Um. Pete. If my sister sees, she'll bite that hand off."

He snatched it away.

"You know something?" he said, slurring just enough to let me know he was about to say something uncomfortable. "In this light, you look just like her. Did I ever tell you that?" He leaned in and took a sniff of my hair. "You even smell like her."

I stood up.

I'd heard Ruby. Something about wine. Something how everyone knew she didn't drink beer, so why didn't they bring wine? How self-centered of them, how rude.

She was mostly teasing—and of course she didn't mean me—but she wouldn't drop it. I edged away from the shore to listen.

"Go get some for me, Lon," she was telling London.

But London didn't seem to be at my sister's beck and call any longer. "Tell Pete to go," she told Ruby. "You know he will."

"Petey's trashed. He's about to pass out." As Ruby said it, Pete wobbled on his seat on the log. He was drunker than he'd seemed only minutes ago.

Ruby set her sights on Owen.

"How about you go, O?" she said. "And none of that gas station wine either. Nothing in a box. I want something good and red and worth every penny. Here, take a ten. You can cover the rest, right?"

"I'm baked," Owen said. "I can't drive."

"London has her parents' car — she's got it parked on the other side of those trees," Ruby said. "She can drive. Can't you, Lon?"

"Yeah, but I don't have fake ID," London said. She stood there, near Ruby, her mouth open as if she wanted to protest more, but then she caved. She caved as my sister knew she would. "But I'll drive," London said. "If someone'll go with me."

Ruby gathered up a sigh, like she was beyond exhausted by this conversation and about to let go of the idea of wine, and break up the party while she was at it, and maybe slash a few tires on her way home, but then she lifted her head, and I knew she wasn't done yet. I felt the heat in her eyes even from where I was standing.

She took her time looking around the circle — from Owen, who was trying to bum a cigarette; to Pete, so falling-down drunk he seemed about to somersault into the newly blazing fire; to a kid tending the fire with a big stick; to London, who was standing there in a shirt as white as the bikini I had on and you could see the fire reflected in it, making it appear like she had a chest full of flames. Then Ruby's eyes landed back on Owen, where she'd started in the first place.

"London, you'll drive. Owen'll go with you. I know he has ID. I've seen it when he buys beer at Cumby's. Says he's twenty-five and some guy named Dave from Georgia. Dave's a Sagittarius. Isn't that right, O?"

His head nodded up and down like she had it on a string.

London, too, was stuck on a pin, legs dangling. The flames covered her stomach, fanned into her face. "All right," she said. "There's barely any beer left anyway. But where? Nothing's open."

"That place east on the highway will be," Ruby said. "Phoenicia Wines. It's open twenty-four hours."

"All the way out there?"

"Yes," Ruby said. "It's not far. Fifteen minutes to get there, tops, if you speed."

I expected Owen to argue, but he only nodded, put his arm on London's shoulder. "Yeah, whatever. Let's just go."

"I'm driving," London insisted as they walked toward the trees.

At first, I thought Ruby wanted Owen out of my face so it would be less painful. But then why didn't she just tell him to leave, and take London with him?

It wasn't until Owen and London were in the trees and couldn't be seen anymore that it hit me. Maybe Ruby didn't know what she'd done, how dangerous it could be to have London in the driver's seat if they were headed outside town.

Ruby must have not realized.

I turned to tell her. I turned and saw she knew already. I was sure she did, by the air around her, the heat of it, the energy crackling in it. By the way she stood beside the fire, watched it grow. I knew in the way I knew all things about my sister—without her having to use words to say. She knew exactly what would happen when London drove across the town line into Phoenicia. Hadn't I told her I'd seen it with my own eyes?

I grabbed her arm and pulled her away from the crowd, toward the water. The reservoir beside us sucked in a breath, listening. "Why'd you do that?" I hissed. "Owen could—The car could—You could kill him."

"*I* couldn't kill him," she said, palms up in innocence, "*I'm* not the one driving."

There was glee in her answer, undisguised delight.

"But—"

"He did something he shouldn't have, Chlo. He should have known better. He hurt you. No one hurts you. Did you think I'd just let something like that be? Just walk away tonight and do nothing? If you think that, you don't know me at all."

"You shouldn't have let him go."

She looked at me as if she could see me quite clearly in the dark. "If you're so worried about him, then why didn't *you* stop them, huh?"

"Because . . . because you said."

"You don't always do what I say," she pointed out. "You didn't wait for me by the car, did you?"

I shook my head.

"And if I told you to swim across the reservoir right now, and bring us back a souvenir while you're at it—would you?"

We both looked out for the other shore across the way. It was too dark to find it, and the moon had dimmed to nothing and wasn't helping, but it was out there, we knew. If I swam a straight line from here to the void of blackness ahead, if I stayed down, and kept kicking, I'd make it there sometime. If they didn't swim up and catch me first.

"No," I said. "Because you wouldn't ask me to. Not again. It's too dangerous."

She didn't respond. I took the flashlight from her hands and turned it on toward her face. I saw how she watched the water, warily, as if expecting a serpent thing to come coil a tentacle around her leg. Yet her eyes sparkled at the same time, and her bare leg was out and waiting, as if daring it to grab her, taunting it to try.

She gave me a nudge. "Move back, Chlo. You could fall in."

I climbed off the rock to the one next to it, farther away from the water.

After a while, she called for me.

"Chlo?" She was only one rock away, but she sounded distant. "What time is it? How long have they been gone?"

I pulled out my cell phone to check the time. Maybe a half hour had passed since Owen and London had left, I wasn't sure. I told her the time.

She concentrated for a moment on this, and then her eyes shot closed. She sunk down on the hard, cold rock, spent.

"What's wrong?" I asked.

"I don't feel so good," she said. "I'm very, very tired."

I knew she'd been trying to do something right then, a psychic burst of energy to warp the world her way. But it looked like the strain of it would kill her first.

"Ruby, stop. Sit up."

She pulled herself up slowly, as if it took great effort.

"Look at my eyes, Chlo. I think I'm getting lines. Can you get wrinkles when you're only twenty-one? Have you ever heard of such a thing?"

She aimed the flashlight beam at her face. It washed her out, bright as it was, but there were visible lines I hadn't noticed before. She'd never looked this tired.

"What's going on?"

"Balance, Chlo . . . Give and take. Push and pull. You for her, her for you. I think they're mad that I tried to have it both ways—to keep you alive and her, too."

"But what're they going to do?" I said, getting scared now.

"Do I have to chop off my own arm and hand it over?" she said, speaking nonsense. "Because I'd do that, I would. If you could keep yours."

"Okay," I said. "But what are you talking about?"

She lifted her arm slowly, the arm still attached to her shoulder, and pointed out at the trees in the distance. "Look," she said. "It's too late to take back."

She was the one to notice it first, but then, all at once, everyone noticed, and they were running toward it, and shouting. Ruby stayed put. I hesitated for a second, and then I, too, started running. We were all converging on a figure in a bright white shirt.

She looked ghostly as she emerged from the trees, her body birch-white, her short hair almost the same color as her clothes, as if she'd rolled around in baby powder to give us a good scare. The palms of her hands were up in the air, waving.

London had come back—alone.

She was a blinding bright spot against a backdrop of dark trees and then she was surrounded. By the time I reached her, there was a small crowd. A friend was propping her up. You could see bits of gravel on London's hands and blackened skid marks on her knees as if she'd crawled down the road and through the woods to reach us.

Questions were thrown at her: "What happened?" "How'd you get here?" "Where's O?" "Omigod are you hurt?"

London took a step away from the crowd, it seemed toward me.

"I must've blacked out again," she said.

I glanced back at Ruby, but she hadn't left her spot at the edge of the water. From this distance, she looked like any other brown-haired girl sitting on a rock under the stars. All that sky overhead made her look small.

"I think there was an accident," London said. "I think. I mean, I don't remember. Where's my parents' car?"

Then more questions, and London's friends surrounded her again, and I couldn't get to her, I couldn't see her face or hear what she was saying. I thought of when I found her in the rowboat, and then when everyone knew, and everyone saw, and you couldn't think with all the yelling and the splashing and the need to get away.

I could see the accident as clearly as if I'd been in the car as it happened, in the back, watching. Speeding down the dark road, no cars ahead, no cars behind, and then the blur of a traffic sign to the right, the town line crossed, and the girl at the wheel gone. The car would keep going even without her frail weight on the gas pedal. The wheel would veer even without her hands there to make it turn.

Owen wouldn't know what was happening at first. He'd shout, "Watch the road, Lon!" The windows would be down, so his ears would fill up with wind. He wouldn't be wearing his seat belt.

When he realized the driver's seat was empty beside him, it would be too late to jump in and take over. Far too late to hit the brakes. He wouldn't know how to stop the car. The last sight through the windshield would be the thick, oncoming trunk of a tree.

Then, inexplicably, by some kind of cruel miracle, the girl would reappear, but outside the car, dozens of yards away.

She'd be back inside the town line, a town — she wouldn't know this — she couldn't ever leave.

Her parents' car gone.

Her friend with it.

And she'd have no idea how.

If you were driving on Route 28 late that night, you might have seen the girl in the middle of the road, looking like she'd dropped from the hatch of a low-flying plane and only just got to her feet after the fall. She would have been dazed. She wouldn't have moved out of your way, so you would have pulled up near her, rolled down your window, called out, "Are you all right? Do you need a ride?"

"I blacked out again," she would have said, and run off — a streak of white into a dark nest of trees.

That was how I pictured it.

Now Pete was rushing to his car, off to find his brother. And Asha was frantically trying to reach Owen on the phone. Damien was crying like a girl. And Vanessa was peppering London with questions. Cate was staring into her flashlight, and Kate, who I'd forgotten was there, was trying to find her shoe. Others had phones out searching for signals, and a boy I didn't know was saying, "This isn't happening, this isn't happening," though it was, most definitely it was.

Ruby wasn't there at all.

I turned around, toward where she'd been sitting on the rock. Did she see what she'd done? Did she regret it? Would she wind back the clocks to set it right like last time? Could she? Was there something wrong with me that I believed she could?

Only, she wasn't on the rock anymore. She wasn't on the shoreline or near the fire that was puttering out to nothing. She was gone.

My eyes went to the reservoir. And out there, drifting somewhere in the dark middle, was what may or may not have been a rowboat, with a person hunched over in it, a person who may or may not have been my sister.

Her arm moved. For a second there, I thought she may have been signaling to me.

If there was anyone in the world I knew, it was my sister. Ruby, who'd been there the day I first opened my eyes. Ruby, who'd raised me. Ruby, who kept all my secrets even if she didn't reveal all of hers. Ruby, whose bathing suit I was wearing right then so I looked more like her than maybe ever.

Balance, she'd said. Something about balance.

Sometimes you look at someone and, if you know them well enough, like really know them, you can be sure to guess what they'll do before they do it. You may not understand why, may not ever understand it, but you don't need to know the whys and the hows of things. Sometimes you only need to stop them.

I dove in. I was swimming like Ruby had told me not to. Swimming so far, I lost track of shore. If you'd been watching from the waterlogged streets below you may have seen the white blur of my sister's bikini—easy to spot against the dark reflected night.

Ruby used to say I'd never drown, that I couldn't, my body wasn't built that way. Slip me under, and I'd emerge with fins for feet. Water turned to air once it reached my lungs. That was one of her stories and we'd all heard it a hundred times.

Another was the story of Olive, one of the nine towns flooded to make this reservoir. What was it that made the people not want to vacate it for some other surface town? What tethered the two girls from her story here and made them have to stay? She'd never explained that.

And after the steam whistle sounded out, did the girls stand with backs straight and eyes closed while the dams were raised and the water rushed in, steeling themselves for impact and then letting themselves get washed away when the wall of water hit? I imagined so. And, after, did they ever wonder what was up here, ever think of climbing out? These were things I'd never know.

All I knew was to keep swimming.

When I finally reached her, she looked into my eyes, which were almost like her eyes but barely half as green, and she opened her mouth and she said, "I'm really going to miss you, Chlo."

CHAPTER TWENTY-THREE

THEY ASKED

They asked me why she did what she did. Only, when I told them, they refused to believe me.

The people in town, they just kept asking, again and again, for weeks and weeks afterward, what happened, how did she get in that boat, how'd she go under? They never found a body; they never found a reason. No one would hear me when I told them about the hands that got hold of her ankle and pulled her down.

No one believed.

I guess maybe they never had. No one in town had ever really trusted the stories about Olive, about the long-lost people still wading its flooded streets. They'd never heard the whistle, or sensed the eyes keeping track of their trespassing feet. The graveyard up above was any other graveyard. The shards of old teapots that sometimes washed to shore after a storm were any old trash and not valuable artifacts, antiques.

So, later, when I told everyone what had happened to her—her friends and my friends, who couldn't meet my eyes; Jonah, who skipped town soon after; Pete, who tore her picture from his wall for what she'd done to his brother, then secretly put it back up; her ex-boyfriends; her admirers; the guys at the gas station; the girls who kept her in sunglasses; our mom, at the bar; our mailman, at the corner; the cops, the news, the homeless guy who barked like a dog in the street—they all refused to believe.

They forgot who she was:

Something fantastic we could never explain. Someone better and bolder than every one of us. Someone to paint murals and build bridges for. Someone worth every ounce of our love.

Someone powerful, but in the end not powerful enough.

When she went under, no one would believe she thought it only temporary.

That she couldn't drown.

That it simply wasn't possible.

Not her. Not us.

How, when the cold hands got a good tug on her ankle, she said, "Don't worry, I'll just have a talk with them."

How she said, "Don't worry, Chlo. You know how everyone always does what I say."

How she was wearing my bathing suit, and I was wearing hers, so, maybe, for a moment, they were fooled.

How she went under and how her breath bubbled up like tiny, translucent balloons cut loose from their strings, and how her arms reached out, and how her hair turned electric, and how her mouth mouthed not to worry, she'll be back in time for breakfast. And then how the reservoir took her, and I tried to get her back, but her fingers slipped from mine, and how I sat there in the boat under her stars and her moon, gated on all sides by her mountains, watching the last bits of her breath float up and away.

AUTUMN

CHAPTER TWENTY-FOUR

I SAID

I said I'd stay in town, even after. I'd stay, though I heard how they talked about me, in the months that passed, the things they said. I couldn't help but hear. With Ruby around, I used to find it easy to go deaf to anything anyone else uttered—it happened with barely any effort, like I'd been listening through an empty water glass held to a wall and all I had to do was step away.

But, without her, every word seeped through.

I heard them in the school stairwells and behind my back in trig and in chem; in the upstairs girls' room, in the downstairs girls' room, by the coolers in Cumby's, on the Green as I drove by in her enormous white car, on the track while running laps in gym. They said things they'd never say out loud, if Ruby were here.

They called me "disturbed."

They called me "hopeless."

They said I needed to get over it, move on. They said

she was gone, and that was the worst, when they said she was gone. They said if I couldn't face the fact that she was gone, someone should lock me up, like on that psych ward in Kingston where they put the cutters and the nymphos and the kids who talked to animals and thought they talked back. They probably would have said far worse, if they knew where I spent my nights.

The thing is, everyone was wrong. There was no need to pump me full of sad-girl meds or fire up the electro-shock machine. There weren't enough talks in Guidance to convince me to let go of Ruby, to stop acting like she was around, because what no one in town could seem to face was that she was still here.

Soon it was late fall, and I'd just turned seventeen, and the nights were longer than they'd been in summer, which I didn't mind, since it meant I could make my visits with Ruby far earlier.

I parked her car where she used to park it, and I found my way to the rocky shore without needing a flashlight. I'd walked the path enough times that my feet could find footing before my eyes had time to adjust.

No one went swimming here anymore—it was too cold. But kids from the high school would come sometimes, for the thrill of jumping the new shock-fences, getting the electric buzz kicking up through their toes. They took the long way in, with the running leap and the high climb; they didn't know how to find Ruby's way, how it was there as it used to be, how all they needed was to seek out the flap in the fence, duck down, and crawl through. I knew, but I didn't tell them.

They'd spill out of their cars, parked where even the laziest cop could spot them, then stomp through the woods, cracking branches off trees, making a mess of the shoreline with their discarded trash.

If I heard them coming, I'd take cover in the trees. But one night they were quieter than usual and caught me out in the open, near the rocks. And worse—London was with them.

She walked differently, with Ruby not around. She walked like she owned the place, had carved her initials in all the tree trunks, then sucked the sap out with a straw. She was reckless, taking hits of E at school. She was sloppy, with her boyfriends on benches on the Green. She was nothing like my sister.

She'd stepped out of the woods with her friends—three boys. They carried bottles of beer and flashlights, which bounced to me and then away from me. As soon as they saw who it was, the lights went far, far away.

Only London came close. The beam of her flashlight revealed the collection of items at my feet.

"What are you doing, Chloe?" she hissed.

"Nothing."

"Hold on. You're not going to—"

She stopped short when a boy called over to her, some boy I didn't know. "What's she doing?" he said; he wouldn't come see for himself. There was something about me that scared people now, like they could see through me to what I carried around inside my heart, that lit and forever-flickering flame. You'd think they were afraid I'd try to burn them with it.

Or maybe they just saw me at the reservoir and thought I was about to jump in.

"She's here to talk to her dead sister," London called out, laughing as she did. The boys didn't laugh; they couldn't believe she'd said it.

I had no reply. I didn't—wouldn't dare—deny it.

London was cracking up. She laughed and she laughed and the way she laughed told me she didn't care about anybody, especially not herself. I knew this from how she laughed at me—Ruby didn't have to tell me.

Even the boys told her to stop laughing. It wasn't funny. I could tell they didn't want to stand in the dark before the depths of the reservoir; they wanted to go, to get away from me and from it. Now.

Then we heard the splash.

It came from deep in, too far from the rocks on shore to pinpoint. It could have been anything, could have come from anywhere.

We were all looking out after it when one of the boys stepped up. He squinted into the dark distance. "Is that a . . . boat?"

The rowboat was white, or it had been, but with rust it looked reddish gold. Burnished by our eyes, roughed up from being out in the open, it drifted there, bobbing in the wind, going nowhere.

"That wasn't there before," the boy said.

"That's some creepy shit right there," another boy said.

Then all eyes on me, and with the eyes came flashlights, and beams of light up and down my body, like I could somehow explain it, had some kind of remote in my pocket that could direct the night and the wind and every free-floating object from here to the Hudson. Like I was somehow in control, someone they shouldn't mess with.

London pulled her light away. "She's just screwing with us," she said.

"I'm not doing anything," I said, holding up my hands to show empty palms. The reservoir curled quiet at my side, not giving itself away.

No one would say her name out loud, though I knew they were thinking it. You couldn't not-think it, not here with her breath on the air, her eyes glowing from the tree branches like owl eyes, her face on the crater of the low-hanging moon.

"O's having that party," one of the boys said. "Let's go."

"Yeah, let's get out of here," another boy said.

A beer bottle was tossed in, but it was empty, so it didn't sink at first. It rolled along the surface of the water without even a message inside it.

"Yeah, the party," London echoed.

No one asked if I wanted to come. Without Ruby, I wasn't invited to parties anymore. I'd heard Owen had gotten his casts cut off and was throwing a party because he could walk again, but no one at school said, *Hey, Chloe, O's having a party, you should go.*

The boys took off, and London started to follow, but then she paused at the tree line, and I saw her shadow waver, her short stick-up hair and her telltale stick-out ears. Did she know how close she'd come to not having this party to go to? To not having these boys to follow her around?

Is this what she did with her life, since Ruby had given it back?

"Hey"—she was stepping closer to me now, talking nice to me, now that her friends couldn't see—"Chloe? Are you, like, okay?"

"I'm fine."

"How could you be fine? You're not *fine*. Obviously you're like the furthest thing from fine." She looked down at the pile of stuff at my feet. "Are you gonna burn all that up or something?"

"What? No!"

"Then what? Bury it?"

"Why would I bury her stuff?"

It was dark, and London had her flashlight held low, but enough of her face was illuminated so I could see that I was making her uncomfortable.

I picked up a magazine. I collected them during my shifts at Cumby's.

That was my after-school job now—they let me take over my sister's old shifts; I barely had to ask. I worked behind the register, carding kids for beer and selling instant cheese pockets, and I'd learned to pump gas the way Ruby used to, keeping the weight of the hose balanced on my hip.

If I nicked a few magazines off the rack while at work, no one docked my pay, but it wasn't due to some kind of powerful sway I held over the guys in the store. I saw how they looked at me when I pumped a tourist's tank—nervous that I'd crack and take hostages. The only person who came on purpose during my shifts to get his tank filled, and looked me in the eyes when I was filling it, was Pete.

I'd kept it secret so far, but there was something about London that made me want to tell her what I was doing here. To hint at least.

I wanted to see if she remembered.

Here we were, on the edge of the body of water where I'd found her that night. That boat was *her* boat.

London slept nights at her parents' house now, and she

was back the way she used to be before that summer, but she was still more connected to this than she realized.

And besides—I *wanted* to talk about Ruby; she was all I wanted to talk about.

"She likes to read magazines," I told London, "glossy fashion ones. The fat, fall ones are her favorites." I flipped through the thick, bright thing in my hands, fanning out its happy pages like it didn't twist me up to do it. "You know, fall fashion—boot season."

"Liked to," London corrected me. "Liked to read magazines."

"Likes," I corrected her.

I looked past her at the water beyond us both, the water that seemed to have no end in the night, and there was no reason to think you could swim it—no one could.

"Only problem is they get wet," I continued. "The pages get all stuck together and it's pretty much impossible to read that way."

London threw up her hands. "I know I should feel sorry for you, but I can't anymore. You put on this show, to get people to pay attention to you, but guess what? It's not working."

She said it with her back to the water—oil-black in the blacker night—close up to it, nearer than Ruby would have wanted me to stand on my own, the heels of her feet practically inside.

She shouldn't have done that. She was close enough to push.

But before I could do a thing—before I could even let myself think it—an answering splash came from the reservoir, close to the rocks now, right where we stood. It could have been a fish, or a rustle of wind, anything really. Still, I wasn't expecting it and the noise startled me, but it shocked London—she jumped and skidded, almost belly-flopping into the frigid shallows, flashlight and beer bottle and all. The shriek she made hit the water and burst back up in our faces. It echoed against the rocks here and the rocks across the way. It flew through the sky. It filled our town and escaped to the next county.

So much noise, all the people down in Olive would have had to hear it—no one could have slept through that. They'd have gathered on their Village Green, boys and girls, moms and dads, the mayor's daughters—the oldest Winchell sister who still looked after the youngest, like I pretended Ruby kept on doing with me—eyes cast up toward their watery night sky that hung below our airy one, to the surface, to London's spindly legs, her bony ankles in striped socks well in reach.

Months ago, Ruby had said something I'd kept thinking about. Balance, she'd said, it's all about balance.

Give and take, push and pull, this girl for that girl, one thing for another.

If not me — Ruby would never, ever let it be me — then would London do? Had they changed their minds and would they take her back now? Would it work if I threw her in? If I did, then would someone I wanted to see more than anyone in the world come walking out in her place? Someone wearing a sundress in the night, drenched through and showing blue shaking knees, a braid of seaweed for a toe ring, hair longer than I'd ever seen it, a new freckle I'd get to know on her nose? Was it wrong to wonder these things? Could anyone blame me if I did?

But London had distanced herself from the water; she wasn't even on the rocks anymore. She was on flat, dry ground, closer to the bank of trees, as if about to make a run for it. She whipped around, eyes skittering. She was hyperventilating and couldn't speak.

"See something?" I asked her.

"I thought — I almost thought . . ." Then she was shaking her head, shaking it away. She wasn't going to say it out loud, wouldn't let me have it, not this one little thing.

A sound came from the woods — one of the boys she'd come here with, shouting her name.

She snapped out of it. There was a party to go to, Owen's party. He could walk again; everyone who was anyone in town would be there.

"Gotta go," she said. And she took off, stepping fast into

a trot, a trot that turned into a full-out run, unapologetically running away from me, as if I'd spooked her.

I could hear her crashing through the woods. Tearing past trees, pitching herself up and over the fence. In the near distance an engine roared; tire skin got lost on asphalt as they hit highway, and I was left alone, here at the edge of Olive.

Alone with Ruby.

I took a step closer to the water. I was always hesitant at first, careful. There were the hands that might make a grab for me, and I knew how strong the people were down at the bottom, how their weight got doubled by the water, but how fast they still were, faster than you'd think.

All it took was one tug.

Then you'd fall.

Imagine tumbling through a dark tunnel, its walls made of mud and nothing to hold on to, nowhere to climb. Imagine distance was measured in cupfuls, and someone just poured in a whole lagoon. Imagine being so drenched, your bones got soggy. Imagine the cold.

It'd be wet like nothing I'd ever felt before, not even that time our mom left me too long in the bath and Ruby came home to find me pruned and greased up with soap, splashing a tidal wave over the bath mat.

Falling would last a day and a night and part of the day

after that—the reservoir was deeper than anyone who dug it in 1914 even knew. And when I hit bottom, I'd look up and up, and there'd be muck in the way—leaves and scum and tire goo, and junk like old sneakers and bottles people threw in—and that's all I'd see of sky from then on.

All that, Ruby used to tell me.

Now, I stood at the edge. I didn't call her name; I wasn't deranged, not like people said. She wouldn't have been able to hear me if I did, not with all the water in the way.

I thought about what happened. She'd tried to save me—twice. The first time, when I almost drowned, she reached out to find someone to give instead and it only happened to be London. But the second time, the worst and final time, she jumped in herself to take my place. I would have gone instead, if only I'd known.

If she could hear me, that's what I'd tell her.

I climbed out to a rock I often sat on, the one that jutted past the others, half-submerged. I felt like one of those kids with a relative in prison, counting off their sentence until the day they got out. A wall of glass separated them, and armed guards were always watching. No touching, not ever. They could bring gifts if allowed: magazines, and pictures to paste on cell walls, but everything would have to be searched first. And once they left, they couldn't send texts.

I was luckier. I didn't have to wait for visiting days—I could come anytime, though that didn't mean I'd get to

see her. And I could stay all night if I wanted to. I lived
with my mother, reluctantly, and even though she was sober
again she wouldn't care how late I was out, even on a school
night. Maybe she knew who I came to see.

I fanned out the magazines and laid out some strawberry
candies from Cumby's. I put out one cigarette—just the one;
because once she was back, she could have one and then
she was officially quitting—and her naked hula-lady lighter.
I was careful not to get any of it wet. I couldn't help but
wonder what would happen in winter, when the reservoir
froze over. We didn't have enough time together as it was.

Then I waited.

Sometimes the time passed quickly, and before I knew it
the alarm was going off on my cell phone to let me know I
should drive back home, since I had school the next morning. But, other nights, time felt light-years long, like how a
star spied through a telescope on Earth is really a sun that
could have died already, years ago, and it took that long for
its light to reach our eyes down here.

That could have been the way with sound in Olive, too.
How I could call for her one Thursday night in Novem-
ber, and three Novembers from now she'd finally hear me. I
hoped it wasn't, but I worried it was.

If you want something badly enough, it can come true—
you just have to make it that way. By believing. I think she
told me this once.

This was what I believed: That one night, it would happen. She'd see me on this rock, see me waiting for her, and she'd swim up.

Maybe she'd make a play for my ankles, get me to shriek. Or she'd try to catch my attention first, like I'd find her in the beam of my flashlight out in the middle of the reservoir, there where the light could hardly reach. But more likely she'd just walk out as if she'd been lounging about down there, wishing for a tan all this time. She'd keep it casual; she wouldn't want to upset me.

She'd climb up on the rock. She'd look the same as always, except her hair would be longer, swirling past her waist. Once up at the surface, she'd be cold, surely; I should remember to bring a sweater. Other than that, she wouldn't look any different—just paler. But if I put a hand to her chest, I wouldn't feel air filling her lungs, now that she'd grown the gills.

She'd be homesick, she'd have to be. I knew she missed me, but I bet she also missed other things, like dry boys she could keep an eye on, because reservoir boys had to be slippery. And things you could only get up top, like fried foods and red wine, and sunglasses, because it would be too dim down there to need any. I knew she'd miss driving in her car down a long, flat road, the kind she used to speed down with headlights off. I'm sure she'd miss sleeping in a bed with an actual pillow, as algae must get so sticky and clump up your hair. She'd miss things I took for granted: sunshine and rainstorms and horribly catchy pop songs, even if she'd heard them a thousand times before. And stupid things probably, too: like getting an eyelash stuck in her eye, or doing laundry and having to fold it after, or the annoying way nail polish chips and you can't get it all off unless you buy the special remover. Things like that.

There was so much she couldn't have down there. She'd want to come back up for good.

It could happen.

All I knew was that she couldn't be down in Olive this long by choice—they were making her stay, punishment for all the things she did. She got too powerful up here on the surface, she stopped being careful, and the people of Olive just didn't like that. I knew that if it were up to her, she'd already be up here, with me.

Even if it took her forever to make it to the rocks on shore, I hoped she knew I'd be here when she got out, holding a bag of dry clothes, her blue boots maybe, or her black ones, and glasses, dark-tinted, to keep out the glaring sun. I'd help her get steady on her legs again. I'd walk her back through the trees, if she forgot the way.

Her car would be parked where she always parked it, and I'd open the passenger-side door for her and say, "Back to town, Ruby?" and she'd say, "Where else, Chloe?" And she'd take a tug on my hair and say, "I know you finally got your license and all, but are you gonna let me drive or what?" and I'd smile, because I couldn't stop myself from smiling, not with Ruby around, and I'd hand over the keys.

That's what would happen, when she got out.

But the reservoir was quiet and still—no splashing, not again. So I decided to wait on the rock a little longer; it wasn't that late.

If I closed my eyes, I could almost feel her playing with my hair the way she used to. Her light touch at my forehead, either her light touch or the wind's. Her fingers as she did the braids she used to put in my hair when I was a girl, working slowly, methodically, at a rate that might take a hundred nights to finish, more nights than I could guess at counting, more nights than she'd want to say.

I felt so sure of it: her fingers moving lightly through my hair, my eyes closed to the wind, the reservoir at our backs, leaving us be. So sure I'd open my eyes and find my hair in braids, and the strawberry candies all taken, and there on the rock, Ruby, my big sister, saying what should we have for dinner, pita pizzas or mashed potatoes, and what day was it anyway and were there any good movies on TV?

It sounded impossible, something no one would believe. Yet I was so sure that at any moment I'd open my eyes and see her. I'd open my eyes and see.

ACKNOWLEDGMENTS

My brilliant agent, Michael Bourret, somehow saw the potential in my pages and supported me through every difficult and dramatic moment to reach this point. I was once advised that working with him would be the best thing to happen to my career; time and again, this has been proven true.

My phenomenal editor, Julie Strauss-Gabel, pushed me to new heights I'd hardly dared imagine with this manuscript. This novel needed her to edit it. It absolutely would not be what it is without her vision, her deep understanding of its characters, and her belief that its author could actually pull through. I'm in awe of what she can do and beyond lucky for the chance to have her skill and attention shine my way.

Grateful thanks to: Lauri Hornik, Linda McCarthy, Steve Meltzer, Rosanne Lauer, Lisa Yoskowitz, Liza Kaplan, Elena Kalis for the stunning cover image, and everyone at Dutton and Penguin Young Readers Group; Lauren Abramo at DGLM; the Writers Room; Think Coffee; the Corporation of Yaddo; the MacDowell Colony; Aimee Bender, and her Tin House workshop the summer of 2008; Sigrid Nunez; Molly

O'Neill; Micol Ostow; Mark Rifkin; Courtney Summers; my brother, Joshua Suma; and my Woodstock friends who swam the Ashokan with me, especially Esme Breitenstein and Christine Gable, and in memory of Carlena Hahne, who was lost too soon.

Thanks for encouragement from: Kate Angelella, Joëlle Anthony, Hilary Bachelder, Jim Berry, Bryan Bliss, Marc Breslav, Cat Clarke, Erin Downing, Annika Barranti Klein, Will Klein, Yojo Shaw, Erin Swan, Christine Lee Zilka.

My beloved mom, Arlene Seymour, has so much Ruby magic in her she's the reason I was able to become a writer at all. And my little sister, Laurel Rose Purdy, was the best gift my mom ever gave me and the inspiration for the heart of this story. Rose: I hope this reminds you every day just how much I love you.

Regional history was altered for the purposes of this novel, but acknowledgment must go to a book of true history, *The Last of the Handmade Dams: The Story of the Ashokan Reservoir* by Bob Steuding.

And finally, I'm endlessly grateful to my other half and my love, Erik Ryerson, who found a way to take a couple of characters, a crazy premise, and a flimsy plot and help to magically bring it all to life one night in a back booth on Bleecker Street—and then read and edit drafts of these pages so many times I lost count. This novel simply would not exist without him.